# THREE SHEET

# THREE SHEET

TIFFANY THAYER

ISBN-13: 978-1-962896-77-1

Published by
Cutting Edge Books
PO Box 8212
Calabasas, CA 91372
www.cuttingedgebooks.com

TO MY MOTHER

# CONTENTS

**PART I**

CHAPTER ONE THE BOOK OF MINNIE     1
CHAPTER TWO THE BOOK OF ROBERT     18
CHAPTER THREE THE BOOK OF HEK     41

**PART II**

CHAPTER FOUR THE BOOK OF EGO     81
CHAPTER FIVE THE BOOK OF LIFE     149
CHAPTER SIX THE BOOK OF PAIN     232

**PART III**

CHAPTER SEVEN THE BOOK OF PEACE     261
CHAPTER EIGHT THE BOOK OF CRIME     273
CHAPTER NINE THE BOOK OF JUDGMENT     288

# PART I

# CHAPTER ONE
# THE BOOK OF MINNIE

## 1

T HE Freeport Silver Cornet Band swung down Stephenson Street playing, *there'll be a hot time in the old town to-night.* The hot time was beginning even then. The crowds along the line of march screamed their cheers. The band finished that song—and only the drums played; rrrrrum, rrrrrum, ahrrrum-tum-ta-t'-tee-de-um! That was for her. The drum beats without any music were Minnie's share. The *hot time* was for the lucky ones.

Then some sickening, impossible maladjustment of their repertoire, reflecting a diabolical sense of the inappropriate in their leader, a streak of sadism On High, caused the Silver Cornetters to blare forth—as they came abreast of her—*when Teddy comes marching home again, hurray! hurray!*—

That the God of Freeport was a sadist—or, that the Marquis' self-indulgence was God-like.

Until she heard that song, Minnie had suspended judgment. It required such a minor sort of miracle, the barest little half-pint bit of wizardry, and something not unheard of. It wasn't as if He would have to make up a brand new loaves-and-fishes business. Mistakes of the kind she prayed for had occurred many, many times. All the War Department had to do was get a name wrong and the trick was done. Was that asking so much? Names were forever being mistaken—on packages, everywhere. It could happen in Washington too.

But—when the band, just coming even with her, at the head of the procession, had chosen that moment to play that song—she knew. How could she help but know? Teddy! *When Teddy Comes Marching Home!* If only *his* name had not been Teddy too. They were spitting in her face. They were throwing salt on her raw heart, torn and beaten and bleeding

In that first line, where he should have been, faces she had not seen before separated the blue parade uniforms from the campaign hats. Company K had been rearranged. The entire company had been changed. Familiar heads had been put in others' places. Of course, Ted was not the only one who had died. But probably he was the only one in Freeport named Teddy. *That* insult, that extra pang was hers alone. *When Teddy comes marching home again, hurray! hurray!—*

Hurrah!—and a tiger!

But the new arrangement of the ranks deferred finality again, made the official error, the prayed-for error, still possible. Minnie searched each file as it passed—eyes front—for that one face they said was no longer alive, until the sticky little hand in hers had twisted and tugged a full minute. "What is it, Bob?"

Robert Ingersoll Knott scowled as darkly as five years can scowl on the balloons a peddler hawked.

"Do you want a balloon?"

The corners of his mouth tugged grimly down. He glared his hatred of the toys in such abundance.

"Do you want a balloon, Son?"

That was the whole trouble. There! See? *A* balloon! He knew it. He had known it from the moment they had come in sight. One was all he could have, regardless of that unlimited supply. But—once in his hand—that particular balloon took on personality, became an individual, grew brighter, fatter, prettier than any of the others—and the scowl vanished.

The street behind the official carriages filled with a milling crowd. Boys older than Robert Ingersoll ran noisily in groups, and men and women on bicycles had collisions and picturesque, revelatory spills.

The families of the marching men followed the parade to Armory Hall, flouting discipline in bolder fashion at every additional fifty feet put between the men and the I. C. depot, until each soldier—or nearly every one—had an arm around his neck, a hand in his, or a female or an infant swinging from some part of his equipment.

Those storekeepers who had not closed for the day left the sidewalk unhurriedly, with back-glances and called sallies as they reëntered their places of business, smiling broadly, even those who were alone. The boys had looked fine. That was a good job they'd done. Now life in Freeport could return to normal— now that the boys were back.

"What was it Grandma told us to get, Bob?"

"Black cotton, number sixty." But once wasn't often enough to say it. He had been silent and good for a long time. "A spool of black cotton, number sixty.... A spool of black cotton, number sixty. A spool of black—"

"That's enough; thank you." They turned in at a dry-goods store.

"A spool of black cotton,—number sixty," she said.

Bob helped his mother by repeating it once more aloud, looking up at her, then, to see if he dared say it—only one more time. It was hard to tell through that thick black veil. He wished she wouldn't wear it; she had others so much nicer. The one with the big fish-net holes—or the other one with little holes like the dining-room curtains—they made mama even prettier than she always was. This one just covered her up so you couldn't see her.

He knew what it was for, of course. This was the veil you wore when papa had been taken in the Philippines. "Taken in the Philippines" should, by rights, have meant something like the abduction of Proserpine in Pluto's chariot, but it didn't. There was confusion somewhere. Grandpa had been "taken" too, they had said, though he lay about the house for days after that, first on a table, then in a very pretty box. A bugle had been blown at the cemetery and soldiers had shot their guns in the air over the hole. If you were "taken in the Philippines", were there guns and a bugle too? But mama looked so sad when he asked about such things that he had not voiced that question. It hurt him to be the cause of bringing that expression to her face, that pained look to her big brown eyes, and he seemed always to be doing something to cause it. Every day or so Grandma reported some misdemeanor which brought that horrible punishment upon him. He would have much preferred a whipping or one of the more usual correctives employed by the parents of his playmates. Going supperless to bed would have been a lark by comparison, but Robert could not explain that, because it was not clear to him. He knew only that it oppressed him, smothered him and made him wish to die whenever he behaved so badly that Minnie had to "talk" to him. The poignance of that ache within, the novelty of each new offense, the appalling number of wrong things a boy could do and this one's too-ready assumption of his own culpability, all united to prevent him from noticing that most of his malefactions occurred while his mother was out of the house, kept him—for a long time—from realizing that often the same acts performed in her presence were not even remarked. This extraordinary fact was brought to his attention from the negative angle, thus: "Do you just wait for me to leave the house, Bob, to do things like that? … You're a good boy while Mother's home. Then the minute my back is turned you do something you know you hadn't ought to. Why do you do it?"

That was a direct question, but Robert Ingersoll could not answer it. It was not true that he waited for her to go shopping before turning criminal. Often enough he did not know she was gone when Fate jerked him up—red-handed. Bob Knott was more than twenty years old before the true explanation of that phenomenon became clear to him, but the old lady, Grandma Elling, was dead by that time, so he could not punch her jaw.

In Stukenberg's, the boy tried to see through Minnie's veil to learn if he had offended. Well, anyway, it *was* black cotton, number sixty, they were supposed to bring home.

The clerk had been a schoolmate of Minnie Knott and, of course, knew of her condition. "When do you expect the new baby?" she asked in a whisper, smiling slyly.

"This week, Doctor Smith says…. I wish it was over."

"I'll bet you do. This week! You'd never guess it."

"No; I know."

"How would you like to have a little baby sister, Robert?"

The balloon came slowly down from its proud height—the length of its stick and the boy's arm. A baby sister! That made at least ten times he had heard that lately. If he wasn't careful he *would* get a baby sister, with everybody thinking he wanted one. Bob glared at the girl as he had at the balloons. It embarrassed him to be addressed directly, especially on that subject.

"Don't be rude, Son. Bertha's speaking to you."

"I want a dog," he said grudgingly.

Bertha tittered, and Minnie lifted her veil, draping it over the front of her hat and dabbing gently at her nose. The clerk saw the red-circled eyes. "You've been crying, Min."

"Eh? … Yes—I guess so."

"Oh—*me!*" the girl said with futile vehemence. "It's just a *shame!*"

Mrs. Knott lowered her veil again. "Don't mind, Bertha. I'll be all right. I shouldn't have come down to the parade, I guess. But I thought—maybe—" She broke off because her voice would have trembled. Then: "Bob wanted to see—the soldiers."

They were in the street again and walking home, down South Galena Avenue toward the Parsonage. Bob ran ahead, tossing his balloon and catching it, going: "Boom, boom, boom-boom-boom" with his mouth.

So—that was over, and without miracles. It had been a lot to ask after all. Miracles, if any, came from the God Ted Knott had flouted, flouted even in naming the boy. One couldn't very well do that. It wasn't consistent. If she were true to herself in embracing Ted's disbelief, in accepting that name for her son, she shouldn't weaken now, and cower, and whimper for Providence to return her lover. Ted wouldn't like that. She could see his eyes again now, narrowing down to hard, fine points at her first indication of timidity before ideas. "Get strong!" he had said. "Stand on your own two feet. Don't blame a wraith in the sky for our stupidity."

Yet, he had been soft too. Soft and tender and kind.... And his slender fingers had gripped her shoulders and his lips had murmured against hers. Must she call this new issue of his after some other heretic—in respect to his memory? Immanuel Kant Knott. That just sounded like bad grammar. She raised her voice: "Turn in the grocery, Son."

## 2

THE Ellings had never assimilated Theodore Knott. In their Embury Parsonage stronghold they had sat like pious wolves alert to rend the outlander who had taken their favorite daughter and sister with an easy, insolent laugh—and a polite cough for their God. They resented that laugh. They resented that cough. They hated his lifted brows and his graciousness in debate. They hated the extra words he knew, knew and *used*, damn him! They hated his books.

But Ted told Minnie—before Bob's birth—that he hadn't married her family. "Your mother and father are one thing. We all get stuck with those; but don't hold it against me, darling, if I maim that ugly brother of yours or break your fat sister's left leg. They have no use for me and the feeling is fully returned."

"They just don't understand you." Min had a way of drawling when they were alone together. Her speech was quick enough at other times.

"Oh, I know what's the matter with them, all right. Tessie's afraid I'll take a notion to go back to Chicago, you with me, of course, before she gets married and gets out. That would leave her with the dirty dishes. And Oliver is scared pea-eyed green that both you girls will leave him with the house and the old folks on his hands.... I know.... But, Chicken."

"Yes?"

"I won't."

"I know."

And he stayed. He ran the job-printing side of the *Standard* and practically supported the family. Oliver was unskilled and he jumped from this occupation to that without profit until he finally married the daughter of a Rockford furniture factory and went there to an office berth.

Tessie never did work at anything except Cedric, and, in truth, he *was* a full-time job. He had been sparking her six years when Ted reached Freeport, and Robert Ingersoll was nearly three before Aunt Tessie finally wheedled out of her prize a question she could twist into the semblance of a proposal of marriage. But—if Cedric was a little vague in his phraseology, Tessie was not, in her answer. Twist what she said as you would, nothing else could be made of it. Yes, thank you. Yes, she *would*.

So, after some delay, they were married and Cedric moved into the Parsonage. This, it should be explained, was the old parsonage (the two-story brick, painted yellow, which has since been torn down) not the bright new frame with the veranda on the corner of Williams Street, the other side of the church. The square old building was set, you may remember, just far enough back from the front sidewalk to afford root-room for a gigantic maple. There were four rooms downstairs and five aloft, not to mention the summer-kitchen—which was by far the best way. The three buildings, Embury and the two parsonages, filled the short block directly opposite the High School and the whole was known by all Freeport as "Trinity Corner". The Ellings took pride in that. Nine church spires could be counted from the windows—and on Sunday morning nine sets of bells called the faithful to be saved by nine formulæ, all in a radius of two hundred yards from Minnie's home. There were other churches in Freeport, of course, lots of them, but in no other locality was the architecture of salvation so variously omnipresent in so short a space.

If William and Letitia Elling had been other than they were, moving with their family to this place could scarcely have failed to make them soul-conscious. If they had arrived, lax, at Trinity Corner, they must have reformed. But they were not lax and had never been lax in their duty to God. The welfare of the spirit was of vital, personal and immediate importance to the old folks, and the children had been raised accordingly. Oliver was furbished and Tessie and Minnie were tied up with ribbons every week for Sunday School; they were *clean*, it was often remarked, if their suits and dresses weren't new. And on other days Epworth

League, Christian Endeavor and Prayer Meeting claimed their attention if not their interest.

Minnie enjoyed it all. She was quick. Sometimes she was a little too quick—to ferret out disconcerting questions to pose her preceptors. But these were guileless and, of the three children, she was the first to memorize the books of both Testaments, fitting the multi-syllables to monotonous, chanting songs.

*Genesis, Exodus,*
*Leviticus, Numbers*
*A-a-a-and Deuteronomy—*

The other:

*Matthew, Mark, Luke and John,*
*Acts and Epistles to the Romans,*
*First and Second Corinthians,*
*Galatians, Ephe-e-esians—*

Slowly, through her childhood, she accumulated a considerable hoard of incomprehensibilities, cache of fermenting small-doubts usually occasioned by observation of a strangely recurring incompatibility of creed and life-practice. Long before Ted appeared, fresh from college, a perennial sophomore, Minnie had ceased to voice her thoughts. She knew "it is not given us to know", and quit asking.

Ted was clever, clear-eyed and forthright, impatient of discretion and tolerance.

He talked, to Minnie, the iconoclasm he was compelled to keep out of his business associations at the *Standard*. He had heard Ingersoll lecture in Chicago, had met the great man and had shaken his hand. Without realizing what havoc he wrought,

Ted answered Minnie's questions, answered and elaborated while she worshiped him. Her God went the way of Santa Claus and she had only Teddy for a pillar of strength.

Their baby was to be made a thinking individual. There was to be no cant or hypocrisy in his education. They planned, plotted the course of a life, thought intensively how best to keep him from wasting his early years in ridiculous beliefs, the faiths of their fathers. How loudly, proudly and readily they would answer his baby questions: "We do not know. No one *knows*. Some say this—some that." And how he would live to thank them for it. This talk filled the period of her pregnancy. It was private talk, just between them.

One day, shortly before the event, Ma Elling looked up from her darning as Minnie entered the parlor. The wattled old face undulated into its mechanically benignant smile which had never fooled any one outside the family and said: "What were you thinking of naming your baby, Min?"

The girl seated herself carefully in the Morris chair and leaned her head against the green plush. "Helen or Robert—whichever is suitable."

Her mother said nothing, but as Minnie closed her eyes she thought the darning-egg came out of that sock with something of a snap.

"Helen's——eh, pretty——" There were more spaces than words, the way the old lady said it.

"I hope it's a boy," the expectant one said dreamily.

"They're less trouble. Land, the time I had with you and Tessie."

"Yes, I know," Minnie hastened.

And another time names were mentioned, but the young culprits kept their awful secret until that last dramatic moment. The story is still told in Freeport. When the wreckers tore the old Embury down—to clear the way for the new—one long split in the main rafter was pointed out by the workmen. "There it is!"

Grandma Elling was responsible. She had been insistent upon baptism and could not understand her daughter's opposition. Minnie and Ted had never discussed their lack of faith with her. She was too old to understand. There was no use taking her belief from her at her age anyway. Magnanimous youth! Finally the youngsters decided, after a week of whispered, pre-sleep debate in bed, to let her have her way. It was only a gesture anyway and could do the child no harm.

Up to that time, "Robert" had sufficed. There was to be a middle name, but they had not yet made up their minds. Then— of a balmy Sunday—with the church filled to capacity, Reverend Harper turned to Minnie, one of his hands full of water and the other full of Bob, turned to her with questioning brows and she held a typewritten slip of paper close to his nose.

"I christen you—Robert—Ingersoll Knott, in the name of the Father, and the Son, and the Holy Ghost. Amen."

Then it was the rafter cracked.

## 3

SOME months before the parade in which Teddy did not march home, Grandma Elling had returned from the weekly meeting of the Women's Relief Corps (ladies' auxiliary to the G. A. R.) with the belittling phrase "Uncle Sam's Picnic". That was what they called it. The "boys of '61 to '65" could not take the trouble in the Philippines seriously. "Uncle Sam's Picnic" they dubbed it—and their wives had echoed the disparagement. It wasn't much of a war, to their way of thinking.

The family was at the supper table, eating in the kitchen as they always did when there was no company. Minnie answered the phrase with her little, one-sided smile. "I'll bet Ted doesn't think much of it,—as picnics run."

"Oh, Min, I never thought you'd mind. Ted seen his duty and he's doin' it like a man. 'Course it ain't no picnic to have to leave your home an' loved ones an' go off somewhere among a lot o' heathens.... It's just the vet'rans' way of sayin' it. It's only a joke."

"Pass the bread," Cedric demanded, loquaciously—for him. "Bread!" usually got him what he wanted.

The plate was at Minnie's hand, but she ignored him. Tessie rose to replenish the supply of boiled cabbage.

"What's the matter; am I eating too much?" the man asked testily.

"Min," her mother said.

"I think Mother wants you to say 'please'," volunteered he who should be seen but not heard.

Cedric's knife hit the table on the right side of his plate, his fork came down on the left. Consternation and rage distorted his features. "What's that?" he yelled.

"I swan," said Grandma Elling, and Tessie stood perfectly rigid halfway from the range.

"Don't yell at that boy," Minnie said quietly. "That's exactly what I *was* waiting for."

"Don't—don't *yell* at him? You—I—are—are you gonna let him t-talk like that to *me?!*"

"Talk like what?"

"Why—why, tell *me* to say 'please'! A man, a grown man!"

"He was only trying to be helpful. A grown man shouldn't have to be told."

The bowl of steaming cabbage arrived with a plump in the middle of the table. Tessie had not yet found the words she wanted, but setting the dish among them with a punctuational bump served to announce that she was by no means a noncombatant.

Grandma sputtered. "He shouldn't be allowed to speak up to his elders like that, Min, and you know it."

"His elders shouldn't speak to *me* like that. One doesn't demand bread; one asks for it."

"*One!*" Tessie mocked.

"Since when have *you* been so all-fired high-toned?" Cedric wanted to know.

"There's nothing high-toned about ordinary decency. The word 'please' doesn't cost you a cent no matter how many times you use it. I'm trying to teach that boy to be a gentleman and I refuse to allow any one to sit at this table and grunt for their food. If you can't ask for things you want and ask to have them passed, you'll never get anything to eat."

Tessie found her tongue. "More of Ted Knott's doing! 'Ted comes from a good family.' 'You must be careful in front of Ted.' Now we have to be careful in front of *all* the Knotts."

"I pay for my board here—and Tessie helps with the work. If you don't *like* that arrangement"—Cedric swaggered—"we can leave!"

"That is entirely up to you.... Are you through eating, Son?"

"Yes, Mama."

Minnie rose. "Run, get your cap.... You'll excuse us; won't you?"

Tessie bowed from the waist. "Yes, Mrs. Knott."

"Min!" her mother fluttered helplessly.

"We're going for a little walk."

"Does she think *I'm* going to do these dishes? I *cooked* this supper," Tessie fussed.

"I shouldn't have told her that about Uncle Sam's Picnic. That's what upset her."

"Oh, she's been upset ever since she married that man."

"Who does she think she is?" Cedric grumbled, spearing the top slice of bread with his fork at two paces.

They heard the front door close behind Minnie and Bob.

"She's spoiling that boy," said Tessie. "The idea!"

"She coddles him," Letitia agreed. "You'd think he was twenty instead of five."

"If I'd of spoke up to my old man like he did to me, I'd of got a back-handed lick in the teeth that'd put me under the stove," the male bragged. "I never heard the like."

"Using the front door!" Tessie said.

On the street, it was a source of wonder to Robert Ingersoll that no matter how fast or how slow their pace, no matter how many corners they turned, the moon followed them. There she was! Back of every house or church they passed. "What *is* the moon, Mama?"

Minnie was boiling the oatmeal next morning when Tessie and her husband came in. "Good-morning," she greeted them. But they had decided not to speak. As a protest against the indignities suffered the previous evening, Mrs. Knott was to be cut. "You two are behaving like children," she said, when she finally comprehended the stupid plot. They sat like wooden images through the meal, speaking only to each other and to Letitia.

Letitia began to sniffle and then to cry softly. "My own daughters," sobsobsobsob sniff. "T-turning against each other over that—infidel's child."

"He's my child, too, Mother."

"No respect for God or man." Sobsobsobsobsob. "Oh, if Pa had only lived. Not a one of you dared to upset me so while he was here."

"I'm sorry, Mother," Minnie said.

Wail! "Oh, I've never had a moment's peace since that Ted Knott came into my house. Him and his city airs. Sneering at us and our ways."

"Ted never sneered at you, Mother. Please try to remember. Ted loves you—just as I do." Minnie spoke very quietly.

"Humph!" Tessie *couldn't* let that pass. "Never sneered at us? I'd like to know what you'd call it."

Absorbed in the conduct of the sortie, Cedric forgot and lit his pipe. This cardinal sin threw Grandma to the enemy camp. She stiffened, held her napkin before her face and began to jerk. Minnie dashed for water. "Put that pipe out, Cedric. You know Mother can't stand the smell of smoke until after breakfast!"

He crept away, abashed.

"Well, that's one thing Ted Knott never did," Letitia called after him. Cedric kept right on going.

The breach widened. While Spain and the United States were agreeing on terms of peace, drawing closer together, the Cedric Haeffers and the Theodore Knotts were drifting further apart. The break came two weeks after that, on pay night. With money on him Cedric was hard to hold. He came home from Woodmanse's foundry, jingling several half dollars loosely in his pocket. It was just possible he had had a glass of beer. "Pack up," he said to Tessie. "We're getting out. I can't take no more of her guff."

They took half of a little house at Miami and Delaware Streets, in the Third Ward, leaving only Grandma, Bob and Minnie in the Parsonage. Through the partition of their effects and for a week after they were gone, Minnie waited for one of the disgruntled pair to mention what they proposed to do toward helping with the support of the girls' mother. Nothing was said. There was her pension, of course. After a protracted correspondence with Washington, at Grandpa Elling's death and for months thereafter, that had finally become an item of income to be depended upon. But it wasn't much. It wouldn't keep her, without a man in the house, a man with a job. Oliver sent twenty dollars at Christmas, but Christmases were a good way apart. If it became absolutely necessary, probably he could do more. Minnie would hate to ask, but if it were necessary——

Letitia was prostrated for three days as a result of the family's disintegration. This was the last straw. She contemplated a barren future in which she would be almost wholly dependent upon the largesse of the infidel. But on the heels of peace with Spain, there came a letter from Washington, a letter which made Grandma Elling wish she had never heard the joke about Uncle Sam's Picnic. The letter was an official communication and, although addressed to her daughter, to Mrs. Theodore Knott, the old lady had opened it. She had not looked at the name on the envelope at all. Official letters from Washington were always hers—every one in the house knew that—always something about her pension. Sight of the official stamp—even the color and shape of the envelope were enough to identify the missive as hers.

All the red tape they went to about that measly pension. Thought she was one of those chits who married Grand Army men knowing they'd get that money when the veteran died. As if she hadn't put up with his quid of Sweet Burley since she was a child of sixteen.

Min found her in the McKinley rocker staring out of the parlor window with the letter in her hand while tears ran down her cheeks.

"What's the matter, Ma?"

Her mother started, turned guilty eyes toward her—then resumed her weeping with new energy. "I—I've—opened—a letter—of yours," she said between sobs, "from Washington."

"Washington—" Minnie tried to misunderstand. Tried with her heart to silence the brain that clamored the truth with a thousand cruel tongues.

"It's not—about Ted?"

The War Department was sorry, very sorry, and said so with some redundance. Typhoid—more deadly than the Spanish rifles or the native *bolos*—had taken Ted Knott.

# CHAPTER TWO
# THE BOOK OF ROBERT

## 1

D INNER was ready and waiting, fried round steak—it being
Friday. Grandma wore apron and dust-cap and the brooms
stood in the corner where she had dropped them to toughen up
the thin slice of meat against the coming of noon.

"Land! you took your good time," she greeted Minnie as they
came in the door-of-all-work through the kitchen. "I haven't
started the upstairs."

"We'll be ready in a minute. I'll do the upstairs. You can rest
all afternoon."

Bob marched toward the front of the house: "Boom, boom,
boom—boom—boom," the rattan stick of his balloon carried at
"Shoulder Arms!" and his knees held stiff as pokers.

"Don't go in that parlor, young man! I just got it swept.... How
much did *that* cost?"

"What? The balloon? ... Ten cents."

Grandma's lips hardened against each other in disapproval
but she turned to dishing up the meal without speaking.

"Come, Bob; get washed."

"Boom, boom, boom—boom—boom."

The paper labels on the enameled face of the new lavatory
reminded Minnie that the plumber had not been paid. Another

item in the long indictment of Ted. She would hear about that sooner or later. The bath and toilet in the house had been his idea, his responsibility. So had the electric lights. None of the pension money could be diverted to these uses.

"There you go, Bob." She sent him to the table with a tweak of his ear lobe.

"What's in that bag?" Grandma asked.

Bob knew. "Apetiza biscuits!"

The old lady raised astonished brows. "Apetiza biscuits!" She looked at her daughter sternly.

"Oh, Ma, they aren't expensive. He saw them on the shelf—and—asked for them."

"Suppose he asked for the moon! Would you give it to him?"

"I told him we couldn't afford them—but his little chin began to quiver and he looked so sad."

"You'll see his 'little chin quiver' a good many times before you die."

"I know that. That's why I got them."

"Why—why, *Min!*" Grandma's own chin began to tremble. "You never used to speak to me like that." The most spurious of throat-catchings, indicative of an imminent sob accompanied a few prefatory tears.

Robert Ingersoll felt very small. He would not have asked for the biscuits if he had known they'd cause a set-to. He hung his head toward the unsavory plate of overdone steak and brittle German-fried potatoes so that Mother shouldn't see that he again wanted to cry.

"*I* don't know what we're going to do.... No money coming in.... You—buying balloons and—and Apetiza biscuits." Letitia had worked up a full-grown sob by that time. She caught her breath with an effort and wiped her eyes with one corner of her apron.

"We'll get along all right, Mother. The biscuits were only ten cents too."

"That's twenty cents, just thrown away."

The two women sat down.

"We got your thread, Grandma," Bob offered the olive branch. They chewed in silence.

Minnie watched Bob sawing at the leathery beef and remembered Ted's comment. "It's no wonder good teeth are an Elling tradition, that cow you eat here every Tuesday and Friday should make you grow fangs."

"Shall Mother cut it for you?"

"Please."

That afternoon the upstairs went unswept. As Minnie dried the dishes a *bona fide* labor pain shot from the small of her back forward and down. It differed from the twinges she had been having for weeks. She recognized its import of finality. She waited an hour, to be absolutely sure, then undressed and went to bed.

Having borne Robert, she knew exactly what to expect. Yet it surprised her to learn—before morning—that it was over.

"Another Republican," Doc Smith whispered to her. "Not a blemish on him."

The question of names arose again—immediately. It required great resolution to renounce "Ted". That was what his mother really wanted to call him. But a series of tear-dampened sessions made this fatherless fellow "Harper Elling Knott". Grandma felt she owed her pastor something for the shock of that "Ingersoll". Minnie didn't see that it mattered. "Harper" didn't sound like a handicap.

The neighbors—and to this remnant of the Elling family in the old Parsonage that meant two-thirds of the population—visited Ted Knott's widow who had just given birth to an eight-pound boy. Minnie wondered why his weight was mentioned so often. She hadn't seen him weighed. She was made to know by force of myriad repetitions that: *Now* she had *two* reasons to bear the loss of her husband with fortitude. She did her best to smile at all these good people.

Her nights were endless dreams of Ted leaning over Bob— then turning to kiss her. He would never see this big boy—this eight-pound Republican.

If they would only stop talking of God and His infinite wisdom. Wasn't the inscrutability of the ways of Providence sufficiently evident? Had they all to point it out to her? At times she wanted to scream at them and claw their faces. Then she chided herself for an ingrate and again forced the weary muscles of her face to smile.

Ted's body arrived before Doc Smith would let her get out of bed. Grandma Elling took Bob to the cemetery—and there *were* "taps" and a firing squad! If you waited long enough your questions were answered without being asked. He was buried from the house.

The day before the services, Captain Schmidt, of Company K, and Doc Smith sat beside Minnie's bed and explained that the casket would not be opened. It would be unwise. Typhoid had a way—It was better not. And—since no one could see him—it would be silly for her to risk her health, jeopardize her future well-being by going downstairs so soon.

She promised to be good. The doctor knew best. But that night, when she heard the little group which was sitting up go into the kitchen to make coffee, Minnie slipped quietly into a wrapper and house-shoes and crept down the dark stairs a few at a time. She didn't mind missing the services. They would be a ghastly farce anyway, performed for Ted. But she couldn't let him go—back to the earth—back to the nothing out of which he had come laughing into her life—without saying good-by. She couldn't.

Formal, stiff, as undistinguished as any one penny in any ten or any fifty, the coffin stretched grayly across the south window. A sealed box, and she must take the word of an official paper, a form filled out a thousand miles away by a stranger, that the contents was her husband, the father of her boys, the only love of her life. They were going to put it in the ground without looking to see who was in it. And Willy Dreyer would ride in the last carriage as he did at all funerals, with his white *boutonnière* and his idiot's smile.

Minnie crossed the room carefully, painfully. They must not know she had been here. She wouldn't make a fuss. She wouldn't make them open it. She must hurry back to her bed, lest her strength fail and they find her.

She touched the ugly box with her finger tips and tried to imagine she clasped his hand. She edged along to where his head might be, and put her cheek against the rough cloth. "Good-by, Teddy," she whispered. "Are you in there—Teddy? ... Good-by." Hot tears welled from her staring eyes. She patted the container— as if it were his shoulder, then she retraced her steps, warily, and got back in bed.

## 2

TESSIE wouldn't have it said of her that she had failed her family in time of need. She and Cedric came back to the Parsonage "until Min could get around". Oliver came over from Rockford for the funeral. His wife did not accompany him. "She isn't well," he explained, "and you folks have enough to do."

Cedric gawked into Minnie's room and extended a horny hand. "I guess we can bury the hatchet at a time like this," he said. "They ain't gonna open the coffin."

"No.... Thank you for coming, Cedric."

"Oh—sure. We talked it over. It'd look funny; Tessie's your sister and all."

"I don't know what Mother would have done without you. I'm sorry it all had to happen at once."

"Oh, sure. It never rains but what it pours."

"It seems that way."

"Well—" Clumsily, he got out of the room.

It was arranged that the door at the foot of the stairs be left open so that Minnie could hear Reverend Harper's address—and the hymns. She thanked them, helplessly.

At the last moment she called Bob to her side. "You stay with Mother, Son; will you? That's going to be very unpleasant down there."

"Yes, Mama."

And when, from the rustling, the clearing of throats and the silences between, she knew the show was about to start, Minnie deliberately prodded Harper Elling Knott into screaming wakefulness—then sent Bob hurriedly to shut the downstairs door. The plan would have come off perfectly if Bill Schraeder had not been seated so close to that door. The Reverend Harper's address was well into its second paragraph. A loose boy running about, swinging on doors, seemed untoward to Bill. He stuck two thick fingers into the waistband of Bob's little pants, hooked them there and with his face utterly expressionless gave the preacher what he hoped would look like his undivided attention. Bob writhed and squirmed and wriggled. Heads turned and brows scowled. Bill took a fistful of cloth and by the openness and bland unconcern of his countenance tried to impress the critical with his innocence as a participant in the scrimmage. But Bob, intent only on performing Minnie's instructions and returning to her side, became more than one hand could hold, even if it was a hand as large as Bill's. In bringing his other arm into play, Bill turned Robert a bit too far to the right and his thrashing legs tangled with those of a folding chair. The clatter halted, temporarily, the patrio-religious eloquence of Reverend Harper. Several people rose.

Bill's hair was mussed, his necktie pulled out of his vest, yet he smiled at those about him as he set the boy on one fat knee and held him like a ventriloquist's dummy. Pop! Robert's little fist caught him squarely in the eye and Robert's treble shrilled keenly through the hushed rooms: "God damn you; my mama wants me upstairs!"

And Bill's worst fears were proved well-founded, a few days later, when gossip brought the story wafting back to him. " ... and Reverend Harper was delivering the most beautiful address when Bill Schraeder started tormenting the boy ..."

Bill owned the Mission Café, Freeport's only restaurant of consequence, and he lived halfway down the block east of the Parsonage. Each of his fingers was as thick as Bob's wrist, and his body was mountainous in proportion. Considerably older than Minnie, he had nevertheless set his cap for her just after she left school. Who hadn't? In all the wide Elling acquaintance there was never a male who approximated eligibility who had not ventured part of the way toward proposing to Minnie.

The list was long, unexciting and predominantly Teutonic. It would be all three, in Freeport. *Long* because the supply of pretty girls who were also slim was always limited; *unexciting* because, outside of a few brakemen on the Chicago run of the I. C., none of the local blades had imagination enough to invent more than one way to kiss; *Teutonic* because you had to be German to vote—in Freeport.

Now, one at a time, those who had contracted no families in the interim, looked again at Minnie's big brown eyes. They had called her "Saucers" in school. Bill stopped in, two days after the funeral. "Hello, Mrs. Elling; how's that Minnie?"

"Oh,—it's Mr. Schraeder." Success, even in a neighbor boy, awed Grandma. And Tessie, standing behind her, felt her hair with repairing fingers, and smirked, "Good-evening, Mr. Schraeder."

"'Lo, Tessie. How's the new baby?"

"Oh, they're both doing fine. Would you like to go up?"

"I would…. Ha! I want Minnie to see my shiner."

"Oh, Mr. Schraeder, we were *so* sorry about that."

"Awph—my own fault. You didn't mention it to *her*, did you?"

"Oh, she knew it."

"Yes," said Letitia grimly. "She knew it…. So far, she ain't done a thing about it."

"Well, what do you want her to do?"

"Well, none of my children was ever allowed to use language like that—under *no* circumstances."

Bill grinned—a Gargantuan grin. "Where is she?"

"Right upstairs. You show him, Tessie…. I hope you won't look at the way the house looks. We ain't had time to give it more than a lick an' a promise for days."

"Bosh!" He followed Tessie. "You better ask her if it's all right."

"Oh, it's all right, Mr. Schraeder."

"*You see.*"

"Yes, sir…. Mr. Schraeder's here, Min."

"Oh, tell him to come in…. Hello, Bill."

"God! just look at you." He towered over her, his eyes filling with details to increase his desire.

Minnie smiled without knowing that the only way to describe its one-sidedness, its charm and color and effect would be to call it "bewitching". This big man's frank worship fed hungry roots of her being. As Tessie fluttered out, mumbling an embarrassed nothing, Minnie's ears repeated: "God! just look at you." … "God! just look at you." This was like old times.

"What's the matter with me? Anyway, I haven't got a black eye."

"Say! He's got spunk!"

Minnie nodded. "He's Ted's boy."

"Yours too. You've got plenty."

"I don't need it."

"I don't know.... Maybe you will, now. It's none of my business, Minnie, but—eh—what—what do you plan to do? Ted—eh—Ted never struck me as—well—did he—did he have much insurance?"

"Not a penny. He didn't leave me a thing, Bill; nothing but memories—and better wits than I had before. He taught me to live."

"And two boys."

"Yes. Two boys."

"Well, I just wanted to tell you—you can call on me. I've got enough for my needs and then some. There wouldn't be any strings attached to it. Any time—"

"Thanks, Bill."

"Well, I don't want to tire you.... Is that the new one?" A trundle-bed stood a foot from hers.

"Yes. Like to see him?"

"Would I?!"

"Just lift that corner.... Nothing much to look at, is he?"

"They're all kinda like that; ain't they?"

"Ted used to say Bob had an 'indeterminate' look as a small baby."

Bill was polite. "Ha, ha. That's good. Ha."

"They take shape a little later."

"Yeah. Look at the shape *I* took!"

"There's lots of you, Bill."

"Plenty."

"You ought to get out of the restaurant, you get bigger every day."

"That ain't the restaurant. That's from eating around in people's houses. When you gonna bake me another pie?"

"Just as soon as I'm up.... That's all right. You can leave his face out."

"That's a promise, Min. I'll be waiting. Next week some time, maybe?"

"Yes, sir."

"Good!" He saw that she was tired. "I'll run along now. Hurry and get well."

"Oh, I'm all right."

"Well—so long."

"So long, Bill."

"Anything I can bring you?"

"No, I don't think so."

"I'll send you a posy."

She smiled. It would be a great deal better if such good intentions could be used to pay the milk bill.

## 3

CHARLIE MARTIN resumed *his* courtship where it had been dropped at her wedding, the second day she was out of bed. He called in the evening with his Buick—a brilliant red one built high in back with a single door in the middle of the rear, reached by two steps. He could not conceal his surprise when she called Bob to accompany them. Why! She was a *widow*.

Robert Ingersoll started to school that winter. One basement room of the high school building was a First Grade, so he had not far to go. Minnie had taught him to read and he could tell better stories than the teacher. He wrote his name, the names of all the members of the family—including all the forebears Grandma Elling could remember, the alphabet and certain common sentences—before he started pasting and weaving colored paper in class. He wrote: *How are you? Bob is a good boy. Mother is thank you*—with fair legibility.

In the schoolroom he learned nothing. In the schoolyard he learned a fascinating law of physics through a painful experience. An iron pipe was threaded through a series of wooden posts, for hitching. At recess on the first cold day of the year, he was dared to lick this pipe with his tongue. A Knott, it developed, never took a dare. He left a goodly area of Knott tongue adhering to the metal. This, it seemed, was not only science; it was also sport. The little inquisitors screamed their delight.

It was, perhaps, characteristic of Robert that he reached the hitching rail ahead of any one else the next morning and conducted a series of experiments. After practically ruining his tongue, he found that his own warm breath would loosen the frost-clamped flesh without pain or damage if he resisted the first impulse to jerk away. Thereafter he enjoyed the distinction of being one of the few who could perform the rite without injury. A very real distinction in that place; in all essentials a feat of magic.

In a dark hallway after dismissal he learned the exterior structural difference of the sexes from a curious baby wanton who offered to show him hers if he would show her his. Bob attached no importance whatever to his findings in this department.

In three months he moved through as many grades and before the end of the semester he was taking examinations that would, if passed, admit him to the Fourth. These new grades were in the Third Ward school, five blocks away and through a square park wherein was a fountain. His school life was an unconvincing dream. He was scarcely conscious of what went on about him and he made few friends. He was hooted as a teacher's pet because, while his fellows were studying their reading, he was posted before them all, next to the teacher, *to tell the others what the hard words meant!*

His memory was uncanny. He never needed to study. When his books were bought at the beginning of the school year, he read them through, then scarcely opened them again. He talked and read with Minnie at night and dreamed the day away in the schoolroom. Arithmetic became his favorite subject, which increased the amazement of all the adults privy to the details of his training. "What," they asked, each with his own inflection, "next?"

What next?

Her course was so esoteric that it was impossible to divulge its aim or its details to any one. The adumbrations which became visible brought nothing but criticism. She was wrong to make this boy into a monstrosity. It was unnatural (they meant immoral) and immoral (they meant precocious or premature). Minnie talked gayly to Ted's picture after each new manifestation of progress with Bob and its concomitant denunciation from a relative or a neighbor. The mere fact that they condemned an act would have made Ted favor it enthusiastically. She was succeeding—alone. What she and he had planned for their first-born was materializing. Bob would become a reasonable individual—a person who never uttered banalities, never thought in a groove—a mental giant, modest withal, since the basis of his wisdom was to be a ready confession of ignorance.

Thus Minnie and Bob were drawn closer and closer together. Neither had any other confidant. They lived for each other, each in the other, in a large sense each creating the other. A psychic affinity grew between them, so harmonious, so refined, that they seldom spoke together in the presence of others, but communicated every nuance of thought by delicate gesture and subtle movement or sound. It was as if an individual had halved himself, yet remained one; as if one mind walked about in two bodies. And this drove the suitors away. It was disconcerting to those ardent beaux to learn that their advances, although made to an individual of the opposite sex, had been noted, and recorded with amusement, by a child as male as they.

While Bob astounded his teachers in the lower grades and gave them ready argument—the small savings of Ted and Minnie dwindled and were gone. Credit was easily obtained, but the mounting bills worried Minnie and she cast about for an income.

Harper was an expensive baby. He burned his hands, had colic and croup, cut his head, and broke out in a rash at the slightest pretext. Doc Smith called no less than twice a week, and although he never sent a bill—there it was to be paid. Diets were ordered for mother and child, and it is so expensive to cook a little dab of something special for one person. When he was eight months old and could be left in the care of the aging Letitia, Min called on Bill Schraeder.

"*You*; a pastry cook! ... You better marry me, Min, and forget about working.... I could send the boy to college, when the time comes." Bill had said that hopefully. He knew that the shortest route to this woman's heart lay through Bob—and probably through Bob's education. At the beginning of the twentieth century, it was still a popular fallacy that colleges educated those who attended. "Contact" was a synonym for "collide".

She took hold of one big paw. "I'll put it this way, Bill, and it's really final: I won't marry any other Freeporter. If I marry any one in town—it will be you."

"That's a peck o' consolation."

"It's the best I can do."

"You got it in for us small-towners. You figure all Chicagoans are like Ted."

"No, I don't."

"Well, don't; because they're not. You got a good one. You were lucky;—but, gosh, Min, another one'd turn out just as wrong as he did right."

"I don't intend to marry any one, Bill.... Will you let me go to work?"

So to Grandma Elling's pension was added a sizeable salary—for a woman, for Freeport—and the doctor began to receive a regular pittance, the plumber and the electrician the same. A new roof was ordered for the house, and new clothing was bought for the growing Bob.

With Harper weaned and beginning to jabber—out of diapers early, as was Grandma Elling's practice—Bob getting on with long division and developing, outside of school, exactly the sort of logical mind they had planned he should, Minnie breathed more easily. If things could be kept going smoothly, the debts kept down and every one in good health until Bob was graduated from high school, her troubles would be over; she would not have to marry.

She was so fair. She detested the idea of contracting a husband solely to be supported. The only difference between that and selling herself on the street was the monotony of having but a single customer. Her body urged its health upon her consciousness, at times almost demanding its complement. But marriage for physical gratification alone seemed shameful to this Minnie who had loved and had been loved. She had no heart to offer, and that, she felt, made an honorable alliance impossible. So long as the pressure of a man's hand, proximity to a man's body, served only to remind her of Ted, she could develop in herself no desire for any sort of intimacy with any of them, not even with big Bill who was so like a Collie or a Saint Bernard in disposition that one forgot there was enough of him to make two men.

Until Bob had outgrown her, had attained the special degree of maturity they had determined should set him apart from his fellows, Minnie would not admit an outsider to their lives. They were two; that was enough. Their years would flow smoothly, side by side, like an unhurried river and—say—a canal, cut approximately parallel.

Those plans had been made so sincerely, so wholeheartedly, so entirely without reservations, that Ted's death was but a distressing incident, in no way affecting the vital necessity of achieving their aim. Renouncing the marriage bed and adding the rôle of untiring and tireless special-tutor to that of mother was less a matter of "keeping faith" with either or both of her two men than it was a fulfilling of a self-imposed destiny, determined upon with a companion, but independent of him. "This shall be my life," she had said, before Robert Ingersoll had been born, embracing the prospect with all its unseen, unknown and unpredictable ramifications, eagerly, and without recapitulation. Thus the demands of their dream became as inexorable as the demand of her lungs for air—and almost as little noticed.

If there had been, in Freeport, a presentable young man possessed of sufficient insight to penetrate the psychology of this obsession, equipped also with a desire for Minnie, a little energy and a spark of inventiveness or the ability to dissemble, the history of the Knotts, *mère et fils*, might—could easily—have been very different. None appeared. Life, for Minnie, became one damn' pie after another.

## 4

UNTIL Robert Ingersoll was seven, that he was "too young to get anything out of it" had served as sufficient excuse for the omission of Sunday School from the routine of his life. To an unbiased observer, leaving Sunday School out of the boy's training may appear to have been no more than noninclusion. It would seem, perhaps, to such an hypothetical observer, that here was a new life, a new individual—and that the inclusion or exclusion of any number of the elements which have made other lives, other individuals, would be subject to the intelligence or, at least, to the decisions of those who passed upon his diet. "Excuse?" such an one might think to ask, "But why?"

There were no unbiased observers within ten miles of Trinity Corner. Not sending the boy to Sunday School was *neglecting* to send him. It was a grave omission, much the same as denying him milk.

Grandma Elling grew restive under the critical inflection of her neighbors' observations that: "Robert isn't being sent to Sunday School yet; is he?" One Sunday morning in his eighth summer she was to be put off no longer.

"It's all right,—you not going to church,—though Cecilia would be glad to run in of a Sunday morning to mind the baby, but the boy is growing up a heathen.... Reverend Harper asked me only last Sunday if Robert was getting the proper spiritual guidance.... Made me feel like a fool. I tell you, Min, it's been put off and put off.... It's high time he started."

Minnie had not expected to have to talk about that just then. It was a glorious day and she had slept uncommonly well. There was just a quantum of take-the-bull-by-the-horns in her mood. "I don't think he needs it. I want him with me," she was astonished to hear herself say.

"Not need it?! Don't need to know about his Maker? Don't need to know the word of God? Why, Min why—why, Min!"

Bob stood comparing the triple chin of his grandmother with his mother's firm, young throat. How Grandma's chins wiggled when she was angry!

"I think he knows those stories, Mother. He's read them."

"*Stories!*"

"Do you want to go to Sunday School, Bob?"

"He should be *made* to go. You were."

"Wouldn't it be better to have him want to go?"

"No child wants to go."

"How about it, Bob?"

"Will you go too?"

Minnie laughed. "I'm too old."

Letitia snorted. "Oh, you make me sick. The very idea of askin' him if he *wants* to go. You know what's good for him and he don't. What kind of a man will he grow up to be without the influence of the church? Min, I can't understand you ... a good Christian girl like you—brought up in a good, Christian home.... People are talking. What *has* got into you?"

From seven metal throats the call to worship was sounding. Embury joined the ensemble.

"You'll be late, Mother."

Grandma Elling left the house, drying her tears. Her black taffeta furbelows jounced as she walked the few short steps to the church next door. This was her reward. This was the fruit of all her care, all her loving kindness through the years. Her own daughter had turned against her. Her own daughter had forsaken the church.

One by one the bells ceased, and late comers hurried to unostentatious seats in rear pews. Organ notes drifted through stained-glass windows and an holy, somnolent peace settled over the deserted streets.

Minnie wrapped the last of the sandwiches. "Where shall we go to-day, Son?"

"Yellow Creek?"

"All rightie."

A rig, arranged for at the livery stable the day before, drew up at the side of the house. Harper and a few books were put on the seat between Bob and his mother and the bay mare, of considerable age, drew them at a joggy pace past wide lawns and fresh-looking frame houses.

Before the gasoline era, every seventh day was Sunday in Freeport. And when it got to be that, everything else turned in to help.

The drone of a minister's voice with its drawling undulations, its sing-song rise and fall—those inflections unique in all oratory, peculiar to the pulpit alone—chanted its way through open church windows. That was the only sound save the more or less even clop of their horse's feet on the macadam. They were the only humans abroad. The maples and elms arching and meeting overhead would wait until Monday to rustle. The local birds had taken themselves without the city limits for the day. One little white heathen, a "cabbage" butterfly, swooped and fluttered in its personal version of flight, toward them and away. Even the sun's work seemed to be effortless and the pale yellow light that dappled the street and the houses had filtered through the trees quietly and without jostling.

"Then mochaderangoforintee. We fulltramaguskrumawdernolis—trafawzonfawzonfawzonoh." The minister.

"Mother,—he's not *saying* anything. He's just making a noise."

And Minnie's heart was glad. What was the man saying? Did he know? In the beginning there was The Word. Logos. She glanced at the books the boy had picked for the excursion. A life of Isaac Newton, Bullfinch's *Age of Fable*, Donnelly's *Atlantis*. Ted's library was the product of a catholic taste.

Harper pulled his brother's hair and gouged at his eyes. "Look, Mother, he doesn't understand eyes yet. See—he wants to take hold of mine."

Under lazy willow branches on the bank of Yellow Creek they ate sandwiches and read their books.

"Gee, it's a good thing Grandma doesn't know this book's in the house."

"Why, Son?"

"Well, it says the sinking of Atlantis probably started the legend of the deluge. Grandma doesn't think Noah was a legend."

"What do you think?"

"I don't know; it says they've found a lot of relics and things."

"But you don't absolutely believe it, eh, Son?"

"You're trying to catch me. Of course, I don't. One must always reserve judgment. Oh, I know."

"You're a good boy—give me one of the peanut butter—"

They ate in silence and watched the water.

"Gee, I—"

"Yes?"

"Nothing."

"Nothing?"

"There's some peanut butter on your chin."

"Thanks ... You said—-"

"Aw, I was thinking about Dad. He was lots of fun."

Her old one-sided smile. "Yes, he was."

"I think wars are rotten.... I had to stay after Thursday b'cause I wouldn't salute the flag."

"What? ... And you waited until Sunday to tell me?"

"Well, there's no sense to it. It's just like that preacher. Look,—the whole class gets up and puts their hands on their head and heart and everything and says this 'salute' and they don't think what they're saying or why or anything. They just mumble sounds. They only do it because Miss O'Connor tells 'em to; and I couldn't. And they all hurry and say it as quick as they can so they can sit down."

"Catch Harper, he'll roll in the creek."

"Stay up here, fatty."

"Tell me about it. What did you say?"

"I got up—like the rest, but I didn't move my hand around and I didn't say anything. Miss O'Connor saw me and said, 'Robert, don't you know the salute?' and I said, 'Yes, ma'am', and she said, 'Why don't you repeat it then?' and I said, 'I wouldn't give my heart and my head and my hands for *any* flag.' And she said, 'Where have you learned this sedition?' and I said I didn't know what 'sedition' was but I'd look it up in the dictionary and then tell her and she said, 'Now don't get smart!' and I didn't mean to be smart at all and I said, 'May I talk this over with you some other time?' and she got red as paint and said, 'There's nothing to talk over. Repeat the salute as I bade you,' and I wouldn't. So I had to stay after and all the kids call me a rebel."

"And after school?"

"She came up to my desk and said, 'Well, young man, what have you to say for yourself?' and I said, 'Nothing.' Then she said, "What did you mean by that display of insubordination?' and I said, 'I asked you to talk it over with me, but you wouldn't'—then she got all red again and angry as the dickens. Why do people get so angry when you want to talk things over, Mother? She couldn't be calm and talk—she just had to have her way."

"Teachers and parents don't usually talk things over with children, Bob. Somehow they figure that your young ideas don't count. You see, Miss O'Connor would have her hands full if she had to discuss everything with each of her pupils separately."

"I never heard any of them ask her to."

"What else?"

"Well, she wouldn't talk about it, she made me write the salute fifty times before I could get out. But that wasn't the same as saying it and I didn't mean it anyway. Then I gave her the paper and she said: 'I hope this has been a lesson to you,' and I said, 'I don't think it has taught me anything,' and then she got out of her chair and I thought sure I was gonna get it. But she said, 'Robert Knott, you are a disgrace to your country, to your father who died for his country, to your home and to your flag. You may report to the principal the first thing in the morning.'

"I tried to tell her it was on account of Dad that I wouldn't salute her old flag—but she said, 'Not another word! Report to Dr. Barbour in the morning.' So I did."

Harper was attempting to dissect a brown and yellow caterpillar. The experiment was stopped.

"Dr. Barbour was more reasonable. He said we shouldn't be bitter about Dad, that we should be proud of him, even if he did die of typhoid instead of getting shot.

"I didn't say anything, Mother, I just looked at him—and he couldn't look at me. Pretty soon he said, 'I know it's hard. But you must learn the meaning of patriotism. I'll try to talk this over with your mother at the first opportunity. '

"Then he gave me a book to read. Hale's *A Man Without a Country*."

"Did you read it?"

"Sure.... But it didn't mean anything. It was all one-sided—their side. If you'll let me, I'd like to take Liebknecht to him Monday and ask him to read that."

Minnie chuckled and shook her head.

"That wouldn't do, Bob. You'd just make them hate you. Here's what you must do, I think. When these things come up—bow to their authority. They have a hard job, these teachers. Most of them do the best they can. School isn't the place for you, but I can't teach you myself. I haven't the academic background and I haven't the time. They have much to give you—mathematics, geography, physics. If they mix a lot of biased history and jingo patriotism with it, we have to expect that. They are making citizens—heroes to die in future wars just as Dad did. We can't get away from it, Bob. Wherever we might go it would be the same. You'll always have to bow to their rules—outwardly, and be glad as you can be that they can't read your mind.

"I never could understand why more Jews and Greeks and Protestants didn't profess the faith of their inquisitors and save their skins. It seems so much simpler. But I suppose a great many did do that, only that kind of people don't make history. It's martyrs and heroes that we hear about in history—not the men and women who baked the bread.

"So, I believe I'd do whatever they say, Bob. Salute the flag and all the rest of it. You may even have to go to Sunday School to please Grandma. Would you mind?"

"No, I guess not. Couldn't you go too?"

"I could. It would be pretty hard. Their sanctimonious faces make me forget to be reasonable. I get to hating them—too actively."

"And Grandma?"

"Somehow it's easier to make allowances for those we love, Bob. It's her training. But then, it was *their* training. It was mine.... Wouldn't you think they'd outgrow it?"

"Maybe they are just pretending—like I will be when I salute the flag."

"I used to think that, Bob. Now and then we find a few who are just pretending. Just sending their shells to church—but not many. No. I've talked to lots and lots of them and most all of them believe.... Some of them who aren't quite sure of themselves, act as if they believed to be on the safe side. They try to fool their own God. That's funny, isn't it?"

"When I'm grown up I won't have to pretend any more; will I? I'll pretend to be patriotic and everything now—until I'm through school, and I'll go to Sunday School until Grandma's taken—but I won't always have to pretend, will I? When I'm big and educated I can say just what I think—can't I?"

"Maybe.... Mother's grown, but she doesn't say what she wants to—except to you."

"But aren't there any people like us anywhere?"

"A few thousand, Son, but they're scattered all over the world. They're hampered and held back by economic conditions and family ties. No more than two or three of them ever get together at one time—and most of them go insane."

"Gee, I wish I was grown up."

So the willows that dipped their leaves in the swift waters of the creek were treated to such words as have seldom, if ever before, passed between mother and son. Each Sunday the little picnic was planned and the country around Freeport was explored. Rain seldom deterred them. They left the baby in Grandma Elling's care when the weather was too bad.

# CHAPTER THREE
# THE BOOK OF HEK

1

In Harper, Grandma Elling saw her opportunity. In him she would instill a righteous heart, and a proper fear of God. Minnie had cheated her with Robert, beginning with his name. In this later case the older woman already had that advantage.

Before he could pronounce the word "umbrella", Harper Elling Knott lisped his way through the Apostle's Creed and the Twenty-third Psalm. Letitia had everything her own way. Save for callers, she was alone in the house with him all day. Minnie maintained a meticulous schedule at the Mission Café further to secure her independence of Bill Schraeder. No hint of scandal could be breathed against her while she delivered honest toil at regular hours for her salary. Arriving late and leaving early, as she might so easily have done, as, in fact, Bill urged her to do, would have made her a "privileged character" to the other employees. They'd have said it with acid voices and a leer of nasty knowing.

Bob ran to the hot kitchen door straight from school. The doughnuts for the next breakfast would be bobbing in the great kettle of grease—and the holes were his—as many as he could eat—almost always *a*great many. He seldom failed to note with an ill-hid satisfaction that his mother left all the things for other, meaner souls to clean up. At home they did the pans and dishes themselves, but here Minnie was a superior being. A man in a grievously soiled and often soaking white apron stood alert and obsequious, waiting for her to lay down the long-pronged fork for the day. This brute never failed to say: "Y'all through, Miz Minnie?" Then they would walk home, hand in hand, leaving all the succulent and delicious *restaurant* food, to partake, some two hours later, of what Grandma called "a real, home-cooked meal".

As they plied their "case-knives" on plates of this home-cooking one evening, unusual sounds came from the high chair between burbles of porridge. "A Lorsa my shedder—Isa wan—" Bob politely stopped eating and looked from the baby to his mother and back again. Minnie smiled and patted a ringlet back from Harper's forehead. "What did he say?" Bob asked.

"I'm not sure," Minnie smiled. "I think it might be a poem."

"He said," Grandma Elling volunteered with hauteur, " 'The Lord is my Shepherd, I shall not want.'"

"Oh, did he?"

"It sounded very plain to me. Go on, Harper, say more."

But Harper only banged with his spoon. The performance for that evening had been concluded.

When Grandma had retired to her McKinley rocker and the table was being cleared, Robert stood before his mother with blazing eyes. "*She's* taught him that!" he whispered fiercely. "She's warping his infantile intelligence!"

Moments such as these were difficult for Minnie. She dared not laugh. No matter how ludicrous his precocities, they were of her making. Bob was sensitive, and one laugh at his baby indignation might never be explained away. She choked, now, and hastily seized the slim excuse for a reprimand to cover her agitation. "You must not refer to Grandma as 'she', Robert. It's disrespectful. Always say 'Grandma'. Do you understand?"

"Yes, ma'am," he wilted…. "But—isn't Grandma?"

The crisis seemed to have passed. She laughed. "I don't think it's serious, Son."

"It might be if we don't stop her."

"He'll be all right. Why, he doesn't know what he's saying—and the minute he begins to think about things we can straighten him out; can't we?"

"He'll be handicapped."

"I wonder … I wonder if it isn't better to let him grow up and become a pillar of the church—an usher, maybe—and marry some nice girl here…. What do you think? Wouldn't he be happier?"

"No!"

"We aren't happy, Bob. You and I can't be happy—looking at things as we do, seeing the hopelessness of all the misery and ignorance about us. Isn't it better for him to be happy, to have a God to blame everything upon,—a God to ask for help in time of affliction?"

This was a little thick going even for Robert Ingersoll. He dried several plates, absorbed in study of her words.

Letitia came to the door. "I'll put the baby to bed, Min," she announced. "Come along, Grandma's little man."

Between the stifled clatters of the dishes they washed snatches of babble came to them from upstairs.

"Listen!" said Bob.

"… If I should die before I wake, I pray the Lord my soul to take."

Minnie dried her hands and held them, one on either cheek, of the young materialist. "Combating that would cause endless arguments, Son … We don't want that. It isn't pleasant to live in a continuous state of bickering."

"You didn't let her teach *me* those things."

"Ted was here then, Bob. When you were his age, there were other people in the house. There were many other things to fight about. Everything was different then."

"It isn't right," he grumbled, and for the next following four years he continued to grumble as Grandma Elling's dominance of the youngest Knott became more and more complete, more and more objectionable.

When Harper flourished his first pocket knife and threatened to cut off the ears of the little girl who came to visit next door, Grandma did not nurture the shock and hoard up her tears against Minnie's homecoming as she always had done when Bob had sinned. She forgave him readily and did not even deprive him of the knife.

When he begged to be allowed to go, *at four in the morning!*, with Mr. Carpenter to watch the circus unload, Grandma was on his side. When the ice went out, after midnight, and Harper had sneaked off to watch it, Grandma not only went to help find him but waited, in awe of the spectacle herself, waited and watched the huge cakes rear high in the air and crash back on the muddy bosom of the Pecatonica. For a while it looked as if Stephenson Street Bridge might go. The flood waters swept over it, across the car tracks, and the ice jammed hard and fast against the piles, span and rail.

Bob and Minnie tired and went home, but Harper and Grandma waited to see them blast the ice with dynamite to preserve the bridge. On their way home, later than Grandma Elling had ever been abroad before in her whole life, she warned Harper about the Pecatonica. Each year it claimed one Freeport boy, each year without fail. It usually turned out to be a boy who went swimming or fishing on Sunday; that was true, but sometimes it made a mistake. He must be very careful. The river was deep and treacherous, having a powerful and malicious undertow.

## 2

As far back as either of the boys could remember, there had hung on a nail in the front-door casing, an enormous brass key which was more untouchable than any of the shells or rocks or wax flowers under glass on the what-not, more dread even than the bottle of water from the river Jordan. This was the key to the Fire Alarm on the corner and it had been the sacred charge of the Ellings ever since they first moved into the Parsonage. It must never be moved from that nail, not ever. Yet, when Harper had measles, Grandma, with her own hands, had taken it down for him to play with. It had been put back at once, the very minute the quarantine sign was taken from the door—and how often Letitia thanked her lucky stars she had put it back just when she did.

The very next Sunday, the coldest day in the history of the local Weather Bureau, the Presbyterian Church caught fire. The sexton, overzealous for the comfort of his fellow Presbyters, had negotiated a miniature hell in the furnace. Shortly after eight o'clock, the overheated flue touched off the old, dry wood around it—and the show was on. Finding the great brass key and turning in the alarm had no effect on the flames whatever. They spread in great crackling sheets and billows, gutting the edifice and bursting the stained-glass windows in spectacular showers of lambs and Christs and Good Samaritans, piecemeal.

As the excitement subsided, late that afternoon, Harper thought of a puzzling question. "Grandma."

"Yes?"

"Why did God let His own house burn down? Because they were Presbyterians?"

Minnie raised one eyebrow so Bob could see.

For weeks the ruin of the church was the favorite playground of Harper and his friends, the chief attraction being the melted and broken colored glass.

## 3

NICKEL shows came to Freeport. Between terrific chasing of Indians and still more terrific gallops of *The Night Riders* there were illustrated songs. At the Superba one heard *Daisies Won't Tell, Dear!* and *The Holy City* sung by a baritone who sometimes forgot the words. There were ice-cream socials on the Embury lawn—between the church and the *new* parsonage. At these festivals, a young sprout Harper's size always got more than his share of pink ice-cream, being plied with it by pretty girls who found him a tension-breaker as they sat with their stiffly upright escorts. "That's little Harper Knott. Isn't he just too sweet? … Come here, Harper.… Would you like a dish of ice-cream?"

Two or three times a week a dramatic show came to the Grand Opera House on Galena Street and played to capacity audiences. With a population of less than eighteen thousand, Freeport was known as a "better show-town" than Rockford. The group of natives which served Freeport for an upper crust attended these performances to a man, but the real money came from the I. C. shop employees, molders and machinists from Stovers', Woodmanse's and the Moline Plow Company, the painters and woodworkers from the Henney Buggy Company, employees of the medicine factory, the brewers and the farmers. Freeport was a live town. There were nearly as many breweries as churches. Saloons were everywhere. Besides the nickel shows and the Grand Opera House there were the *Bijou* and the *Orpheum*, in which vaudeville could be seen, *and there was Germania Hall!*

Another periodic entertainment was "local option" agitation, but not even the drys took it seriously, they were so hope-
lessly in the minority in a town built and controlled by jovial
Germans. B & O beer was famous. Vast quantities of it in kegs
were shipped to Chicago, and the bottled variety was drunk all
over the world. The coal man—Hill—gave bags of candy, fruit
and jumping-jacks every Christmas morning to every child who
applied. The Knott boys were forbidden to join the line, since that
gratuity was "for the poor".

Raleigh, the "patent medicine and sheep-dip man", was
elected mayor, and tiny enameled pins the shape of hatchets were
displayed in jewelers' windows with "Carrie A. Nation" lettered
on them in gold. Huh! She better not come to Freeport! She'd
sure get all that was coming to her.

*The* Teddy, of course, was President, but the sting had gone
from the name. Minnie's Teddy was only a dream now, a dream
of six exquisite years that had embodied a lifetime.

Cedric, quite suddenly, developed a ranching uncle in
Wyoming—and joined him there, dragging Tessie with him.
"Dragging", that is, as one drags a boy to fire-crackers or a kitten to cream. It was pitiful to see how much she wanted to leave
Freeport, no matter what her destination might be. She tried to
hide it, of course, crying and making a fuss about knowing no
one there, leaving her friends and family behind! But it almost
killed her to come back, two years later, when Cedric's uncle hack
had enough of him.

*The* Teddy was President: *Perdicarus alive or Raisuli
dead!* The Big Stick. No race suicide. The Trusts. The twentieth
century entered its second decade.

Harper Knott came home from school with three front teeth
missing. Grandma Elling, after some preliminary questioning,
learned that the grandson of another Civil War veteran had

called the Spanish-American War "Uncle Sam's Picnic", declaring it but a mild fracas—really no proper war at all. Harper had resented that, declaring also that the Chicago Cubs was a far better ball team than the White Sox of the same city. Whether Harper knew his adversary's baseball leanings before the battle or not, he learned them then.

"But yotta see him, Grandma. I gave 'im a dirty one in the eye.... They are a better ball team, ain't they, Gramma? An' it wasn't a picnic either, was it?"

Grandma Elling remembered the phrase. "It wasn't no picnic, Harper; you bet it wasn't. They seen lots o' fightin' and your father was one o' the bravest.... Don't you let none o' them smart kids run over you." Ted Knott came nearer to a posthumous initiation into the Elling clan with every breath his second son drew. Seldom if ever before had a child played parent to an adult with such marked success. From a whining and cantankerous despot of the Christ-like-humility school, Letitia Elling changed completely as the development of Harper absorbed her more fully and ever more fully. She displayed Harper's scars proudly to his mother and Bob when they came home that night.

Bob, deliberate and mature, his face already lined beyond his years, looked down at his young brother and asked, "What made you fight, Harper, the remark about war or the baseball business?"

"Well, he had no business sayin' it. I guess my father wouldn't go to no—to any picnic war. And I bet he was a better ball player than his old man too."

"But which thing were you fighting about?"

"Well, gee, he said he could lick me anyway."

Bob shrugged and the horizontal ridges in his forehead deepened. "It seems to have been a matter of general principles."

"Gosh all Friday, didn't *you* ever fight? I guess you'd fight too, gosh.... Pa was a good ball player, wasn't he, Ma?"

"I don't remember. Maybe he was."

"Didn't you ever fight?"—turning on Bob.

"I don't remember fighting—ever. Maybe I did."

"Huh, seems to me you'd remember if you ever did. You ain't—aren't so old. You're only six years older'n me. I guess you'd remember.... Sam Keller's brother is a pug.... What are you gonna be? He's only twenty.... You're old enough to train. If you want to be a pug you gotta train early."

Their mother interposed. "Would you want your brother to be a prize fighter?"

"Huh, fat chance! That old stick-in-the-mud. He's a greasy grind.... Teacher's pet. He walks all the way up the street with a high school teacher—with glasses.... Naaaah—walked home with a teacher with glasses."

"Hush, Son; what have the glasses to do with it? And what is a 'greasy grind'?"

"A nut that studies all the time.... Always readin'. Some fat chance of him bein' a pug ..." contemptuously—"him! ... You know what they call me now?"

"Prize fighting is not Christian, Harper." Even Grandma Elling opposed her favorite's choice of occupations for his brother.

"No; what do they call you?" Bob asked.

"They call me by my initials."

"By your initials."

"Yeah, 'Hek'; see? Harper Elling Knott. If your initials make a word like that it's a sign you're gonna be rich."

"Is that so? And what word do yours spell?"

"Hek, like 'Where the heck you going?' See?"

"I see."

"Well, is there anything wrong with that? I wish you'd call me Hek at home too. Harper's a goofy name."

"Why, Grandma gave you that name, Harper," said Grandma.

"Ooh … Well, it's too much like a Sunday name. Hek's good enough for school." He looked at her sidewise, apologetically.

After supper Bob took his schoolbooks upstairs to the spare room Ted had shelved for his library. He was taking the "Scientific Course"—concentrating on mathematics. His senior year in high school would begin in a few months. After that he hoped to go to college, if his help were not needed at home.

Minnie was not sure. "Ted used to say he spent the first two years out of Northwestern, unlearning all the dogma they'd tried to teach him. Maybe it's different now. Do you want to go very much?"

"I think so, Mother. Mr. Andrews, my trig teacher, says I'll get a lot out of it. He thinks as we do about most things too."

"Well, that's a year yet. Maybe we can arrange it. If you still want to go when you're graduated—I'll help you. Is that a bargain?"

"You're a peach."

## 4

HARPER could be heard yelling some catch-phrase that was part of his game with the other boys on the corner. Grandma and Minnie sewed in the parlor.

"Patty Shirtleff was in to-day."

"Yes?"

"Her brother sold his eighty acres near Cherry Valley to the shoe man,—Carson."

"Yes?"

"Turned a nice profit too. Sometimes I wisht Elling hadn't give up that piece we had in Wisconsin.... Land is a terrible good investment—to hang on to."

"Yes, real estate is a good thing."

"Half a section, it was. Right good land.... I remember when we moved onto it. I was carrying you.... Mostly prairie—a little timber. We put up a cabin,—me helpin', sick as I was. We had two horses, a yoke of oxen and a Jersey for milk.... Them were winters! I ain't seen the like since you've had your growth. Don't you remember none of it?"

"Very little, Mother."

"An' I used to give the Indians a dime—to go away.... Oh, there; I 'most forgot. I ain't filled in my pledge card yet .... They're goin' to rebuild Embury——"

"Yes? They've been talking about that for some time, haven't they?"

"Yes, but they's been a faction that's held out to finish payin' for the organ before they started the new church. Reverend Harper has persuaded them, though, and it looks like we'd have the new building after all.... I got a pledge card but I thought I'd ought to talk it over with you before I signed it."

"Well, Mother, what do you think? What are others giving?"

"Well, they all give as they can. Those that have it gives freely and all others in proportion. I hadn't set on no definite figure.... You support this home,—don't think I lose sight o' that. There's my pension, but it ain't much, an' you work hard—what with the two boys and all—"

"Would a hundred dollars be enough?"

"Why, Lord bless you child—I hadn't thought of any such sum.... Why, Minnie, we can't ... A hundred—"

"We won't have to pay it all at once, will we?"

"No, no;—and none of it right away. It's only a pledge—to be taken up within a period of time—I forget how long."

"Put down a hundred then. We can put it by, a little now and a little then."

Again the old lady's eyes filled with tears as she rocked and attempted to sew. She had hardly known how Minnie would take this. The pledge card had been hidden two weeks, waiting for the most auspicious moment to discuss it. One hundred dollars—from Minnie to the church! It must mean a return to grace! Her daughter reborn! Timidly, between little sobs of joy, Letitia said:

"Why don't you come to church Sunday and get a card of your own? Then we can each put down fifty dollars."

Thread, scissors, thimble, spilled from Minnie's lap as she rose. "Oh, mother—" but the worn, old face, tear-stained and yearning, stopped her. What was there to say? If she were prepared to endure privations, prepared to face Bob with the fact that *she* was helping to build a church, to give her mother this moment's happiness, she must not destroy the effect she had achieved. In a voice that was harsh and strained she said: "I can't do that, Mother.… You pledge it all yourself …. I'm going upstairs—excuse me."

Bob heard her door close and wondered why she had not come in to talk. It was too early for her to go to bed. He tapped gently.

"I'll be in in just a minute, Bob.… Anything special?"

"You're crying!"

"Well, I won't be in a minute. Go on with your work."

He descended the steps. "What's the matter, Grandma?"

"I don't know, Bob, I don't know. Your mother acts so strange sometimes. I can't for the life of me understand her."

"Well, what was said? Why are *you* crying?"

"I just told her about the new church.... She offered of her own free will to give a hundred dollars toward it, and then I asked her to offer fifty of it in her own name and you'd 'a' thought I'd struck 'er."

The boy smiled grimly. "I should think you had."

"What? ... What do you mean?"

"Nothing." He climbed again to his books and sat gazing at them silently—not seeing.

Minnie entered and squeezed his shoulder. "See? ... never a tear.... I'm a fool to be upset so easily."

"Yeah,—it is silly."

"Did you talk to Grandma?"

He nodded. "Uh-huh.... You didn't drive a very sharp bargain—but we'll make it.... You were right, of course. We've got to—play the game.... I got two jobs to-day"-—at her start—"after school, of course."

"Where? What?"

"I'm going to keep books for Sheehan, and for Hahn at the racket store."

His mother went to the window.

"Don't take it to heart. It's only temporarily. I thought it would help toward coll—eh—collaring the bills."

She turned to him without speaking.

"Oh, that smile! ... Well,—what?"

"Bob—we're the chumps." She dropped into a chair across the table from him. "You and I, and others like us, read and think and theorize. We decide to be Supermen. We call pity and love 'emotions' and spit upon charity for a fraud—but when we try to practice the tenets of our philosophy—no matter how thoroughly satisfied we are that our theories are right—we can't do it. When it comes to *living* the ruthless creed that we preach we aren't up to it. The Christians have it all over us when intelligent action is required. They act as we theorize. And, *vice versa*, we act, as they theorize and hate ourselves for weaklings as we do it.

"They preach brotherly love and live like jungle beasts; we preach the survival of the fittest and weep like paid mourners at every beggar's bogus sob-story. Truly, man is the most inconsistent animal in the pack."

"Human, all too human."

She made a little puff with her breath, a sort of concentrated sigh. "What is that you're doing there?"

The clock struck eleven as Bob tried to explain an intricate problem in calculus to his mother. "That's beyond my depth. Is that school?"

"No, Mr. Andrews is giving me this stuff on the side.... You'd like him, Mother."

"Would I? Why don't you have him over? What time was that just struck?"

"Eleven, I think ... Harper? I beg your pardon—'Hek'?"

"Yes. Isn't that silly? ... I haven't heard him come in."

They investigated and found the boy still abroad. "I'll go."

Bob called from the front stoop—then from the side yard—then from the back. The street corner was deserted. The noise of a game of robbers-and-police had been stilled a long time. Bob walked around the house again, calling as he went.

From an old woodshed in the rear he heard a faint answer—almost a groan. The door of the place was open. "You in there, Harper?"

Unmistakably, a groan from the far corner of the inky interior. Bob struck a match.

With the odor of a recent illness there was mingled the stench of a black cheroot.

"Mmmm. Lesson number one in manhood."

He lifted the green-faced boy and carried him to the house. "Young man, you've been smoking!"

Between hiccoughs, Hek answered: "Don't you—suppose—I know it?"

## 5

It was Hek—coming home from school with a shrill whistle—who found Grandma Elling unconscious at the foot of the stairs that led to the second floor. She had been there some time. The boy tugged at her shoulders without moving her many inches—then bolted for the restaurant and his mother.

Minnie took a taxi and tried to learn from the excited child what had happened.

"I'm afraid she's dead, Mother. She looked all broken and hardly breathed much."

Grandma regained consciousness in bed and said with an apologetic smile: "I fell."

A worn spot in the hall carpet at the top of the stairs had caught the old lady's common-sense heel and she had pitched, head foremost, down the stairs. Old bones knit slowly. Her clavicle and her left arm were broken. Grandma Elling, for the first time in her long, active life, was absolutely helpless.

She fretted and fussed from her white pillow, blaming the accident upon her own carelessness, calling herself a lazy old woman, threatening daily to get up and do her rightful share of the work. Her first week in bed, Grandma played her favorite rôle of the pioneer wife who had brought her family westward in an ox-cart; she was, for the time being, the woman a little boy, Harper Elling Knott, had made of her at sixty-five.

"Don't you quit your job, Min; you just tell Schraeder you'll be back to work next week, Monday. I'll be perfectly well by that time and able to do for myself."

But the improved exterior, the shell of warmly human tolerance, the fortitude, the veneer of that characteristic which a glib age has learned to call "regularity" began to peel. A week in bed had Letitia right back where she'd been at Harper's birth. The inactivity, the barrenness of long days in bed and the extra number of callers—such callers—such sympathetic callers—worked to destroy what improvement there had been.

The week dragged on into a month and Minnie finally relinquished her job. Bob left school and entered the accounting department of Stover's, full time. His face and manner made it easy to lie about his age and, although acquaintances in the office knew better, he was accepted for twenty-five.

Henry Andrews, his mathematics instructor, called at the Parsonage to learn, from sheer unselfish interest in his charge, if it were as necessary as Bob had said for him to quit school.

Grandma was sleeping upstairs.

"I love the boy, Mrs. Knott. I don't know when I've had a student who affected me so much. He's mature. You see, we teachers get to feeling pretty much the same way the scholars do about school. It's only the few, rare personalities such as his that make the game worth the candle. If some one like Robert hadn't turned up in my classes from time to time—not often, but once in a while—I'd have quit teaching long ago.

"And he tells me his father died before he was five. That's astonishing."

"You know how happy that makes me feel. Bob thinks a great deal of you, too."

"We get along like brothers."

Minnie raised her brows.

"Well," he laughed, "like *some* brothers."

"His father was a great student too, a great reader."

"A Northwestern man, he says."

"Yes,—but he was opposed to universities. He always said Bob should not go."

"I know.... Perhaps he's right. But I should like to see him continue his work. He is so serious."

"Serious? Yet he has a fine sense of humor. A real one, I mean, not the sort so many people brag about."

"What an analyst you are! You give his father too much credit for his mentality, I'm sure."

Minnie smiled proudly.

"I came to-day to see if it were not in any way possible to keep Robert in school. He told me frankly that his help was needed at home. Graduation is so near."

"Do you think the gesture of graduation means so much to him?"

The teacher pondered, then shook his head, his eyes again full of respectful astonishment. "No. It does not. My thought has been superficial after all. The act of graduation means nothing to him—and no matter when he quits school he will never quit studying—not that boy."

Minnie crossed the room to the upright piano and moved the picture of Ted which stood there so that his ear was turned directly toward all this fine talk.

But the necessity which took Bob from his academic studies was finally apparent to the instructor and he rose to go. Minnie was loath to permit it. She wanted to hear more of this, and more and more. It was only the beginning of the recognition her boy was to receive from people who really mattered.

Mr. Andrews' leave-taking was blurred and confused with a faint call from upstairs. Minnie hurried up.

"I feel terrible, Min. I'm all faint like and I can't move my left limb.... You—I guess—you better call Doc Smith."

Minnie thought the doctor would never come. Then she thought he'd never go. She met Bob at the door.

"Grandma's had a stroke, Son," she said quietly. "That fall hurt her worse than we thought."

"The doctor here?"

"He's been here four hours."

"Gee, it must be pretty bad."

Doc Smith was in the hall, gently closing her door.

"She's resting easily now. Her heart has been weakened by that fall. She has an even chance. We have to fight paralysis.... She's not so young as she was once. She mustn't be excited or worried ... Keep her absolutely quiet ... I'll call again in the morning."

He called again in the morning, and again the morning after that. His visits became a feature of every matin, the official opening of the day. Hospitals were in ill-repute among these, people and it was their pride that they could care for their own. You couldn't expect proper attention from strangers. Even Minnie felt toward nurses, paid for their services, as many a king must have felt toward mercenaries in his army: that they filled a need but that a better accounting was rendered by those who served for love of their homes.

At first, Grandma improved. Doc Smith, who was an Elling-Knott tradition, brought something more than a country doctor's skill to this case. He was aided by their collective blind faith. He had pulled Grandpa Elling through pneumonia and a broken leg; he had delivered Minnie, and then Bob and Harper in their turn; he had cured measles, chicken pox, whooping cough and mumps as easily as you could shake a stick; he had saved Grandma and Ted from diphtheria and it was beyond equivocation in the family that if *he* had been in the Philippines, Ted need not have died. Now, he was curing Grandma Elling of paralysis, the while he mended the two broken bones. It was, of course, perfectly simple and easy for him to do this. It was just a matter of time. But something went amiss, because it took much longer than any one had expected.

While her condition was still a novelty, fellow-members of the church were with her daily. The minister stopped for prayer two or three times a week. Flowers she had, and fruit and potted plants (they last so much longer); Bill Schraeder looked in every evening or two for a moment and every Friday he left his *Saturday Evening Post*. "Like to look at this?"

Her appetite was good, her mind as clear as ever. Her arm mended, and, to all appearances, the collar bone, too. The doctor gave her exercises to keep the arm from stiffening. Only her left "limb" was useless.

She couldn't understand that. "If it was the arm there'd be some sense to it. But the limb wa'n't even bruised."

The dread word "paralysis" was never mentioned in front of her. Her "stroke" was a "spell" and the useless leg was only "stiff".

All payments upon improvements in the home were suspended. Oliver was somewhere in Italy with the daughter of the furniture factory, at his father-in-law's expense. Minnie could expect nothing from that quarter and times were terrible in Wyoming.

Bob was the sole support of the household and regardless of the high opinion of his intelligence held by Henry Andrews, Minnie and others, he was only a junior accountant to his employers. His salary was small and although the rent of the Parsonage was low, it required expert management to keep their debts within hail. Slowly the expenses increased, despite Minnie's frantic attempts at economy. Bob bought no new books. Harper was sent to school with second-hand texts. The boys' clothing was mended at Easter instead of being cast aside for new. Minnie never bought dresses or coats. "I never go out; what do I need new things for?" She made her own hats from bits of goods, fur and feathers that had accumulated in the attic. Dessert was eliminated from all meals save Sunday dinner.

Every evening their regular reading or studying was prefaced with a discussion of ways and means between Minnie and Bob. Their battle-cry was "Keep Harper in school!"

Time, as it passed ever more wearily, grew accustomed to the sight of the old lady in bed. Despite her exercises, her left arm stiffened and finally died, as had her leg. With that, Grandma grew still more fretful, still harder to please, more picky and importunate. Minnie only smiled at her and redoubled her efforts to be perfectly attentive, loving and kind. If the boys and their mother were denied delicacies at table and the luxury of new clothing, Grandma Elling wanted nothing. Her diet was kept rigidly as prescribed and every comfort that could be devised was procured for her, regardless of cost.

Her second stroke came at night, about eight months after the first. Bob had been studying late. He went to the bath after midnight, and upon passing the old lady's door, looked in. She lay gasping for breath, her eyes glazed and staring, her body rigid. He called the doctor, then woke Minnie. "Grandma's worse, Mother. I've called Doc Smith.... What can I do?"

"Put some water on to heat," she said, struggling into a worn kimono, "then bring me the ammonia."

His eyes heavy with sleep, Hek poked into the hall. "What is it, Mother?"

"Grandma, dear ... Go back to bed."

He returned to his room but not to bed; instead he dressed. If there was going to be excitement, it should never find him asleep. He stood just inside the shadow of his door watching the activity in the hall.

Just before dawn the doctor said: "I think I'd send for her minister. She is conscious now." The all but lifeless eyes looked their thanks. Grandma could not speak.

"I'll go," said Harper, and he sped down the steps before Minnie realized that he had not gone back to bed. As he ran the short block to the new parsonage, he was a courier despatched by Napoleon. He crossed the enemy's lines and gained the veranda, bleeding from countless wounds: "Nay, I'm killed, Sire." As he held his thumb on the button of the bell, he became a very small boy abroad alone on a very dark night.

"What is it, Son? What is it?"

"Gramma's worse. Doc Smith says you better come."

"Certainly, certainly.... I'll be there directly."

Again a courier sped through the dark—this time an enemy of Napoleon's—meeting and conquering the Corsican single-handed under the maple. He raised a thoughtless clatter on the stairs. Shhhhh!

Grandma was asleep, breathing easily.

When the Reverend Harper arrived she had not wakened. Loosely clad, he looked from face to face about the bed, then put his Bible on the table.

"The crisis is passed," Doc Smith said. "Sorry we got you up. She has a marvelous constitution. She'll probably sleep a long time,—all day."

The minister took Minnie's hand. "This is your cross, young lady—let us pray."

"I think I'll stand it better without that, Reverend Harper.... It was my mother who needed you, not I." She withdrew her hand.

"Not pray?"

"You must not think we are ungrateful—" Bob was watching her closely. "Oh, very well—let's pray!" Easier—that was so much easier.

She listened to the droned supplication of the sleepy pastor and looked at Bob for forgiveness. Dr. Smith had moved silently to the bedside and was once more taking Grandma's pulse.

Hek hung on the bed, jiggling it. Minnie lifted him to his feet beside her. She wanted to shake him and say, "Pray, you little fool. This is the stuff you've learned—now use it." But she said nothing.

The Reverend Harper concluded by assuring God that it was the wish of all present that His Will be done. Minnie asked herself what need there had been for prayer if it were not to ask that He change His Mind about taking the old lady, but only to assure Him that He might do as He pleased.

Doc Smith and the minister talked in low tones on the walk before the house as the eastern sky lighted higher and higher.

"I'll sit up, Mother. You get a couple hours sleep. You'll have a hard day.... Back to bed, Hek."

Napoleon's courier sulkily disrobed. He disliked orders from Bob. The six years' difference in their ages was not worth considering, and about the same number of inches difference in their height gave Hek confidence that he could "lick the tar out of the mutt", if it ever came to *that*. He was a punk kind of brother anyway.

When Bob had gone to the office, Hek began badgering his mother to let him get a job. He could earn some money too. He bet he could earn almost as much as Bob did. He was fourteen and if she'd sign a permit he could get a job as easy as pie. Feel that muscle. He could earn a lot of money. School was no good. Couldn't he, Mom?

Planning to disappear completely and forever from their lives, he pushed his heavy feet back to the blackboarded prison.

How different this child was. Did he belong to her? You couldn't doubt it very much with that mouth, still curved in an almost baby pout, those enormous eyes. His skin was fine-grained, pink and white and smooth. His hair was wavy, lighter than any of the Ellings. Lighter than Ted's. Minnie watched him scuff out of the yard. It would all be forgotten by night, forgotten in an hour. He took punishment so easily—bouncing back without rancor, ready and anxious to sin again. How *normal* he was—and how little it mattered! Mentality, then, had nothing to do with mother love. She consoled herself that Harper's was no basic deficiency; that his training might still be altered in time. She had been so busy. Now she would bring him up sharply. She would have more time with him, and Grandma could no longer interfere.

Could, no longer—

Minnie realized suddenly that she had already given up hope for her mother's recovery. Without thought, she was assuming that Grandma would always be an invalid, always be confined to her bed, always be helpless.

"So … That's where pessimism leads," she muttered as she put away the last of the breakfast dishes. "Then, Min, let's see you do some constructive thinking."

Her reading had acquainted her thoroughly with "New Though," "Mental" and "Christian Science". Minnie began to apply those principles of each which her gelid logic admitted possible. She "held the thought" of a perfectly well mother—again at her household tasks. She printed a picture on her brain of Grandma again lifting her skirts to her shoe tops and executing the few comic dance steps she remembered from her girlhood. She filled her mind with an *active* mother, as the directions said she should. She tried—tried everything—even verbal prayer. "It's no good without faith," she told herself. "I wish I knew how to get that."

Minnie looked into the room for the hundredth time, in the middle of the afternoon, and thought Letitia still slept—then one lid opened. One eye looked at her. "How are you now, Mother?" The eye rolled. "Do you feel easy now?" That single eye refocused. "Could you eat a little soup?" She smiled—like a salesman. She must sell her mother this soup—good soup. The eye seemed to agree to the soup; her mouth did not move. Then Min noticed an odor and the food was delayed while the linen was changed.

Grandma Elling was paralyzed. She could not move; she could not speak. One eye would not open; the other appeared half mad. She could control no bodily function, and if she thought, she was incapable of making it known.

Gruel was ordered, chicken broth,—tea. She was fed a spoonful at a time. She could not hear or smell or feel. She saw but poorly with her single eye; what she tasted none could say.

The task of caring for her grew daily more difficult. She communicated only one sensation—that of hunger. When she wanted food she found a low, animal moan in the back of her throat—which she could raise or lower at will. Minnie learned to listen for that sound and in a vain effort to lighten her work attempted to teach her mother to call her thus when she needed other attention. When this failed Minnie asked the doctor if there were any gauge.... There was none.

## 6

So the unremitting vigil of love beside a husk of what had been a mother continued. Day in and day out—in darkness or light, the infidel daughter served that spark of life as vestals are said to have tended their sacred fires. The doctor called twice daily and for a time pretended to hope. But that pretense thinned like smoke in a breeze under Minnie's direct questioning. There was no hope. She would linger—in about the same condition—for a long time. How long? He could not say. By a series of minor miracles she might be given the use of her tongue—perhaps even the use of her arms. There was a specialist in Chicago——

By painful economies the services of the specialist were procured. He gave Grandma Elling the use of her tongue. Then the miracles stopped. He gave her the use of her tongue—and only the most gracious of gods will ever forgive him for that. The mind that controlled the tongue was gone. It fabricated neglects and built hatreds.

Callers were told of her daughter's abuse,—how she was maltreated by her own flesh and blood.

She contrived diabolic hoaxes,—calling Minnie from steaming wash-tubs where sheets were being laundered for her, to say that she would like a small piece of meat for lunch.

"But the doctor says you can't have meat, Mother. He knows best."

"He told *me* I could."

"He did?"

"He certainly did…. It's a wonder to me you don't listen to him when he's here. If you got his directions straight, I'd prob'ly be up and around in a few days."

On the telephone Doc Smith denied her meat, telling Minnie she must expect these mental lapses.

Another day great sobs would emanate from the sick room. And Minnie would be told to go away—to send her daughter to her. "If Minnie was here I wouldn't be made to suffer so…. Please send for my baby."

Tears and sighs and hardships—for months and months and months. Labor and pain and filthy drudgery, while Bob brought home the means of a meager livelihood and Hek continued to pass examinations only because the teachers were fond of him, and could deny his big eyes nothing.

Evening found both Bob and his mother too worn for much study. He would read a little, but his eyes closed against his will. Minnie often fell on her bed—half dressed, exhausted by her labor. Bob, finding her thus, would loosen the balance of her clothing and tuck her in, open her window, kiss her sleeping face and go to his own bed.

Hek sometimes helped his mother with the supper dishes—then left the house, not returning until the others were asleep. Minnie's plans for his education progressed but slowly. After climbing the steps to her mother's room fifty and more times a day, besides doing her housework, she was too tired to cope with his youthful buoyance and twisted concepts. Out of all the books in the house, only one series held his interest; these were the adventures of *Si Klegg and Shorty* which had come with Grandpa Elling's *National Tribune*.

"Liars go to hell when they die, don't they, Mom?"—as Hek dried a platter.

"No! Where did you get such a notion?"

"Everybody says so…. Gramma told me."

"Hell! … Where is hell?"

The boy looked at her amazed. "Why, it's down under the earth, ain't it, Mom?"

"Of course not. That's ridiculous."

"But it says so, in the Bible."

"I don't believe it."

"It does so. Gramma read it to me an' I read it myself."

"But I don't believe it is true."

"Well, ain't the Bible true? Ain't it the word of God?"

"I doubt it."

He dried three plates. "Ain't there no hell, then, Mom?"

"Isn't——"

"Isn't there any hell, then?"

"I think not."

"Well, then, what do people go to church for?"

"I have often wondered."

"You and Bob never go."

"No. Is that why you go? Are you afraid of going to hell if you don't go to church?"

"Sure.… Grandma says I have to go to save my soul."

"You needn't go any more, if you don't want to."

"And I won't go to hell?"

"I think not."

He dried the knives and forks and fled to his companions. "Say, you know what? There ain't—isn't no hell! You know that! My mother says so."

And soon Freeport knew that Minnie Knott was an "Atheist", that she taught her children apostasy, that she was an unnatural daughter and probably old lady Elling wasn't as crazy as she was made out, but was telling the truth when she said she was starved and beaten.

This came back to Bob from Florence Mitchell, his girl, if Bob can be said to have had a girl. She worked at Raleigh's. They had gone to school together. In these years of Grandma's illness they met almost every evening, as if by chance, at the corner of Spring Street and Chicago Avenue. They walked a few blocks together— and there were other rare and random half-hours they managed to squeeze in. Florence was a tall girl, just the right size for Bob, and they'd have gone to shows together, and elsewhere, if things had been different. Without once discussing it, an understanding had grown between them, and each—held rigidly emotionless by inner mailed hands—knew that eventually, when the hurdles and barriers and débris of previous generations should be cleared from their path they would marry, if both lived.

Bob didn't mention this to Minnie. She had other plans for him, Marriage, when it did come to Robert Ingersoll at a long-deferred last, should be an event. By that time, he should be a personage and his union should be with a lady of somewhat similar stature. The Mitchells were no great shakes. When Bob mentioned Florence at home at all, he made his voice as casual as his remarks, as if he spoke about some male acquaintance. This was less to deceive Minnie than to drug his own perception. Bob did not know it, but—in effect—he said: "See? I'm not in love with her. Why, she's just a schoolmate! I can think about her and talk about her without a tremor." He was a potential drunkard, bragging in a voice too loud, that he could take it or leave it alone.

"I heard something—to-day."

Bob stooped to pick up two horse-chestnuts beside the walk. "Yes?"

"About you.... Well, about your mother."

"Yes?"

"I don't believe it, of course."

He looked at her quizzically. Something a respectable girl should not believe must have been an unpleasant thing to hear. "What was that?"

"Oh, the girls were talking. It isn't true, of course."

"No? Well, what was it?"

"Bob—do you believe in God?"

Oh! That was different. He smiled a little. "What's that got to do with it?" His thumb ran over the smooth brown shells of the buck-eyes.

"Well, that's what was said. They said your mother taught you and Hek that there wasn't any God. I just told them right out I didn't believe a word of it.... You *do*, don't you?"

"Believe in God?"

"Yes."

"The phrase doesn't mean much—that way. I don't think you're asking what you want to know."

"What?"

"I say, you imply too much. I can't answer your question because you haven't really asked one."

"Why, it seems to me I did. I asked you if you believed in God. That's a question, isn't it?"

"Which god?"

"*Which* God? Why, Bob, do you believe in more than *one?*"

"You become more and more obscure. I can't answer because I don't know what you want to know."

"Oh, you do too."

"I don't. Look, Florence: if you study comparative religions, you will find forty or fifty gods to choose from. I don't know which one you are asking about. I don't know what you mean by 'believe'."

"Bob!" She was hurt. "You don't! ... You don't believe in God!"

"I give up, Florence. As long as you keep repeating that meaningless phrase, 'believe in God', 'believe in God', 'believe in God'; I just can't talk to you. I don't know what to say."

They had reached her home and stood uncomfortably where the walks joined. "A meaningless phrase! Oh!——" Florence was going to be offended by that. "I'm sorry.... Of course, I should have known that I couldn't talk well enough to suit *you*. After all, you know so much more than anybody else."

"Florence."

"It's all right. Good-night."

"Good-night."

She disappeared around the corner of the house, walking fast. Bob watched the corner for a moment, smiling faintly. Wasn't that silly? Getting upset about that! He didn't know he gave people the impression that he thought he knew it all. He didn't mean to.

The rest of the way home he planned how he would tell Minnie, making her laugh. He would burlesque the incident; come in tiptoe, shshsh! "It's out!" he would whisper. Her eyes would dance a moment. "It's out! … We don't *believe* in 'God'!— and *the whole town knows it!!!*" Perhaps she'd laugh again. It had been an unconscionable long time since he had heard her really laugh. But the Minnie who faced him from beside the kitchen range when he opened the door shot a bolt of ice into his breast. He opened his mouth to breathe. Thus gasps are caused. "Oh, *mother!*" he said and closed his eyes. He folded her in his arms and buried his head in the crook of her neck, kissing the familiar flesh too tenderly for description. >

"This apron's greasy," she complained. "You'll get it on your suit."

He hugged her tighter. "God damn it!" he said through clenched teeth. "God damn it."

"Hey! … What's the matter? Do I look as bad as that?"

He held her at arm's length. "This must have been a day," he said slowly. "I've never seen you look so tired."

"Mm," she smiled. "Callers."

"Oh, I see."

Minnie nodded and turned the potatoes in the pan. They sizzled viciously and spat grease in stinging drops.

"They know better than to take Mama seriously, but there's always that partial doubt."

"One of *those* days."

His mother nodded.

"I'll go see her."

Grandma Elling did not recognize him. Her lids narrowed as he approached the bed and spoke. "Good-evening, Grandma. How do you feel to-day?"

The chronic disapproval that had rested on her face so many years was now almost commemorated there in the stiffening features. Slowly her clumsy tongue framed words. They issued in so low a whisper Bob had to lean close to hear. "Take me away from here," she said. "Take me away."

"Where do you want to go, Grandma?"

"Take me away from that woman."

"What woman?"

"Take me away. I can't stand it any longer. I can't stand it."

"Are you in pain, Grandma?"

"She hurts me."

"Who hurts you?"

"Take me away from that woman."

Bob started to leave. He paused at the door. She was trying to call him. "Can I get you something?"

"I want a drink of water. She never gives me water."

Bob held the glass tube in her mouth as she sucked a futile mouthful. Most of it ran out of the corners of her stiff lips. He wiped her chin and neck on a cloth and hastened from the room.

"Her speech is worse, isn't it? I gave her water."

"Oh—"

"What?"

"Nothing."

"Was it wrong? Shouldn't she have had it? Oh, damn me! Blundering idiot. I didn't know. Oh, darling, I *didn't* know."

"Of course not; forget it. She didn't drink much, I'm sure."

"Hardly any."

"It'll be all right. Come. Eat."

"Where's Hek?"

"At the Opera House, I suppose. He usually is."

"Oh, yes, Fiske O'Hara's here."

"He passed out bills."

"Will he eat?"

"I think so. He goes over to Bill's."

"Do they pay him?"

"For passing out bills? They give him a ticket or two. He sells them."

"And then helps back-stage."

"*Helps!*"

"I'll ask Charlie the next time I see him if he's in the way."

"He wants to take out an 'apprentice card'—be a stagehand. At his age."

"They won't give it to him."

"Of course not."

"Do you hear from school?"

"No, nothing. I guess it's going a little better or I'd have heard."

Twice Minnie's meal was interrupted by groans she could not ignore although she knew them to be meaningless.

## 7

THEY washed the dishes together.

"Lots of visitors?"

"No-o.... Five or six."

"You say that strangely."

Minnie looked up at him quickly with a proud smile. "I didn't mean to."

"But you did."

"You read my thoughts."

"Harper?"

"No, he didn't come to-day. You know, they come and perform their Christian duty and get away just as quickly as possible now. But they aren't running from the unpleasantness and pain; they're running from me.

"They barely speak when they come in. Their mouths are set. The air about me is contaminated. It wouldn't surprise me one day to see even one of these Protestants cross herself to ward off my evil eye."

"As bad as that?"

"Three of them were up there at one time; Mrs. Snyder, Mrs. Shoemaker and Aggie Kramer. They didn't hear me until I was in the room."

"Yes?"

"They were discussing a committee they might form to call on Doctor Harper to tell him what is going on here."

"To tell him what is going on here?"

"Uh-huh."

"Uh-huh.… *She-devils!*"

"Hek has let it be known that there is no hell—at least not here—and they resent it."

"No,—no, there is no hell here."

"Hush."

"Florence mentioned that. I'll speak to Hek."

"No, I'll speak to him."

"You! You do it all."

"I do it all!" She leaned wearily against the sink, but her eyes were bright as she caressed his face with them, touching his jaw, his ears, his hair. "You come home so tired you fall asleep with your arms on your books. I've seen you.

"You never see a show, you never go to parties. Other young people have parties, Bob. You didn't even know that; did you? You walk a few blocks with Florence for diversion.

"I do it all! ... I've ruined your life. I've done that."

"Now!"

"Let me talk. This has been in my heart for months. Some day I'm going to have to beg your forgiveness. You don't feel that yet, but you will. I wonder if that *can* be forgiven."

"Mother, stop."

Minnie shook her head. "I taught you to see and to think. You'll live to hate me for that. I had no right to do it. I taught you to love knowledge—then I put you to work to support me and that insensible responsibility, that dead thing upstairs."

"Mother!" He grasped her in his arms. "Mother!"

"Let me go, Bob. Let me go. I can't bear to be held like that. Get *me* the ammonia. Oh, God, I'm going to scream!" She wrenched away from him and ran sobbing into the parlor.

*"Mother!"* He followed futilely. Minnie stood in the middle of the room, her fists clenched at her sides, her face contorted, while scream after ghastly scream tore her throat and Bob Ingersoll's heart. Then her eyes rolled out of sight—and she sank in a limp pile.

## 8

"THAT won't happen again, Bob," Minnie assured him quietly an hour later, and he was puzzled by a strange, new expression in her eyes. He sat on the edge of her bed, stroking her hair.

"I'm sure it won't."

She slipped into a lethargic state between sleep and wakefulness. They two were not quite enough, perhaps. She might not be able to stick it out. Hysterics! Imagine! These were loving hands in her hair, but they were *Bob's* hands.

Hek came in from the theater. "What's the matter? Ma sick?"

"I'm all right now. How was the show?"

"Aw, gosh, it was swell."

"Fiske O'Hara?"

"Yeah—Sarah Padden day after to-morrow. Gee, I wish you'd let me get a card an' go to work. I'm tired o' takin' charity from you."

Bob's laughter was too spontaneous to check. Minnie took the younger boy's hand. "Are you taking charity, Son?"

"Sure I am. I don't know what else you'd call it. Anyway, I'm gonna get put on as assistant property man, evenings, anyway."

"After school."

"Ye-e-es.... Gee whiz, I'm gonna quit school."

"Not yet, Hek."

"Are they going to pay you for being assistant property man—anyway?"

"Sure. I get at least three dollars every time there's a show."

"What do you do for your money?"

"Help set, wash dishes, sweep the baiz and the ground-cloth; dust."

"Sort of housemaid."

"Pete's gonna teach me to build a pair o' stairs and make a vase and stuff out o' papier-mâché so's I can pass the examination."

"You think you'd like to work at that, do you? I mean when you grow up."

"Oh, gosh, I'd *love* it."

Bob shrugged.

"Why not?" Minnie murmured. "If he wants to."

"No reason; if he wants to."

"Well, I don't see it's any worse'n bein' a bookkeeper. *The Lion and the Mouse* is coming next week too."

Bob rose. "I guess I'll work a while, Mother. Will you be all right?"

"Yes, I'm fine now."

"*I'll* stay with her," said Hek.

When Doc Smith called the next morning, Letitia had again lost the power of speech. Each inhalation of breath, however, was a rasping moan. For three days her condition was unaltered, then Minnie told the doctor about the tea. "I make it very, very weak, but that doesn't matter. It stimulates her so. Could it be hurting her? She cries out, groans twice as loud, every time I give it to her—and it's practically the only thing she'll take."

"It doesn't hurt her," the doctor assured Minnie. "She feels absolutely nothing."

"Tell me this, Doctor; is there the slightest hope of her ever recovering? Could she possibly be well again?"

He took his time. He was drawing on his gloves. "A case of this kind sometimes gets out of bed, but it never regains normal mentality."

"You mean—that after a period of—of years—we might make her well enough to sit up in a chair—an imbecile?"

He nodded.

"Thank you."

That night Minnie was not tired—yet she could not read. "It's no use, Bob. I can't think.... Can't keep my mind on it. I'm going to take a walk."

"Alone?"

"I—think I'd rather. If Grandma calls, just whistle out the window. I won't go far."

He kissed her and returned to his books. As she passed under the window, outside, Bob heard his mother humming *Rock-a-bye, Baby*. He wondered what new disturbance had come to her. She never hummed like that except when she was distraught.

The next night was the same. She wanted to walk, alone. He watched her out of sight, head tilted, looking at the stars, and humming.

The next night and the next.

"What is it, Mother?"

"Don't mind me, Bob. My eyes are going back on me and it's a sign of age, I guess. No one likes to grow old."

"You can get glasses ...."

"At a minimum charge of eight dollars!"

But Bob knew her eyes were not making Minnie hum and avoid his company.

When Hek had gone again to the Opera House: "Have I done anything? Have I offended you? You have always trusted me, Mother. Can't two decide easier than one?"

"Not this. I've already decided. You haven't offended. I'll tell you soon.... I'll tell you—soon."

The following night she sat opposite him at their table piled with books and papers.

"I'm letting Grandma die, Bob. She hasn't taken anything but warm water for three days."

The solitary walks were explained.

Bob looked at his mother steadily. Neither spoke for a long time.

"Have you told Doc Smith?"

Minnie shook her head. "No.... He might not understand."

"Hek?"

"No."

A week later Grandma Elling was buried.

Then they tore the Parsonage down to make room for the new church. Minnie and her boys moved into a small apartment near Schraeder's café and Minnie went back to work.

# PART II

# CHAPTER FOUR
# THE BOOK OF EGO

## 1

A KISS, to Hek, was a flat-faced, tight-lipped pressure, not particularly thrilling. His experience with girls had been limited to the games one may play in a hammock, the naïve, although strenuous, explorations of inquisitive hands, balked and impeded and held back in a sort of contest in which the prizes were unseen, ill-imagined and markedly tasteless when attained. Still one strove for these unwanted boons, all for the sake of the striving. This was an healthy, cublike sport, differing from a wrestling with another boy only in its details, its objectives, and a few of the rules; the spirit and the motivation were identical. In shinny, the point was scored when a battered tin can had been knocked between two goal posts; in this hammock pastime, the winner was he whose finger tips should advance through and under and between labyrinthine entanglements of lace, elastic and knit-goods to a point however little further, higher or lower, than they had gone on the last previous encounter. Time was invariably called by the referee-mother of one's opponent.

An indifferent player—or one old enough to wish to lose a bout—would have terrified Hek. Like the little boy with the willing tot in his red wagon, Harper Elling would have looked to heaven, likely, and asked: "Oh, God; oh, God, what do I do *now?*"

The younger boy had given considerably more of his time to all games, including this one, than Robert Ingersoll. Bob had had no proper boyhood at all. From a baby he had become a man almost at once, a man, at least, if no further proof of manhood than an adult body and a mind cluttered with erudition be required.

A kiss, to Bob, was a salutation. He had never kissed Florence Mitchell, had never held her hand. When their knuckles brushed in walking, they drew self-consciously apart. Yet they had been—psychically—engaged to marry for years. Their tiff on matters of faith was forgotten at Grandma's funeral and something akin to hope, definite, concrete hope, involving kitchen curtains and no more sheep-dip labels, came timorously to dwell in Florence's breast. He could marry her now. But Bob did most of his thinking *en famille*. How could it be otherwise? He who was to have avoided the channels and ruts of mental mediocrity had been forced by circumstances to become utterly dependent upon the needs and wishes and ambitions of others for his most petty decisions. He whose mind was to have freed him from the clay had become mired in the slough of unselfish consideration.

Minnie and Hek were his first responsibility; nay, they were he. There was no such person, no such individual, as Robert Ingersoll Knott. His mind had been forced so wide open that it had become a plain, an expanse, an area for their tilling. This was clear to no one. Bob did not realize that he had become a member, dependent upon an organism and upon which an organism depended; a mere appendage with less will of his own than any of the burghers he had studied so hard to surpass; less independence, less individuality than almost any one of the great mass of men his reason had been nurtured to despise. It was not apparent to Minnie that beyond some point in his development there must be a divergence of their paths for either to realize more than a vestige of his ambitions. Her vision had stopped, short of the necessity for a life of Bob's own. Vaguely, she had known he would "outgrow" her, but that had meant only that he would advance intellectually beyond her capacity, that he, being a man, would have greater opportunity for the use of the talents she shared with him in part. At maturity he would soar, after their climb together, leaving her on a peak, looking up. That, at maturity, he might decide to swim instead of fly, or might—at the very least—decide to decide, had not occurred to her. She was not informed now. Her eyes still searched the clouds, so Bob looked upward too, right over Florence's head.

Hek regarded his brother as his one, preeminent, natural enemy. His *alter ego*, his only major misfortune. From Grandma and from the attitudes of his playmates, Hek had acquired that thin and baseless regard for Minnie that inheres to the word *mother*. What *his mother* could see in Bob was beyond him.

And here again that breadth and scope and reach of mind that was Robert Ingersoll's curse reacted to his detriment. He "allowed" for misunderstanding in the youngster and tried to disabuse him of his misconceptions. He tried to make Hek love him and respect him—not because they were brothers, but because he was in some measure admirable. He worried for the boy's entire lack of confidence in him. He gave of his own life to seek his brother's intimacy.

Thus, the matricide did not much alter the life of the person Minnie had intended it should free. Bob couldn't very well quit Stover's with all those bills hanging over their heads. He couldn't go away to college with Hek threatening momentarily to leave school. Cedric had returned from Wyoming, feeling no responsibility toward the funeral expenses and Oliver could adduce no reason why he should contribute more than a third. "What have you been doing with her pension?" he asked.

So Florence Mitchell remained unkissed.

But, Hek—

Hek, with his mother's sensuous mouth, wheeled trunks into the dressing rooms of the Opera House. *Babes in Starland* was the attraction Saturday, matinée and night, "with a chorus of thirty (count them) beautiful girls" direct from its six months' record-breaking run at the La Salle Theatre in Chicago. Count them!—well, up to twelve, anyway. Hek counted up to three, the first three in the theater. At the third he smiled—and unaccountably blushed, as he let the big trunk slide from his truck.

The girls had been looking for a place to iron, but Ruby decided to go on in wrinkles if that blush had been genuine. She spread her arms in mock restraint of the other two—and stared at Hek. "Don't shove," she said. "It's mine."

"Have you got an ironing-board?" asked she of the least imagination.

And the other: "Nix, he's only a kid."

Henna had done what it could to hide the Terre Haute in Ruby; mascara covered a mole, but her features had been well thought out and assembled with honest intent to create the face beautiful. "Can you do that again?" she asked Hek.

His feet shuffled and color rose on his neck, his ears.

"Thanks."

"Do what again?" Hek was not aware that there were practitioners of love as a fine art. He did not know that his lips and eyes were incredibly innocent, almost unbelievable in so bad a world. He did not know that his unruly, curling hair made feminine fingers itch to tousle it that they might later smooth it down.

Ruby crossed the dressing room and took his hand. "Come on," she said. "Bring the go-cart with you."

Her fingers sent new raptures up Hek's arm. Her heavy perfume raised a mist before his eyes. She helped him drag his truck through the door, then closed it on her sisters. Without another word, her hands slid up his back and the fullness of her body pressed his overwhelmingly. Slowly—delicately— she started to touch his lips with hers, and stopped, tantalizing herself. Then Hek recovered sufficiently to squeeze her a little closer, as an experiment, and her mouth grazed his again. When he *pushed*, she drew her head away, making a low sound of reprimand—and for the first time the tip of a thin, living passionate tongue entered his mouth, entered his life, entered what might be called his soul. It was withdrawn almost at once from between his lips; it remained in his life from then on—and the scars we shall see on what might be called his soul all date from that first wound which never healed, that first exquisite, immortal stab.

When she tilted back her head to look at him, he followed her hungrily, blind as a kitten who has misplaced a teat. "Piggy," she said, and her breath seared his ear.

"What the hell are you doin' down there?!"—the trunks.

"I—I gotta go."

"One more." She crushed him again—and the living quality of her mouth impressed him still more. Heretofore he had been kissing dead women!

"Hey—*Hek!*" the bellower was out of sight.

"There," said Ruby, pushing him lightly away, "let that be a lesson to you."

Hek opened his mouth to answer Pete. Only a squeak came out. He cleared his throat. "Yes?"—in a treble.

"*Yes,*" the voice minced an imitation. "Whaja do; take a physic?"

Aghast, he looked quickly toward the chorus dressing room. Ruby waved at him and smiled as she went through the door.

## 2

"DJA get an ironing board?"

"I got a cherry."

## 3

HEK trundled the rest of the dressing-room trunks into their places a little louder than usual. He dropped them with unnecessary noise. She would hear him, and, perhaps, come out again. He looked at each chalked number hopefully. A "10" would send him in there——

"3" … "7" … "4" … "6" … "Where does this one go?"

"Look at the number!"

"There's no number on it."

The company property man stuck his head over the edge of the well. "Leave it outside."

Hek took it to the door of number 10 and let it hit the wall hard.

"Drop your watch?" a voice asked, but it was not hers.

Finally another "10" came down. He knocked at the door. "Come."

"Where do you want this one?"

She was unwrapping make-up from a towel, stiff with the residue of countless performances. Her eyes were limpid acknowledgment that she had been waiting as impatiently as he for that other trunk.

Some one pointed and he threw the heavy object with flourishes into position. As he turned to see if she had watched his strength demonstrated, two more girls arrived—and behind them more. Hek searched their faces as they passed, to substantiate the presumption that she was the prettiest girl in the show.

"Hello, cutie," said one remarkably sharp-featured creature, pinching his chin without slowing her pace. The others acted as if he were not there.

Aside from their height, which was nearly uniform, these girls had scarcely a feature in common. Their hats and coat collars were so much a part of their faces that what Hek saw was not a scant dozen different women but that many replicas of their different ideals of beauty approximated. That jaunty, slanting feather, that tam, that toque, that severely simple, military line— meant that its wearer wanted to look like Rosalind, Celeste, Mrs. Millions or a sister of mercy, each according to her own temperament. One dark girl, quiet and detached, preoccupied, stunned him with her simple loveliness. He watched her narrowly, but she passed within six inches of his nose without a glance.

He looked again at Ruby, as he left, but she was jabbering with some of the newcomers quite as if she had forgotten that entirely unforgettable moment.

*Babes in Starland* was a heavy show in all departments. The crew worked right up to one-thirty, then dodged out for a quick lunch and returned to set for the matinée. Hek was all thumbs. Every time the stage-door opened, he turned. Every time a girl laughed, he looked. He made a thousand pointless trips up and down the stairs leading to the dressing rooms. She got out, somehow, without his seeing her, and in again. Not until their stage manager called *overture* did he see her again—and then she was something dazzling beyond belief. She was in tights. He noted that incidentally. It was her face which held his fascinated gaze. Make-up at close range was not new to Hek, but this make-up was. There was no fooling about that; Ruby could give lessons in the application of grease paint.

She let her beaded lids droop to greet him, then adjusted the ribbons and stays of another costume on the floor in readiness for a quick change. Other girls were doing the same, on a long strip of muslin spread for the purpose. The orchestra began to play. Hek tried to be very casual about walking up to her. Bent over as she was, the fleshings were rather more noticeable. His breath was just a little short and labored.

"Did you have your lunch?" he asked.

"I didn't want any. Where were you?" Her inflection implied that after searching the theater for him—for hours—she had hunted elsewhere, her appetite dulled by longing—for him.

"I was looking for you."

She straightened and looked for a secluded corner. Other girls and one or two principals jostled past between them and a backing. She drew him into a narrow opening in a jog, out of the light. He was trembling before she faced him. She was going to kiss him again. God! Her bare arms were open. The hollow between her breasts, her rounded thighs;—her abdomen arched to meet him;—all this delicious sweetness, this scented, tinted beauty, this living picture was there for him to touch; *more*, it wanted him to touch it. She liked him, loved him.

"I'll get you all mussed up," he whispered as she almost cradled him in her arms and began nibbling at the baby mouth no one else had quite appreciated.

The stage manager's voice came up from downstairs: "First act; places. First act. All right, girls."

"You'll spoil your make-up," he objected. Ruby only shook her head, and applied herself once more to his lips. Then she did it again—so sweetly, only the tip, only a suggestion of what she might do—and Hek's sharp inhalation, his fingers suddenly clutching her back were the response she wanted.

"Jesus!" she said—and quickly joined the line forming on stage.

The music changed. "Let's have these bunches," some one called. Hek heard the switch go in. "On your toes."

Music…. "Take it away!"

Hek thought she sang much better than any of the others; there was no question about her dancing. He stood well back out of the entrance, tasting her lips again, waiting for that other …

He scrubbed around his mouth with an handkerchief, but Ruby's make-up did not smear.

The comedian talked to the *prima donna* in low tones until a cue carried her on. Then the stage around him was full of flounces, full of girls. They shed their costumes with three lightning gestures, regardless of who or what was about them. Hek was too amazed to move. He should have known it would be like this—but he hadn't thought. Which was she? Which flying arms, which flashing legs were hers?

"Getting an eye-full, Kid?" the nearest girl sneered.

"I—p-pardon me." That time he *knew* he was blushing. He hadn't meant to be watching them. They were stripped before he knew what was happening. He stepped between the tormentor and the proscenium with his back to them. They'd never believe it was an accident. How nasty that sounded! "Getting an eyeful, Kid?" He hated that girl. Which one was she? *Kid!* He hated that too.

Ruby'd think he had stood there—just to watch the girls undress; to see *her* almost naked. He hadn't. He could explain to *her* that he hadn't.

Some one was behind him. Ruby's hand drew him back. "You're the sweetest kid I ever met," she said very seriously. "I can't stay away from you. I want to be loving you every minute."

"Look," said Hek, like a very small boy, "I didn't mean to——"

"Listen, Jezebel," a sister from the line said close to Ruby's ear, "Mac is watchin' you like a hawk. He saw you kiss this—eh—kiss—*him*, just before the opening—and he's sore."

"He can go to hell."

"Don't be a nut."

"Are you married?" Hek asked.

"We're *on*." The informant sped away.

"Not exactly," said Ruby on the run.

*Not exactly!* A tall fellow in make-up, the company stage-manager, ambled up to Hek and stood silently at his elbow. Would this be "Mac"? Hek looked around and grinned. The other's face did not change. Hek watched the chorus. Ruby shot them a glance from her place in the line. He *was* Mac!

Unconcerned, casual, Hek circled the set near the wall to where Pete watched the performance from the right.

"The next is in one," Pete told him. "You stand there with the two umbrellas."

"I know."

Mac had come around too. "Who is that kid? He work here?"

"You bet," said Pete. "He's my first assistant."

"Has he got a card?"

"Sure."

"Sure," said Hek.

"O. K.... My men won't work with him, you know, if he ain't got a card."

"He's got one."

"Want to see it?"

"No. That's all right." Still he had not smiled. He walked away.

"Whadja do to him?"

"Is he 'Mac'?"

"Yeah."

"I stole his girl."

The oleo hit the stage.

"Haw!" Pete laughed. "Go on home an' dry your ears!"

## 4

HEK dallied, after the performance, upstairs and down, but, always, wherever he went, in a moment or two, Mac would appear. Finally the boy went home.... But—he had heard her say: "He can go to hell." He would see her again that evening. If the man were not her husband, what right did he have to tell her what to do? "He can go to hell."

Hek saw Bob bent over the mission table in the front room as he entered the flat. "Hello, Son," Minnie called from the kitchen. Her voice made Bob look up. He waved. The odor of parsnips was strong in the air. Hek hated them.

"Hello." He kissed his mother, dutifully, and went on to the bedroom he shared with Bob. In the dresser mirror, he studied his face, the unruly mop of taffy hair that curled over his temples in fretful disorder. She had found him desirable. He looked at his mouth.

"What kind of a show is that you've got at your Opera House? A good one?" Minnie asked over the cooking noises.

"It's the best one they've ever had. It's wonderful." ... What would they say if he went on and told them the rest of it? "What's more," he might put it, "the most beautiful girl you ever saw is in love with me. She can't stay away from me. She wants to love me all the time—and her steady fellow who wants to marry her is going to kill me if I don't let her alone, but he can go to hell!" What if he told them that? He wouldn't, of course. Keeping it to himself gave him the upper hand, for once, in this house where all authority was leagued against him.

He washed his face a little more thoroughly than usual, as befit a young lover, and went in the front room to enjoy the vicarious thrill of knowing something, even silently, which Bob did not know.

"Hello, Hek."

"Hya." He sat down. "Gosh! Don't you *ever* get tired studyin'?"

"Nope."

"Supper's about ready."

"I know.... Thanks."

"Gosh, *I* get tired. What's the use of it?"

"Well, the more you know, the more money you can make."

"You don't make so much."

"I'm going to make more."

"But what's the use of it to me? I'm going t'be a stagehand, or an actor, maybe."

"An actor, now?"

"Well, maybe. They make big money."

"Yes, I guess some of them do."

"*All of* 'em.... An' y' don't have to study to be an actor. You just do it."

"You'll have to study to be a good one, Hek.... In the first place, you have to study to be a gentleman."

"Whataya have to study? ... I'm a gentleman."

"Supper's ready!"

"Hek is going to be an actor, he tells me."

"No!"

"All right; you'll see."

"What makes you think you could be an actor, Son?"

"Well, I bet I can."

Minnie patted his hand. "I'll bet you can too, but not for a while yet."

He *ought* to tell them! Right now he ought to tell them that he wasn't a child any longer, that a full-grown and beautiful woman was in love with him, and he had known about babies for ever so long. He wondered if Ruby would marry him if he asked her—now, right away. They could travel—and be on the stage together.

"Do we get to see your show, Impresario?"

"I could only save two. They're at the box office." An allotment of tickets, varying in number, was assigned for each attraction to the property department. These were exchanged with local tradesmen for props the show did not carry. They were tendered as rental for furniture, saddles, pictures, rugs and guns and garden rakes, anything needed in the course of the performance; sometimes they bought fresh flowers, cigars, sandwiches, beer. Usually Pete had some left—the first three went to Hek.

"That's all right," said Minnie. "I don't care much about going anyway."

Bob smiled at her broadly. "You and I'll go," he said. "I didn't ask Florence."

"Oh, but, Bob. She expects it. She looks forward to it."

"She shouldn't ... We'll go."

"Gosh, yes," said Hek. "Don't waste a ticket on that long-shanks."

Bob scowled at his plate.

"Why, *Hek!*" his mother remonstrated. "That's disrespectful. You mustn't say things like that."

"Aw, well——"

"I'm serious, Son. You must *not* make slighting remarks about people's appearance. It isn't Florence's fault she's so tall and slender." Because this might be too subtle, coming from her, Minnie patted the back of Bob's hand.

"Slender!" said the youngest Knott. "She's skinny."

"Harper!"

Bob's grin was not entirely forced. "Never mind," he said. "But I'll tell you what: I'll go get her and you two go. I've got a lot to do. I really shouldn't take the time."

"You know I don't like to go without an escort, Bob. And I'm sure Florence doesn't either."

"Walk over with Hek when he goes. You'll be all right."

"I gotta get back early to-night. Pete needs me. I hafta run as soon as I'm through supper."

"More?" A dish was held before him.

"No, thanks. I've had enough."

"Well, I don't want to argue about it, Mother, but I can't take Florence and leave you sitting home alone. I just can't do it. I wouldn't enjoy the show a bit."

"All right," she assented. "I'll go."

Bob wondered a little that he was not more pleased. Did that mean that Florence's importance was increasing? Did it mean that he was falling in love?

Hek was leaving.

"Son! You haven't eaten anything."

"I've had enough. It's a heavy show. They're using every bat in the place."

"What are 'bats'?"

"Bats?! Don't you know what bats are? Battens! To hang drops on."

"How would Mother know? She's never been back stage."

"Well, gee. I thought everybody knew that. They're wood."

"Sit down and finish your supper. The bats aren't so heavy that you have to go without your meals."

"I've had all I *wanted*. Gooood night."

Minnie indicated his plate. "Look—he scarcely touched it."

"Probably piecing this afternoon. Let him go."

"So-long."

"You come right home after the show," Minnie called as he went down the stairs two at a time.

## 5

BOX-WAGONS and surreys, spring-wagons and buggies, a few high pooped motors—as many "steamers" as gasoline engines—filled Galena Street in prophecy of traffic jams to come. On Saturday evening, farmers came from as far as Ridott and Cedarville, Pearl City and even Pecatonica, to buy supplies, to see a show, to drink a glass of beer. Buffet doors were in constant motion. Hek glanced in each saloon as he passed. Great waves of husky gayety, dyed a thick yellow by primitive carbon incandescents, surged out of each door and clung to the shoulders of exiting groups. Hek's nostrils and ears filled with it. He had never been in a saloon. Swathed and stuffed with bunting and kept always out of sight, the Elling skeleton obliged with a circumspect rattle only on demand. It seemed, if one was alert, a little pitcher with good large ears, it seemed that Grandpa had once had—the craving. Shhhh. The *taste* for it. That was why Grandma had always put local-option placards in the Parsonage windows.

Hek hurried on. He was going to taste beer some day, just to find out what it was like—a little later, of course, when he was older. Nobody in Freeport would serve a minor.

Boys and girls hailed him; adults asked after Bob and Minnie. Hek answered between strides. He was racing now. She would come back to the theatre early, avoiding "Mac", if what she had said were true, if she couldn't stay away from him, couldn't keep her hands off him, wanted to love him every minute.

She would be leaving Freeport in the morning. *Babes in Starland* played Dubuque, Sunday. His heart ached so bitterly at that thought that he could not breathe. He had only just met her—and to-morrow she'd be gone. All that beauty, all that sweetness! There was no one like her in the world. She *wanted* to kiss him. She didn't fight and struggle and hold his hands. *This* was love.

The stage was utterly black. No one had returned from dinner. He found the pilot over the switchboard and then turned on the work-lights. The enormous, barn-like interior never failed to welcome Hek. He could have come in through the stage door thus, a thousand, five thousand times, and always when that little cluster, or a single border, of lights limned the angular outlines of a set, all mistily revealed the gridiron—*'way* up there—with its pendent lines, the drops, the sandbags, the fly-gallery, he would relax subconsciously, breathe easier and feel at home. Somewhere, behind the Parsonage Ellings or behind Ted Knott, there may have been a mountebank, at least a strain of clown. Some Christian martyr, some Puritan, in one of those families had lived or died with a gesture, for the very mechanics of make-believe fit comfortably in Hek's hand. Stage sounds, stage odors exhilarated him. The crack of a lash-line, the scrape and easy bump of a flat being struck, coming to rest with a swoosh against the back-wall. The cries: "Heads!" when a set of lines came down, weighted. "Up on your short ... Tie it," as a drop was trimmed; the voice of the candy-butcher mixed with the orchestra, both muffled by the asbestos; all these things found chords to set vibrating in the youngest remaining Knott.

Now a lady of this sphere, a Ruby from Terre Haute, had struck other theatrical chords on this untuned instrument, basal chords. Like an harp in a storm, Hek's self was set in tremulous motion. A proper ear held close to him would have heard the tones of his ego, his psyche, what might be called his soul.

It would be so easy to say of Hek that he was a born actor, a born theatre hanger-on, at any rate. It would be just as simple to

say that all this fascination for the show world, for the high shad-
ows of a deserted stage and for the sharp-colored, the bedizened
ladies of the chorus was the perfectly normal reaction of youth,
of puberty, to the greatest of all adult toys, the theater and its
women. His enthusiasm could readily be attributed to the contrast between this life, this environment and the stuffy, stifling,
God-besmeared and Christ-infested atmosphere with which
Grandma Elling had surrounded him.

Eh,—but this would be careless. First; we are all "born-actors".
But deck us in a Sunday suit and set our legs in motion—to see
Booth put to shame. Nor was his reaction "normal"—since—he
was not awed, he was not impressed, he was not overcome by the
theater; he *blended* sympathetically, he stayed out of the way, he
never whistled, he never sat in the props, never walked through
a set, never crossed the stage except at the back-wall. Not once,
from the first day he had earned a ticket for distributing broad-
sides, had Hek committed an unprofessional gaucherie. The test
was this: It had never occurred to any of the crew to send Hek for
the key to the curtain.

Third—or fourth; his enthusiasm was not the extreme
of *a* swinging pendulum's arc away from Grandma Elling,
because he was not loud, exuberant or boisterous. There was
nothing of the freed-man about his comportment. On the con-
trary, in movement, expression and manner, Hek appeared
about the theater to be an old, travel-worn philosopher,
returned now to the best-loved scenes of his boyhood. Except,
of course, that he looked a little too much like a curly-haired
Buster Brown.

Incline this way, if you please; incline toward the explanation
that far, far back, Hek's great-great-grandmother, many times
removed, was part barrel-jumper, and her husband—perhaps—a
court fool.

Hek threw on the dressing-room lights and went down stairs. She wouldn't be there—in the dark—but, there was no harm in looking. He heard the stage door open and close above him and he blushed. The musicians' cards were scattered on a felt covered table. He sat down and began shuffling them. He had a right to play solitaire in the Opera House if he wanted to. Not even *Mac* could find fault with that.

The stage-door began an almost uninterrupted squeaking and banging. A few at a time, crews and company were arriving. They nodded and spoke to him as he dealt. All these people knew each other now. Another season, returning, they would be recognized and greeted heartily. "Oh, yes! You were here with *Babes in Starland.* What ever became of that comedian of yours—eh—oh, what *was* his name?"

"*That's* right, *Babes in Starland....* Oh, *this* is the house where——"

That night the Freeport Grand Opera House became "the house where——" to this extent:

Ruby came in with three other girls. "Hello, there," she said.

Hek *couldn't* control his voice. "Hello."

"Playing solitaire?" The other girls went on into number 10.

The orchestra boys began to arrive.

"Yes, I was; but I've got to get to work now." He arose. "I got some work to do in here." *In here* was the locked prop room across the wide cement floor from the pit. The musicians bantered about past games and took their favorite places around the green table. None of them paid any attention to Hek as he opened the padlock and pawed around in the air for the swinging globe. Ruby stepped in the room after him and half closed the door. "Come here," she breathed. He had.

Nor had anticipation enlarged upon this joy a single atom; nor did this repetition stale the thrill. Hek's plan to be more adept, to be active in this play, to use his hands in an improvement on the games he knew, were abandoned, forgotten, when her arms enclosed him. He had meant to show her he was not an utter dullard. He had imagined his fingers seeking out her contours with kneadings and pressures. Poof! The chemistry of her obliterated will. Completely enervate, he lay back in her arms and ate and drank the fare she gave him. For this his supper had been left on his plate.

Mac knocked on the door of number 10. "Ruby."

"Ruby's not here."

"Didn't she come in with you?"

Ruby withdrew her lips and listened. Hek put a protective arm around her shoulders.

The man ran quickly up the stairs and the chorus dressing-room door opened, a black head came out, then was withdrawn. "I gotta find her, damn it." In a moment the same girl who had warned them at the matinée stood in the hall half made-up, a torn wrapper clutched loosely at her breast. Her knowing eyes glanced over the card game and around the rectangle of numbered doors.

"He must of been blind," she muttered, and crossed directly to the prop room. "Mac's lookin' for you, Jezebel," she said into the aperture. "Let the kid up."

"Let him look."

"Y' damn' fool! Is it any o' *my* business? He'll kill you again."

"Not while I'm around, he won't," said Hek, and wondered immediately if it was laughter which shook Ruby's diaphragm.

The other girl let a scathing grimace of scorn drop at their feet and an inelegant sound of disgust rattled in her throat. Then she walked away without another word.

"I've got to make-up, sweetness."

"Does he hit you?"

"Mac?"

"Yes—Mac."

"Well——"

"Does he?"

"Well, once. He gets excited. Don't bother about that. Kiss me just once more."

"When will I see you again? When will I *ever* see you again?"

Ruby did not speak for a moment, but took his hand, gently, and smoothed her dress with its palm. "I don't know, Baby. Maybe never."

"Don't say that. Oh, I've got to see you again, often. I love you, Ruby. God, how I love you!"

"Shhhhh." She shut his mouth with hers.

"Now! … You stay in here until I get out."

"If he hits you, I'll kill him."

She kissed his finger tips and was gone.

Hek waited a moment. A door closed; then he sauntered out of the dark room in shamefully apparent guilt.

"Pssst!" said one poker player. "Get the kid."

"Hello, Hek," the drummer called. "Just come up for a little air?"

They'd seen him! He smiled sicklily.

"Want a towel, Hek?"

Every one laughed except the *Babes in Starland* musical director who had opened the pot.

"Jesus, look at his mouth! What she try to do to you, Hek? Eat your mouth off?"

At the top of the stairs, Mac called: "Half-hour …. Half-hour," and came stalking down. The musical director rose and put his cards face down on the table.

"Half-hour!" Mac repeated.

From within the dressing rooms the call came back: "Half-hour." …. "Half-hour."

The leader spoke quickly in Mac's ear. Hek started for the stairs.

"Ain't that lousy?" one of the Freeport musicians asked at large.

"Thanks," said Mac. He was at the door of number 10 in two strides. "Get into somethin' quick, you molls, I'm comin' in."

"You stay the hell out o' here an' mind your own business," said she who invariably pronounced R-u-b-y "Jezebel'.

He turned the knob.

"We ain't decent!"

Mac went in.

"You get the hell out o' here, Jack MacNab. I don't give a damn if you *are* the stage manager of this turkey, you can't bust into my dressin' room!" This was the same girl.

"Shut your head! You ain't got nothin' I ain't seen a thousand times." He reached Ruby's side without a glance at the other girls in the room. She drew an insolent line with her eye-brow pencil, as if he were miles away. With his open hand he cuffed one ear, then the other. "Mealy-mouthed bitch," he spat. "I honest-to-God ought to kill y'."

Hek had crossed slowly to the door of the room. "You—you come out o' there!" he called after some deliberation. "That's a *ladies'* dressing room."

Mac leaned over the girl who sat perfectly still, looking at herself in the wall-glass. "We're sold out or I'd bust y' inta pieces…. Go on, make-up, but wait'll I get you home!" His legs scissored twice and he slammed the door behind him.

"That's a ladies' dressing room," Hek repeated.

"You'd never guess it!" Mac grated, then turned to the group of musicians and stage hands who formed a semicircle around him. "If there's anybody here thinks anything of this kid, they'll take him home *now*before I lose my temper. Y' hear?" He pushed Hek roughly aside and ascended the stairs.

Then, unaccountably, from nowhere, a fist that is not even to-day identified, caught the upper lip and a good-sized section of the cheek of the company's orchestra leader, cutting him and streaking his chin with blood.

## 6

PETE took his young assistant's arm. "You better go home, Hek. The old man wouldn't like it if there was any trouble."

Hek scarcely understood the property man's words. He walked to the girls' door despite the restraining hands. "Ruby! Did—did he hit you?"

"Make him go home, Pete," some one advised.

The leader wiped blood from his face and sputtered his rage. "Ruby!"

She appeared in the door. "Listen, baby; you get out of sight. I'll see you again,—but you get out o' sight now. Mac's nasty."

"Did he hit you?"

"No!"

"Y' sure?"

"I'd tell you."

"All right. I'll go then. I'll come down to the train in the morning."

The group of men moved awkwardly, with side glances and winks at each other.

"He can't afford to get into a fight," Pete told Ruby. "He's just got his card and the union is tough about fightin'."

Hek blanched. "Would—would they take my card away?"

"Quick as that."

"So-long," said Ruby, her eyes very sad. "I'll see you later." The door closed, shutting her from view.

"Would they, Pete?"

Three or four men added their assurance to Pete's. The union would take his card for fighting in the theater quicker than for any other reason on earth.

"Do you think you can handle the show alone, Pete?"

"I'll make out. You go on home."

"All right. Gosh, I wouldn't want to lose my card!"

Mac was pretending to investigate some crates at the extreme right of the stage. As Pete sent the boy into the night, the big man straightened and—without obvious purpose—walked to the door. Four members of the Freeport local arrived there at the same time. Pete shook his head. "You called half-hour, MacNab. You better make-up."

The stage manager looked from face to face around the group. "Yeah," he nodded, "thanks. Watch fifteen for me; will you?"

"Sure."

Hek turned away from the front of the Opera House lest he meet his mother and Bob. He didn't want to see any one he knew. He didn't want to explain. It would be all over town in the morning. All over town that he had been driven out of the Opera. House. No one would understand about the card, how strict the I. A. was. They'd only know he had had a fight and run away. A fight over a woman!

There was that much in it. They would all have to say the fight had been about a woman. He *had* stood right there and told the big gorilla to get out of her dressing room. "That's a ladies' dressing room," he had said. And what had Mac answered to that? "How'd you guess it?" Something like that.

But—they'd laugh at him anyway. He "wasn't dry behind the ears yet". They'd probably tell it that he was watching the girls make a quick change—and that this Mac had caught him and chased him. That's the way those things got around. He wasn't running from a fight. He'd take his chances with that big ape any day.

He skirted the business section and came to the flat from the less populous side of the street. What hurt the worst was being driven out of the Opera House. That was a disgrace. It might get back to the old man—and he'd fire him.

As he climbed the steps, Hek plotted escape. Why *didn't* he run away as he had so often planned to do? No more school. His card was sure to get him a job. Women liked him. Look; even that hatchet-faced one had pinched his chin and called him "cutie". He didn't have anything to worry about if he could avoid the disgrace of that story, if he just wouldn't have to face any one who knew him. He found the key under the doormat. No more orders from Bob. No more parsnips. He'd get a job—send money home! He'd show them how to make *big* money. He'd pay off those old bills in a hurry.

A closet yielded an old telescope and a worn, brown valise. No one would think he had nerve enough to go to Chicago on the midnight train. *Could* he go, without waiting to see Ruby again! In the note he left for Minnie there would be misleading hints of his destination. They thought he was just a kid. He'd show them. He'd show Ruby too. How her heart would ache when she looked for him at the depot in the morning—while *he* was in Chicago!

Raiding the change purse in the sugar bowl swelled his capital to four dollars and sixteen cents.

Hek began packing. There was plenty of time. They wouldn't be home for hours. He looked thoughtfully at two knickerbocker suits. The gray he had on was the only one with long pants Minnie had bought him so far. But there was no use taking those *short* ones. You couldn't get a job even as an apprentice in short pants. And all those stockings! He owned only two pairs of socks, those on his feet and a pair in the dirty clothes. He'd better take a few pair of those stockings. Nobody was going to roll up his pants legs to see if he had socks on.

A familiar rap sounded on the front door. Who was it rapped like that? Some one who came up pretty often. His pulse stopped entirely and he held his breath. Who *was* that?

Rap—rap—rap, rap—rap—rap, rap.

If he stayed perfectly still they'd go away. They didn't *know* he was here—unless they'd seen him come in.

The door opened. Florence!—of course. That was her rap. "Anybody home?" she asked, entering. "Hello, Hek."

He stood stiffly before her with a handful of long, black, *boys' stockings* dangling from his grasp.

"Hello, Florence. Nobody's home. They've gone to the show."

If a shadow crossed her eyes it was gone at once. "I saw the light and thought there must be some one here. Why aren't *you* at the Opera House?"

So far, she hadn't noted his occupation. He put the stockings behind him and crumpled them swiftly into a loose ball. "I'm—I'm going right back now. I had to come home to get something."

"Is that your room, Hek? Yours and Bob's?" How often she had longed to peek behind that door. It had always been shut when she had been there—for Sunday dinner, several times. She needed to see that room if only for a moment. She needed walls and furniture to house and support Bob's sleeping figure in her imagination as she lay thinking of him before going herself to sleep.

Hek put himself clumsily in her way. "Yeah," he said, "it *was*."

"What do you mean? Isn't it any more?" Florence was more interested in peering past him than in the interpretation of his emphasis.

"Oh, yes; sure." He mustn't tell her he was running away, although he did want to. He wanted to tell some one. Wouldn't she be surprised if he did tell her?

It was obvious that Hek concealed something, that he was trying to obstruct her view of the room, trying to keep her out. "What are you hiding in there?" she asked playfully, smiling and squinting suspiciously.

"Oh, nothing."

"You *are*. What's that on the bed?"

"That's just some old stuff." Then he pretended to play too. "Come on! You get out of here. You go in the front room."

What *was* that on the bed? It looked like a valise, half packed—and an old telescope beside it. Florence tried to push past, holding the boy with her hands. "I'm going to see what you're doing in here."

"Oh, no, you're not." Hek grappled with her and they turned and twisted in each other's arms a moment.

The boy's grip relaxed a little. It astonished him to find that Florence was a woman too. He had not thought of that before. He pretended a renewed interest in the scuffle, pushing and pulling with one forearm across her breasts, the other around her waist, his hand tight-pressed on her abdomen.

"Hek!" she said, every inch the adult, "you're packing your clothes! Were you running away?" Her body was suddenly entirely relaxed. She did not hold his arms, but began a steady pressure away from her on his chest. "Answer me.... Were you running off?"

Hek released her and stepped back into the room, stooping to pick up his stockings. He hung his head. His mouth was surly. "Well?"

"You *were*."

"Well, maybe I was."

"Hek! without telling your mother, without telling Bob. Just going——"

"Oh, *you* don't know what's happened. Gee whiz … I gotta go."

"You don't have to go like that, no matter what has happened.… Aren't you ashamed of yourself? Look at me. Aren't you ashamed?" To be thus parental, thus castigatory, emphasized the difference in their ages—a difference which needed emphasis in Florence's subconscious after that stirring contact with Hek's strength. A healthy young female of Florence's repression is not responsible for the activities of her subconscious. Tell not your beads for her. Yet in the middle of her attempt to regain emotional equilibrium, that "Look at me!" had injected itself in spite of her. The phrase, of course, was in her head from the schoolroom. Teachers said it. But it left Florence's lips with intent she did not realize, even when she followed it up by taking his chin in her hand and turning his head up slowly until their eyes met, until she could look into the hurt and troubled depths of his—very like Bob's, but with longer lashes. Not even then did Florence know that what she wanted was to look thus into his eyes. Not even when, looking, she forgot what it was she intended to say, not even then did the biological basis of her action show itself to her. In a great wave of tender, mothering pity for the pain she saw on his face, Florence put her arms around him and held his head against her bosom. (He was such a child.)

Sympathy had always affected Hek. He weakened before it. Usually he cried. Tears started now—and his chin and lips trembled. "I gotta go away, Florence," he said. Longshanks was nice after all. The warmth and softness of her caressed his ear, his cheek; the odor of womanly cleanliness without perfume played a part Hek did not know. He moved his head back, tilting his face up toward hers. "You wouldn't understand," he said haltingly.

Florence looked into those eyes, glistening full with tears—and turned giddy. She watched that very red cupid's bow of a mouth trembling there three inches from her own—and reached for it. The first, soft impress was electric. Still she found her voice. "Don't feel so badly, Harper. Whatever it is, it can be fixed up."

He started to say *no, it can't*—but she was kissing him again, so he waited. *She* kissed pleasantly too; differently from Ruby, but very satisfyingly. Of course, she didn't put out her tongue. Maybe she didn't know about that. *He* hadn't known about it. Maybe—maybe he should do it to her to show her what it was like. Probably girls liked it just as well as boys. Probably it would make her feel as good as it had made him feel when Ruby did it to him.

Apparently he had got *nothing* out of the pretty practice at all. He had only thought he enjoyed it.... Florence's middle slumped quickly toward him; a low, caressing groan sounded deep in her throat. She grasped his head in her hands and kissed and kissed and kissed—like a starving woman.

Only an innocent of the innocents could have retained the hallucination of tendering motherly comfort after that. Florence achieved it. She achieved it in a somewhat roundabout fashion, aided by these considerations:

That Hek was innocent too, genuinely.

That she assumed he was even more innocent than he was. She believed that he was unsophisticated to a degree not perceptibly removed from feeble-mindedness. Not that Florence thought in those terms. Not that Florence thought. In the madly whirling mélange of half-ideas, split concepts and stifled murmurings of conscience which filled her mind through these hours of a memorable evening, in the very midst of all else that was going on, sandwiched in between ecstasy and a frantic mental search for a moral defense, this sequence occurred.

It's wrong! (For the merest fraction of a second of time she knew that clearly. Then something drove it out of her head.) It's wrong! But Hek's the only witness. And—*Hek's too young to know how wrong it is.* He's too young to know that I know it's wrong and that I'm going on anyway—in spite of anything.

Oh, that raging, racing, chasing kaleidoscope of nameless verbal-mental figures! Name me that dance, that struggle, that combat. Universes are born with less travail. Here, in a single mind, a single head, are: a theft and a giving, dishonor and bliss; pain of the flesh and pleasure transcendent; anguish of spirit and peace after long warfare; disgrace and a coronation. Here are self-loathing and matchless pride; hate and a joy that deserves a better name than "love"; shame and a glorious courage. Here are all these things and a thousand more—nadirs and zeniths all; coming, going, flashing, biting, crushing, pummeling, rending, pinching—until—until it is no wonder Florence fell into an exhausted sleep with her arms around Hek. No wonder.

## 7

WHAT I mean to say is—that Hek and Florence cohabited.

Minnie and Bob found them both asleep on the boys' bed and a new world's record for innocence was tallied. For the theater-goers saw nothing amiss in the juxtaposition of those two bodies. They thought it remarkable, of course, that Hek should have so soon overcome his aversion to "long-shanks". It certainly was unusual that he should be sleepy before midnight. Further than that Minnie, at least, had not the time to delve before her eye caught the traveling paraphernalia, overturned on the floor at the side of the bed, and the scattering of Hek's apparel. "Look at *that*," she said.

Bob nodded, perplexed. "Funny; isn't it?"

Minnie laughed—a gay peal. "Well—it's silly to stand here guessing. Let's *ask* them."

Her laughter brought Hek's body bolt upright, his eyes wide and scared. Florence woke smiling.

"Hey—sleepy-heads!" Minnie continued to laugh. "What's going on here?"

From his mother, Hek turned his gaze toward Bob. "I—I fell asleep," he chattered. If Minnie thought it was a joke—perhaps it could be passed off as one. He shot one fearful glance at Florence's skirt. It covered her neatly.

"Who's traveling?" asked Minnie.

"Aw—"

"Hah? Who's traveling?"

Florence, too, noted Minnie's geniality with relief. She looked guardedly at Bob. He grinned at her. "Why," said she, "Hek intended to, but I think he's changed his mind now." The note of tenderness which sounded in that speech was lost on that group. It was oddly incongruous too. It is practically impossible for a big, bony woman to be wistful.

The situation was becoming a little clearer. "Were you running away, Son?"

Hek got off the bed. "Yes."

"What for?!"

"What for?" Bob spoke for the first time. "Does he need a reason? He's been running away as long as I can remember."

Florence stood up too. "I'm so tired," she said a little pointlessly.

"Have you been asleep long?"

"Not long. I was passing on the street and saw the light"—steady, Florence, they haven't asked for an explanation—"and here he was, packing." It was a great deal to expect, but she hoped Hek would understand that their salvation lay in her telling the story as an adult, amused at his childishness. If she could only squeeze his hand, wink, anything—so he wouldn't feel she was playing him false.

Hek dropped sullenly into a chair.

"I said: 'Where are you going?' and he wouldn't tell me, at first. Then I got it out of him that he was running away." As she talked, Florence felt an increasing nervousness. The need for invention appalled her. She lied so seldom, so poorly; yet a fabrication must be voiced in Hek's presence so that he would know what to say. "I told him he mustn't do that—to you—after all you'd done for him."

Hek squirmed. All three of them stood over him, looking down. Gosh! Wasn't she making it easy on herself? After loving him like that! Going right on pretending to be Bob's girl.... *After all they'd done for him!* ... He looked up at her and let the tip of his tongue slide meaningfully over his lips.

In a panic, Florence hurried on: "I shamed him. We sat on the bed—and he—he cried a little—I think."

Insult *added* to injury! Had to tell that.

"He—he's promised me not to do it again; haven't you, Hek?"

He wagged his head, jerkily, as if preparing some devastating retort—but finally sniffed and did not answer.

"Not until next time," said Bob.

Minnie squatted beside his chair. "There isn't going to be any next time; is there, Son? You don't really want to go away—do you?"

He wanted to cry then, but he couldn't, very well, in front of Florence. He permitted his hair to be stroked, shaking his head negatively, not trusting his voice lest it break.

"Well,—I've got to be going."

"I'll take you home."

Yeah. He'd take her home. He'd walk along the dark streets with her and leave her at her door. Shake hands—maybe. He wouldn't kiss her; wouldn't touch her, love her,—wouldn't do *that* to her. Slow as molasses. Gosh! Probably Bob had never kissed any girl. It was a sure thing he didn't know about tongues. How could anybody be so slow?

Florence held out her hand toward him. See? Nobody could see anything wrong in that. "Good-night, Hek."

"Good-night." He wanted to hold her hand longer. He liked her now, liked her lots. Her fingers contracted convulsively on his. The innocents didn't notice.

Bob did what little talking was done on the short walk to the Mitchell home. Florence had retired for self-communion. Then this bugaboo, this dreadful thing, this one unforgiveable act of girlhood was no more than that! Over and done, with a pleasant tingle and a glow of memory; otherwise everything was the same. It made a difference, of course, who the man was. Just anybody wouldn't do. But *Hek* seemed almost as if it had been—Bob. How strange. Had she wanted Bob that way? Now— before marriage? She had never thought of it before. It seemed a little ludicrous; staid, calm, studious Bob. She turned and looked at him, involuntarily. No, he—he *hadn't* inspired any such ideas. Of course, that might be because he never touched her, never kissed her. She thought she would feel a little foolish kissing Bob.

It depended on the man, the boy. The fact that Hek too would have a definite need for secrecy mitigated one phase of the situation. It would be dreadful to have committed this folly with a boy who must depend only upon his honor to keep him silent. Life, her life, wouldn't be worth living under those circumstances. But Hek's youth and their relationship would hold his tongue in check.

It had been—what was Bob talking about?—it had been—delightful.

## 8

SUNDAY—and Hek awoke with a swagger. Lothario, Don Juan, the fauns, must have greeted days like that; smiling, glad, with secrets. He felt so superior. From knowing one thing Bob did not know, he had advanced in a few short hours to an eminence that brother would never more than approximate. He counted the favors women had shown him between suns.

Kisses, chin-chuckings, the ultimate; and in his mind's eye all three women became of an uniformly superlative degree of beauty. Ruby, in retrospect, was well nigh divine; she of the sharp features suffered a nose-dulling and a chin-rounding operation without ether; Florence, magically, lost all resemblance to a horse, taking on—instead—qualities of the rose, the doe, Christmas morning and white mice.

As he bathed, Hek's internal strutting stubbed a toe. This was against that moot topic of babies. None but married people had them—he knew that—but then, what was this about being "knocked-up"? His data on the subject were scant. One couldn't ask. The facts must be gleaned. Soon, too, now that he was a man. Probably it was nothing to worry about. His confidence returned—and with it his manner.

Bob still slept. Minnie heard him in the ice-box. "Hek?"

"Yes."

"What are you doing?"

"I'm getting something to eat?"

"What are you doing up so early?"

"Oh, I don't know. It's after seven."

"I know,—but it's Sunday."

"Well——"

"Are you going out?"

"Yes."

"Where?"

"I've got to go over to the depot and help load the show." If Minnie did not know what a "bat" was, this falsehood would not be liable to close scrutiny.

"You do? … I should think they'd have *men* enough to do those things. I don't like to have you lifting and straining."

"I won't hurt myself, Mother."

"You be careful."

"I will."

Not only did he possess knowledge neither of these people had, knowledge and experience, but he had also come upon a time when he could deceive them both consistently. This was an absolutely new order, the change abrupt and the prospects fascinating. It was only yesterday that either Bob or Minnie could detect one of his smallest prevarications instantly. Closing the door behind him now marked the third successful major deception in half a day. He took long steps and distended his chest. Childhood had been left behind. Only see his occupation at the moment. After enjoying the utmost personal intimacy of one woman just before sleep, he arose and kept a tryst with another. He watched this devil-may-care fellow pass in a few show windows. He practiced several gaits, tried his cap different ways, swung his arms and kept them fairly still. It didn't matter much what he did, the result was invariably pleasing.

The depot platform was deserted. He was hours ahead of time. That didn't matter. With all the things he had to think about, he could just sit still—indefinitely. He walked over to the bridge and leaned on the rail watching the swift water. He'd just stand here and think. It was better than sitting in the station. Some girl he knew might pass. If one did——

If one did, how differently he would act *now*. Hek smiled in tired contemplation of the boy he had been.... But—it was more pleasant to think of Florence, or Ruby. He'd start at the beginning of it—the first moment he had seen Ruby—and go through the day.

Hek was in the midst of his fourth defloration of his brother's sweetheart, and he had taken it slower each time, when he saw Mac and Ruby coming down Stephenson Street.

As a matter of factual record, the girl had her arm linked in his and her face turned up at him, happily. What Hek saw was that she carried her own traveling bag and that the brute beside her had one free arm! The boy hadn't needed that to show him what sort of man Mac was, but it brought his hatred to a focus.

Before the couple got very near, Hek went around the depot on the Northwestern side and hitched himself to a seat on a baggage truck. The meeting must be casual, especially if Mac were witness to it. If that beast dreamed she had made a date with him, he might beat her. He waited, gauging their progress from the unhurried pace they had been using. The corner.... The tracks. Then slowly across.

They must be on the platform now. Hek's tongue clove to the roof of his mouth, thickly. Probably she would start to look for him alone. He waited what seemed a long time. The soubrette and two of the principal men came through the passage and crossed the tracks to throw stones in the river. A little later four chorus girls followed, and began trying to span the stream with pebbles. The two groups did not mingle. When several other members of the company passed his perch, Hek shifted his weight to his elbow and crossed his leg, hoping his movements would attract their attention. If they actually saw him, they would go tell Ruby where he was.

It was almost train time. If she didn't come soon they wouldn't have a minute together. The baggage man passed with a loaded truck, moving it up the platform to where the proper car would stop. Hek knew him. "Want a lift with that, Dad?" He could be helping his old friend. Mac couldn't criticize that.

"Oh, hello, boy."

"Want a lift?"

"What?"

The truck had passed. Further pursuit of that angle was impossible.

Hek slid off the truck and walked toward the tracks on the I. C. side. Ruby and Mac and at least five others stood in a group, most of them picking their teeth. Some were talking, others just standing. No one looked at him. He leaned against the corner of the brick station and started down the tracks toward Chicago. She was bound to look that way sooner or later.

"There's Ruby's mash," some one said.

"Where?"

"There."

Ruby took Mac's arm. "Come on, Honey, be nice to him."

Hek turned and saw them coming,—*both* of them.

"Hello, Son," said Mack. "Down t' see the folks off?"

" ... Uh, yeah. I came down."

"Swell day," said Ruby.

"Yeah, great," Hek looked toward the sky.

"Do you have much cold weather around here?" asked Mac.

"Gosh, yes. Lots."

"That so? That river freeze, does it?"

"Freeze! Gosh, yes. Jeeminy."

"Then you take your girl and go skating," Ruby said.

"Well, not on the river. We skate at Taylor's Park; that's way over, down Stephenson Street; that way. It's the fair grounds too." Let her think he did take a girl if she wanted to.

"Good skating there?" Mac asked.

"There hasn't been any this year. Probably won't freeze much any more now."

"No, winter's about over."

The train whistled.

"There it comes," said Ruby.

"Yeah,—I'll watch the stuff on. Seen the boys?"

"Bill went in the can a minute ago."

"I'll get 'im.... Well, so-long, Son." Astonishingly Mac's hand was out before him.

"So—so-long," Hek pumped the man's arm twice.

"I thought you weren't ever goin' to see me."

"You been here long?"

"About five minutes."

"Do you love me as much as ever?"

"More. But I don't like him. What did you bring him over here with you for?"

The train thundered up to them, bells ringing, brakes screeching.

"Good-by," she said.

"Gee, I wish I was goin' with you."

"J do too."

"Do you—honest?"

"Honest."

"I don't know—I guess I'm goin' to Chicago next week—get a job."

"What! You?"

Hek nodded. "Why not?"

"Do you live with your folks?"

"Yes; my mother and brother."

"Father dead?"——

"Yes. He was killed in the Spanish-American War."

"You stay right here with your mother, Baby. Don't you go to Chicago."

"Why not? I hate Freeport."

"Yeah? Well, wait ten years and tell me what you think of the Windy City. Do *that*."

"Don't you like Chicago?"

"I don't like any place.... I gotta go now, Baby.... There's Mac."

"Oh——"

"Sorry, I can't. Mac's lookin'. I'll see you again sometime, Baby. You stay right here with your ma."

She ran to her grip, and up the steps into the day coach. In the vestibule she turned and waved.

"*A—a—all* aboard!"

Hek drew his hand through the air weakly several times. Tears were at the very edge of his lids, She had not *kissed* him. There was the train, carrying her away—and she had *not* kissed him.

## 9

AFTER *that* week-end, school was unthinkable. So Hek tried not to think about it. That's pretty difficult, suddenly to break an habit, interrupt a routine of years—and not *think* about it. It becomes almost impossible when one cannot move freely about; not anywhere, inside or out, without fear of detection. Not thinking about school was as hard for Hek as not thinking about jail would be to an escaped but cornered convict. He felt considerably

like a convict, too, those first two or three days. He hung around
the theater and the depot, gliding around corners every time an
intimate of any of the family appeared, jumping out of his skin
at every sharp noise.

Several hours each day he spent in "diner" lunch-counters,
eating hamburger sandwiches and apple pie, and listening. This
source of education, it seemed to Hek, was a vast improvement
over the schoolroom. Here he could listen to lecture and debate
upon every conceivable subject, every field of human inquiry,
every sensible interest of mankind. The principal studies were
baseball and women. The instructors were all men, men of experience, vision, understanding.

The study of medicine was pursued here too—each lecturer
being a specialist, all specialists in the same disease. Hek knew
the disease by name. It appeared in the washroom of the depot
and in the men's room at the Opera House, printed in bold letters
on a little tin sign advertising a patented cure for "all cases, of no
matter how long standing".

"Hell, it's *nothin*'," one day's lesson had begun. "It ain't a bit
worse'n a head-cold."

"Oh, no—o—o? ... Me, I'd rather have a cold."

Other loungers had laughed at that. "*Me* too," several had
said.

"Say—I never seen a head-cold that'd make me bite a ten-
penny nail in two."

"Oh, it *hurts* worse; I mean it ain't no more serious."

"It'll blind y'."

"It *won't* blind y'."

"The hell it won't. You get some o' that stuff in your eye
an' it'll blind y'! Don't tell me. I been to big men. I know. A
specialis' in Chicago tol' me: 'Be careful your family don't
use your towel. It'll get in their eyes an' blind 'em.' He was

one o' the biggest clap men in the Middle-West. Don't talk to me."

"Ah—them birds 're jus' after your dough. They donno what they're talkin' about. They're—eh—they're whadayacallem?— quacks! That's what. They're quacks."

"A bartender in Cleveland taught me how to cure it. I never go to them quack bastards."

"Jever hear the one about the guy ast the doctor couldn't he of got it in a toilet?"

All nodded their heads and laughed. They'd heard it.

"An' the doc says: 'Sure. I s'pose you could. But that's a hell of a place to take a girl.'"

Every one laughed again, the narrator loudest.

On Thursday evening of that Sabbatical week, Hek's teacher called at the flat. Harper, it seemed, had been absent. He was not home then, but this was important enough to make them seek him. Bob walked up to the theater while Miss Murphy and Minnie talked. There had been a show the night before. Hek had worked. To-night the place was dark. Bob went on, looking in several possible places, but returning without the malefactor.

Miss Murphy did not wait. When Hek came in, a little after eleven, one glance informed him that he was found out. He sat down before them with a resolution to remain determined in spite of everything. He was a child no longer.

"Where have you been, Hek?"

"Out with the boys."

"What boys?"

"Oh—a bunch of them."

"What have you been doing?"

"We sat around and talked."

"Where?"

"What's the matter? What did I do?"

"Never mind. You just answer my questions one at a time."

Hek sneered at Bob openly and turned to Minnie. "Do I hafto, Mom?"

"Yes, Hek, every one."

"Well, I'm not goin' back to school, no matter what he says. I won't go."

"You'll go if we tell you to, young man—and we *tell* you to. Miss Murphy has been here to-night and you report to her in school at the regular time to-morrow."

Just at the moment it did not occur to Hek that the most expeditious way out of this unpleasantness was to agree, to assent, to allow them to think he *would* go back. Then, when the time came, he need not go unless he cared to. The odds were terrific that he would not *care* to.

He glared at his older brother. "I won't.... I'm not ever going back to school again."

"You'll go, Hek, if I have to carry you every step of the way in my arms."

"You couldn't."

"I am not going to have to."

"If you did I wouldn't stay."

"Hek, what *has* come over you?" Minnie demanded. "You've always been a good boy. What's happened? Whom are you running around with who upsets you?"

"Nobody, Mother. It's just that I'm grown up now and——"

"Grown up!" Bob interrupted. "Why, you're only fourteen."

"Oh, am I?"

"Of course you are."

"Well, I'm not goin' back to school."

Minnie rose. "Go to bed, Harper. We won't discuss it any further. Go to bed at once."

"I'm——"

"Not another word. Go to bed."

Neither foot wanted to follow the other, but he finally reached their room.

Minnie and Bob looked at each other in silent perplexity. The shadow of defeat had fallen on them but they were not ready to recognize or to acknowledge it.

"I don't suppose there's really anything unusual about it," Bob mused aloud, speaking slowly.

"No—of course not. Probably conversations like this have occurred in a thousand homes—to-night—simultaneously."

Bob smiled at the ceiling as if he saw there a projection of Minnie's efforts and his.

She nodded as if he had spoken. "Yes. That's just it."

"We got started pretty late."

"Oh—I wonder … I wonder. Sometimes I think it doesn't matter when you start. Sometimes I think—in some cases—it is always 'too late'."

"You mean, one has it or one hasn't—and training, education, environment can't change the individual much? … That sounds dreadfully smug, doesn't it?"——

"And quite mystical."

"I don't know how you're going to explain the original difference, then. We had the same father—and your outlook was the same through both periods."

"Until the last few weeks of his. It was quite tragic then."

"Do you suppose that's important? Might the finishing touches be applied to the brain just before birth?"

"They are; don't you think? It's the brain we begin work on almost immediately after birth. Does he notice light? Does he smile or laugh? Say 'mama' … But I don't see the connection in Hek. Suppose I was desolate, crushed; how does that account for this utter normality? I should think, rather, it might have made him moody, brooding, say."

"Oh, no, Mother. The essence of your reaction to Dad's death was futility. What was the difference? What mattered? ... You relaxed. If it's true that his mind was receiving sympathetic impressions—you relaxed at exactly the wrong time. You gave him nothing. His brain came out a blank—like the brains of the millions, all blanks, all receptivity. Then circumstances hit us and that plastic mass took *Their* impressions instead of ours."

"That's right," said Minnie, "blame it on me."

Bob laughed and rose to kiss her. "He blames *me* on you!" He held her head against his body and stroked her hair, actually thinking of the action, watching his fingers, intending that she should feel his love, his admiration, his respect.

"I'm getting gray as a mouse, Bob."

"You are not!"

"I am. Look here, over the temples."

"Where?"

"Right in here," her fingers showed him. "Just dozens of them."

"Not a single, damned one."

"Bob, you're blind."

"There isn't."

"Well, perhaps I got them all. I've been pulling them."

"Seven new ones grow in," he warned.

"Then I'll pull *those* out."

But the shadow of defeat had fallen on them. Minnie and Bob were whipped. Whether Minnie's were the fault, through improper prenatal psychology, or Grandma Elling's, through her misrule of his baby years, or theirs mutually, through laxness of discipline that was the result of their study and imprejudice—whatever the cause, they had failed. They were helpless before Hek's normality whether they admitted it or not. They were vassals to his welfare while he chafed and galled under their imagined dominion.

His future could and probably would be bright, successful and supinely happy. If it were, it would not mitigate their shame. There was this difference between Minnie's aims for Bob's attainment and the ideal those two held for Hek's; that the first had been a concept of an all but final effect, a picture of a complete man—the result of a course of training, whereas the second had been a more abstract hope that by precept and manipulation, the *desire* for a similar end and fate could be instilled in the object of their ministrations. In this they had failed. Hek's desires were the desires of a billion other fourteen-year-olds—a billion.

"Well, Bob,—what can we do about it?"

"I don't know." He resumed his chair.

"If we do get him back to school, it won't last. Every week or so we'll have this same battle over again."

"And how much good will school do him?—driven to it like that; ten can't make him drink."

So they went into the room where Hek studied facial expressions in his mirror, scowling, laughing, being frightful, haughty, adoring—by turns.

From their smiles Hek gathered that their mission was not unpleasant.

"We've been talking about you, Hek? How'd you like to get a job?"

## 10

THE Sunday the *Babes in Starland* played Dubuque, Florence spent at home. She got her father's breakfast and ate it with him

silently. Mitchell never had anything to say. He folded his pan-
cakes and surprised Florence with every bite—even after years—
by getting the corners past his walrus mustache without daubing
it with syrup. Florence cut hers daintily with a fork.

A certain reaction had set in in Florence's case, a depres-
sion. She was different now, that much was exhilarating, but not
even the novelty of getting acquainted with this new self was
fun enough entirely to dispel her memory of the old Florence
entirely out of control. She was not ashamed of what she had
done. She was ashamed of having been so much affected by passion. Until her death, when Florence was eleven, her mother had
instructed her in lady-like restraint. A lady was never hungry.
She ate only in deference to the hour and to the appetites of others. A lady was never thirsty. She drank only half of whatever
was offered to her in a cup or a glass. Thus, from picking at her
meals and sipping at her water and going home early from picnics and parties, it was a short and easy step to loving without
avowals or contacts or emotions—as she had loved Bob. Giving
way to a surge of a desire, actually "going all the way" under
the influence of an animal craving was very like putting one's
elbows on the table, like relishing a chicken leg in both hands,
like drinking enough water actually to *quench* one's thirst.
Pretty bad! Pretty bad!

Mitchell took his stinking pipe and the Sunday paper into
the parlor and Florence did the dishes. She was a different girl
now; what would this new person do about—things? Truth to
tell, she didn't feel very different; but she *should*. She was supposed to. Aside from a vague and almost indescribable sensation
of *sturdiness*, a solidity, a strength in the region of her lower belly,
she felt very, very like the Florence Mitchell of yesterday. She had
seen an old German, one of the fat ones, once, at a picnic, down
a scuttle of lager and leisurely clap his protuberant midriff with

well-satisfied hands. That was the way she felt. What was the word? *Robust.* That was it. Down there she felt robust.

Poor little Hek. Probably he was frightened to death. He hadn't meant to do it any more than she. How bravely he had taken the story of his running away, her twisted version of it. Now, he was probably afraid she would tell on him, tell exactly what had happened. He was too much of a child to realize that she didn't dare say anything. Where do you suppose he had learned to kiss that way? Who had been kissing him? Some of those girls around the Grand Opera House? … Could—could he—have done *that* with some of them? Oh, that was loathsome. To be one of many! Suppose he had; from girl to girl around there (every one knew what show girls were) and then to her.

Suddenly Florence was very angry. Dirty little snipe. Running around sticking himself in just any place. The dish she was washing collided with the faucet. Thank heaven it wasn't one of the good ones.

Florence hoped above all things that Hek would not misunderstand that evening and expect it to be repeated. She hoped he wouldn't get the idea that he was in love with her—or she with him. He was so young you couldn't tell what strange notions he might get. It was a good thing he was young. She gave the dish cloth an extra hard twist. If he were any older she might have something else to worry about. There was that reason for never repeating the offense of that evening—that reason in addition to the one of decency. Every day he grew older and the danger increased. In another year such a thing would certainly have serious consequences. She put the dishpan away with very deliberate, stiff movements. Imagine such a thing! She, of all people! Florence Mitchell with a fatherless baby.

The smile that Florence carried to her dressing for church was just a shade too dogged to be said to reflect a mind free from care.

But nothing happened. Tuesday evening she walked home with Bob and their relationship was entirely unchanged. Thursday morning—a day ahead of time—she sang: *Jesus bids us shine, first of all for him*—as she took the pins out of the cushion.

The first time she saw Hek after that, Florence experienced another new sensation, something that had absolutely never occurred to her at sight of Bob. Gladness, so piercing it stopped her breath, smote her in the region of the pancreas, where classic writ hath it lies the spleen. "Ooh—" she said, "Hek!"

He was across the street from her. Friday noon. He looked both ways carefully before trusting himself off the curb.

"How are you?" she said, holding out her hand. "Where have you been?"

Hek shook her hand and dropped it. "I been around. Where you been?"

"Home."

"Yeah? Gee, I—I thought prob'ly you were mad at me."

"Yes?" She wanted him to talk about it.

"Gosh, yes. Aren't you?"

"Why should I be?"

"Oh, I donno.... Lots of girls *would* be."

"Hek."

"Yeah?"

It wouldn't come.

"What?"

"Hek."

⚜ ⚜ ⚜

"Hek—haveyoueverdonethatbefore?"

Maybe he *was* a born actor. Hek smiled faintly and looked away. "Why?"

"You *have*. Hek Knott, you *have!*"

"Not very often."

"Oh—I'll bet you have a dozen times."

"A dozen!" Hek was incredulous.

"Hek," Florence was driven to her last defense trench in utter rout, "I'm a lot older than you. You listen to me." Then suddenly her mind was barren. What should he listen to? What had she intended to say? … "Hek, we—we mustn't *ever* do that again. Not ever."

"No," he agreed to that.

"And no one must ever know."

"No."

"It's our secret; isn't it?" She took his hand again and Hek looked quickly up and down the street.

"I quit school," he told her. "I'm goin' t' work at Wagner's."

"You are?"

"Monday."

"My goodness. Bob let you?"

His look was mingled exasperation and pity. "Bob—*let* me? A lot he's got to say about it."

She saw she was wrong and tried to apologize with her eyes. "You're not going back to school at all?"

"Nope. One guy that's swallowed the dictionary is enough in one family."

She nodded quickly. "Do you think he's still going to college, Hek?"

"I guess so. He keeps talkin' about it. Wouldn't you think he'd get tired, studyin' all the time?"

"*I* should think so."

Hek didn't bother to analyze her manner as she spoke; she meant something by it. "I better go. We got a heavy show Saturday. You better come see it."

"Maybe I will."

"I'll make sure there's three tickets so you can come with them."

There was no mistaking the little hurt that caused.

"Oh, maybe—maybe I'll come with some one else." Bob Knott didn't *own* her.

"Would—would you come with *me*—if I could take you?"

"You mustn't talk like that," she chided him quickly.

"*Would* you?"

"You *know* I would."

## 11

CAME the War.

Came the "Late Unpleasantness". Came the "Grand Fracas". Came "this man's army" and "this man's town" and silk shirts with barber-pole stripes.

Austria, Serbia—Russia, Germany—France, Belgium, England, Turkey. The world went mad! Hek too. What a chance! Say, didn't he wish he was over there? Sides didn't matter much. Two-thirds of the people he knew were Germans. Every day a few more Freeporters went back to fight for the Fatherland. Boy, wouldn't *he* like to go?! What soldiers those Germans were! A perfect military machine. It wouldn't last long; it couldn't. The Germans were too good.

Headlines screamed advance and retreat. America was not interested. "They" were always fighting over there. Let them fight it out. The United States had no quarrel with any of them.

Boom, boom, boom—boom—boom! Just as a little boy had said it in the Parsonage kitchen.

Then the British were searching United States ships on the high seas, and a German submarine sank American citizens. They were trying to drag us into it.

Atrocities in Belgium. The Germans were poisoning wells, burning and raping children. "A scrap of paper." Germany over all. We won't get into it. We can't stay out of it. A U-boat crossed the Atlantic—landed at New York. The Battle Cry of Peace: "In time of peace prepare for war!" If Teddy were only President.

Gas—shrapnel—trench-warfare. It won't last. The first hundred thousand.

Poor Belgium! H.C.L., the Princess Pats, visiting generals, Papa Joffre, he kept us out of war, the *Lusitania*, overt acts, freedom of the seas, Save the World for Democracy!!!

"*Can't* you keep that damned Knott kid out of here? ... Sergeant!"

"Yes, sir."

"Detail a man to stand at the door until otherwise instructed. His only duty is to keep Hek Knott out of this office."

"Yes, sir." Salute. About face. Pace through door. "Hek!"

"Yeah? Yeah? Will he take me?"

Sergeant Heinritz wagged his head. "Not a chance.... Y'gotta stay away. I can't let y' in no more. He'd jerk my stripes. Be reasonable, willya?"

"Aw, Christ, Heinie, I gotta go. Honest to God.... When's it gonna be another war? I'll prob'ly be an old man. Lemme see him just once more, Heinie; just once."

"I can't.... I know how you feel, kid, but you're too young. Y' ain't even eighteen—jeez. Y' couldn' even go *with* consent."

"I gotta go."

"Private Wells!"

"Yes, sir."

"Stand at this door from now on. If this kid gets in line again or busts in on the Captain—I'll kill y' an' y'll *never* see France."

"Yes, sir.… Beat it."

"Heinie!" The Sergeant walked rapidly away.

## 12

IN the flat it was even worse. Meals, sleep, day and night were made hideous with his wailing.

"Oh, God, I wish they'd take me. Please give your consent?"

Weeks before they had ceased to answer him, but it was farcical to pretend they did not hear.

"I look eighteen, Mom; *please* let me go?"

"*No*, Hek! It isn't civilized."

"Oh, Mom; how'd you like to have those Huns come over here?"

Bob laughed and looked up from his book. "Huns, eh?"

"Yes, Huns!"

"Ordinary Germans, just like everybody here in Freeport.
Now—all of a sudden—they're *Huns*."

"It isn't necessary, Hek. The whole thing is hysterical. Won't you please be quiet and let Bob and me read?"

"Read, ya—a—ah. Whyn't *he* enlist? He's old enough. All he does is read."

"Bob—enlist?!"

"Yes, *Bob*; he ain't too good to fight for his country."

"Me? … Join the army! Why on earth should I?"

"You mean to tell me it don't make any difference to you how they kill and burn and treat the helpless women and children?"

"I doubt that the 'Huns', as you call them, are any worse than the English and French. That is war."

"You better not let anybody hear you talk like that. They'll put you in jail.... Don't you think Americans have any rights? Should we let our citizens be murdered without raising a hand?"

"Let the fools stay home."

"You're a hell of a brother! You're afraid to go.... Honest t' God——."

"Hek!"

"Well—he's old enough, Mom. There's nothin' *wrong* with him. I can take care o' you."

"But it's so childish, Son.... Bob doesn't believe in war."

"Maybe he'll believe in it if the Kaiser comes to Washington. How'd you like to be a German subject? How'd you like that?"

"I can't see what difference it would make to me."

"I guess it'd make a difference if they started bombarding American towns."

"That's silly, Hek. That will never happen. Don't let the newspapers sweep you off your feet, Kid." Then to Minnie: "I take this war as a personal affront. You'd think it was aimed right at us. See what I mean? Fate's killing a million men over there just to show us up. He thinks with his emotions."

"But he's happy, Bob. He has enthusiasms."

Hek screamed his exasperation: "Oh, will you stop talking about me as if I was a bug or something? What if I do 'think with my emotions'? I guess I got guts enough to defend my country. If you won't let me go I'll run away and enlist. I'll go to Chicago and swear I'm an orphan,"—almost in tears—"that's what I'll do." He stormed from the house, then his head reappeared in the door. "Anyway—the draft's goin' through. Then we'll see whether you'll go or not." Slam!

"I hate to have him think I'm yellow."

"He picks up such twisted notions. I'll have a talk with him to-morrow."

"I get that kind of thing outside, too. I haven't mentioned it before. It didn't seem important."

Minnie studied Bob intently. "What kind of thing?"

"Well, when that last bunch left from the office, Jerry Loeke said: 'Well, when'll you be leaving us, Knott?' I don't know what I answered, but it must have been the wrong thing because old Wilkerson said: 'You don't seem to care much for this scrap, Knott. You waiting for a *big* war?'

"You see, I'm about the only one left in that section who is—strictly eligible. Hans and Fred both have families; Fred has three children.

"Then, just yesterday, they were telling about Hek getting thrown out of the recruiting office some seventeen times in one day. Wilkerson said: 'How many times have they thrown you out, Bob?'

"It doesn't mean anything. But, you can't talk to them intelligently. They're like Hek. Creel and the rest have convinced them this is a holy war and nothing can change their minds."

Minnie did not trust herself to comment, and when she went to bed, sleep eluded her.

After one, Hek came home, dirty and torn. Bob squinted at him from his pillow. "What the devil?" The boy's eyes were blackened, his cheek cut. His coat was heavy with mud and his shirt hung in shreds.

"You been fighting, Hek."

"Yeah, I been fighting.... I been fighting 'cause two guys said you were yellow."

"Said *I* was yellow?"

"Yeah.... Said there wasn't gumption enough in the family to stop up a rat hole. Said the Elling-Knott blood was sure getting thin."

"So you defended the family honor?" Bob supported himself on one elbow.

"Well, I tried at least. They licked me, I guess. But at least, I tried." The boy threw himself on the bed and grabbed his brother's shoulder. "Bob, honest to God, are you scared? Are you scared to go over there an' take it—with the rest? ... Are you, Bob?"

"I don't think so, Hek. No. I don't think I'm afraid. I never have been afraid—but there's no sense to it."

"Aw, Bob. Gee whiz, they're killin' women an' children. They're bombin' hospitals.... They need men, Bob.

"I wish to God I could go.... But I *can* support Mom, if you'll go. That's the next best thing. She can quit workin' and I'll support her. Gee, you ain't scared, are you?"

"How would you support Mom?"

"I got my card," eagerly. "I could go on the road with a troupe. The scale's gonna be raised. I could easy make enough——"

"If you went on the road, she'd be alone."

"Well, I don't have to go on the road. I only said that because I can make more. We can get along on what I'm makin' now. Oh, gosh, Bob, don't you *want* to go? Don't it mean anything to you?"

"Not a thing, Hek. Not that much. But I hate like hell to have you think your brother is a coward."

"Aw, *I* don't really think so. But some other guys talk."

"I don't care about any one else. The whole town can call me anything it likes. That doesn't matter.... But I don't want you to think I'm afraid."

"Well, you *ain't* afraid, are you?"

Bob looked thoughtfully out of the window. "I wonder if I am."

"My God, don't you know?"

The older boy shrugged and shook his head. Did he know? Was he sure that he could face poison gas, shrapnel, typhoid? He climbed out of bed and scrutinized his face in the mirror.

"No. I guess not. After all, there's nothing to be afraid of. Physical pain—I can bear that. Death? ... No, I'm not afraid."

"Then why don't you go, Bob? Gee——"

With sudden resolution—"Let's see if Mom's awake." As Hek rose eagerly from the bed, Bob stopped him. "You better stay here. I think I want to tell her alone."

"Are you goin', Bob? Are you honest-to-God goin'?"

"Yes, I'm going. You stay here."

Minnie held her knees in her arms on the bed and let her older boy talk. Going to a war in France to show he wasn't afraid. Going to a war that did not interest him in the least, to show his brother he could do it. Going to war. Going to enlist before they drafted him. Going to leave her alone.... Well, Ted had gone. Ted was a rational individual and he had gone. After all, men went to war; yes, regardless of their intelligence, *men* went to war.

"You'll be a good soldier, Bob."

But Teddy had not marched home. Would this big boy come back? "When are you going, Son?"

"I'll give notice at work to-morrow. Now that I've made up my mind I might as well go ahead and have it over.... Are you sure it will be all right with you?"

"Why not? I can keep up this little place and whatever Hek brings in will be just that much extra. I'll get along a lot better than you will on your dollar a day."

His proficiency in mathematics almost damned Robert Ingersoll Knott to a permanent mahogany trench in Washington. He fought that. If he was going to prove anything, it had to be done thoroughly. "They also serve" was not enough. He knew that the moral courage and fortitude required by a daily battle with columns of figures was his in abundance. Of the other sort, the sort that sustains a man in a rat-infested, water-filled trench, the sort that handles rotting bodies and attempts to kill men—of this sort of courage he was not so sure. He doubted the value of such a possession. Suppose he had it. What matter? Suppose he had not. Would he be ashamed? *Should* he be ashamed? Was it so important that he or any other man possess the ability to go heedlessly forward at a command, when prudence and reason bade him go back? Knowing that he could not face rifle fire, would he be unable to look his fellow-man in the eye as the village blacksmith could? He could not eat cabbage soup and he wasn't ashamed of that. Was there any difference? One lacked this sort of courage and possessed another. Why should a "coward" be scorned? Or even pitied? It really didn't matter. Coward—hero; they both looked alike from Betelguese.

What strange standards the tribe had created! How man had burdened himself with an elaborate moral code which grew heavier for each generation to bear! Was there an acre of soil in the world where an entirely reasonable man might live out his days and die—without hysteria, passion or the oppression of public opinion? It was nobody's business if he *was* a coward. He didn't want to be a soldier. He wanted to study. He wanted to go to college. He wanted freedom and leisure in which to think.

But, perhaps it was important. Perhaps bravery was a part of the complete man. He remembered *The Red Badge of Courage* and thought he would take a copy with him to France, if he ever went to France, and they would let him. It might do him some good, might arouse his pride, might make him feel that physical bravery was important, after all.

After a great many false starts he was assigned to an engineering corps attached to an artillery unit and ordered to report at Newport News on a certain Saturday.

His last evening in Freeport, they had the Mitchells in for dinner. Old man Mitchell clapped Bob soundly on the back and shook his hand—man fashion. Old man Mitchell was proud of him. God, how he would like to go. But these things were for the young. All the glory, all the opportunity for achievement, the rare chance to die for one's country—all, all given to youth. Well, he'd stay at home and do his bit by buying twice as many Liberty Bonds as he could afford. How he wished Florence was a boy! How glad he'd be to send her! How proudly he'd hang a flag in his window with a star on it! Florence's father hadn't talked so much in twelve years. Having delivered himself of this red-white-and-blue bombast, he subsided—stiffly the guest—in a comfortable chair and sucked on his poison-gas pipe, reflecting that he had been wrong in previous appraisals of Bob. The boy really had it in him after all.

That dinner deserved prizes for strangeness and for strain. Florence helped Minnie carry dishes forth and back from the kitchen in spite of protest. "No, you sit down and let me do this."

"I'll help. Your dinner will get cold."

Seated, those five had two things in common. They were all bent at approximately the same part of their anatomies; they were all chewing. What else? Hek alone seemed to have any enthusiasm for the occasion and he was very conscious of Florence's nearness. Old man Mitchell had on his party manners which roused the old school in Minnie and Bob, and made Florence very embarrassed. They could not talk about the war because the three Knotts had no views on the subject which had not been exchanged a thousand times—and Mitchell wouldn't talk. The fact of Florence's and Bob's affinity had never come into the open. Minnie looked at the younger woman once or twice to see if it was hurting her to lose what had passed with her for a sweetheart. What she saw did not make her break her long silence on that subject.

What little was said concerned the food; stewed chicken, dumplings, peas. Dumplings held the two women some time. Their manufacture was so technical.

Hek helped them clear the table, while Bob went into the front room to entertain the old man. With his belly full, Mitchell's party manners passed off and he grunted only monosyllabic answers from around the evening paper to Bob's conversational sorties.

In passing along the hall from the dining-room to the kitchen, Florence carrying dishes in both hands, Hek returning with none, they looked at each other, paused, scrutinized both ends of the hall—and snatched an hasty kiss. Hek also took advantage of her laden hands and held her right breast—the larger—in his palm as he kissed her. Her eyes reproached him for behaving thus on this of all nights.

Mitchell left soon after that, and the four played euchre an hour. Then Bob took Florence home and Hek pleaded an errand.

Minnie, left alone, put away the cards and went over Bob's things, packed since early that morning. She stood a moment looking down at the boys' bed, then went to her own room where Ted's picture sat on the dresser. She remembered creeping down the Parsonage stairs to say good-by to a box, more than seventeen years before. She went into the front room, lined with books, and sat in Bob's study chair.

Some little boys passed on the street below, singing:

> *I didn't raise my mule for army corn-beef;*
> *I brought him up to be my pride and joy.*

## 13

MITCHELL had let off a little more patriotic steam at parting.

"I wish I could feel that way about it," Bob said as he walked home with Florence. "I can't work up any enthusiasm. I'm going because other people have opinions. Not because I want to at all."

"You're so peculiar, Bob. I guess that's why I love you.... You never say the things other people say. You never think like any one else. Don't you really feel that it's your duty to go?"

Love! Florence had said "love". She *loved* him. "Do you really love me, Florence?"

"Love you?"

"Yes."

... "Yes."

"Don't you love me?"

"Yes."

Her fingers twined in his.

"Will you—wait for me, Florence? We'll be married when I get back."

"Yes, I'll wait."

"You've waited a long time already.... It hasn't been all my fault."

"It hasn't been your fault at all. I know that."

Their steps slowed as if an intelligence were in their feet. Under a big tree they stopped. "May I kiss you, Florence?"

Her eyes looked at him brightly. Back of her calm brow she frowned. *"May* I kiss you?" Bob actually waited for her nod before starting.

He *was* tender. This was more what love should be. Of course, the sidewalk was no place for it, but—a lady and a gentleman speak of their fondness and regard, each for the other, then their mouths press and their arms embrace and they walk on, thinking of the future. Yes,—now the rules were being observed. She felt easier. That other thing had frightened her. It had been just possible, there for a time, that this would not come off according to Hoyle. If it hadn't, she'd be in a nice mess, with only that other to look back on. But it was settled now. When Bob came back they'd be married.

"If—if I don't come back——" at her inarticulate exclama-
tion—"Oh, that's all right, but this is a war to kill men. They can't
all come back; and if I'm one that—that get's it in the neck—will
you—help Mother with Hek? Just do what you can? He's pretty
wild."

"He's your brother, Bob."

What did she mean by that? "Yes."

"He'll—calm down—as he gets older." Florence was afraid
she spoke the truth.

"Yes, I hope so."

"He'll get to be—more like you." God fend the day! But she
did not wholly think it.

They had reached her home. "Won't you come in a
minute?"

"Oh? ... Do you suppose your father's home?"

"I think so." Yes. Much more as it should be. *All* the rules
observed. All decorum acknowledged.

"I'll say good-by to him," though Bob dreaded any more
flag-waving.

The rooms were dark. "Father?"

"Not here?"

"I'll see if he's in bed."

He was not.

"Well, I'd better run along, then ... I'd like to kiss you
good-by."

She gave him her body to hold, her lips to bid farewell.
She was herself surprised that he could be so fervent. This
Bob belied the years she had known him. She responded in
kind, without sham. Very abruptly he stopped—and backed
away from her. "Good-by, Florence.... I'll be thinking of
you—constantly."

"Good-by, Bob!" She was sobbing.

# 14

THE following Sunday, *Marry for Money*, a farce, was billed at the Grand. Saturday night, in Dekalb, there'd been trouble. Charlie Grainger had gone to the hotel between matinée and night and hit up the veronal, like a damned fool, until he wasn't fit to go on. It wasn't the first offense, nor the tenth. Tom Helton was tired of it.

The rest of the cast turned in and carried the dopy comic through the show, but it must have been obvious, even to a Dekalb audience, that this was not what it had paid to see. By the middle of the last act, Grainger could understand English and Helton gave him a choice thousand or so words of it to mull over. Filtered through the murk of his brain, the essence of these words was that he was being left in Dekalb. No notice. No transportation. Here was his salary—which he didn't deserve—and to hell with him. Helton had reached the end of his very long rope.

The trouble with being so precipitate was that the Chicago agencies, those last two outposts, lost colonies of the drama, one of which might have got a man to Freeport in time to go on Sunday night, were closed for the business day by the time Helton wired. Freeport was too good a date to cancel. He could do one of two things. The part was a flip bell-hop, all comedy. It could be cut, by rewriting a few scenes on the train, or—with luck—he might find a "home-talent" star in Freeport who could get up in enough of the lines to provide a laugh or two. It was poor policy to permit a house-manager to know your show was crippled, but Tom had known Dave Sanford in Freeport for years, having played the old Opera House with a dozen different attractions, from midgets up; up to Gertrude Bondhill.

He wired Sanford—and Sanford talked to Charlie Gibbs, the stage-manager.

"Hek can do it."

"Minnie Knott's kid?"

Charlie nodded. "Made to order."

"Where is he?"

"Back stage."

Hek said he could. He didn't know what he had let himself in for. Professionals would have quailed before that bargain. The train arrived at ten. They shoved a part in his hands and strewed chairs around the stage to indicate entrances and exits. They walked through the show three times.

"Now—*go* home and study."

He had to memorize twenty sides in less than four hours. They would rehearse again at six.

Joyce Killfeather, who worked opposite the bell-hop through most of the show, offered to help him before six, after he'd studied a while, if he liked. Hek looked from her dazzling hair to her lips, then at the part, and decided his art came first.

"Thank you very much," he said. "If I think I know it, I'll—I'll call you."

"I'm staying at the Senate."

"Yes—thanks."

He scooted into the kitchen of the Mission Café long enough to show Minnie his part and to tell her the news. He was gone before she knew clearly what he had said. He was going to *act* that night. That much she gathered.

At four, Hek was sure he knew the lines. He had recited nearly all of them twice with only occasional glances at the book. He called Miss Killfeather and she joined him at the theater. In practice, everything left him. It was one thing to memorize words without cues, business, crosses and exits. It was quite different to know what to *do* as well as what to say. Over and over and over again, they repeated their scenes together, Hek's mind scattering like blown ashes at the hugging business and the kiss. How in the name of heaven did an actor keep his wits about him with a beautiful girl in his arms?

Some one offered Hek a drink but he declined. "Gosh, no; none o' that."

Joyce went to her dinner and Hek kept on rehearsing alone. He *had* to make good. Minnie and Florence and hundreds of people who knew him would be out in front. Miss Killfeather and Mr. Helton who was giving him his chance would be on the stage with him. Over and over and over.

It was six before he realized it—and the company arrived in a body. They cut down to his scenes and repeated them again and again. Mr. Helton crouched on the apron and yelled at him until the boy's tears very nearly spoiled the show. At a quarter of eight they gave him his costume and Dad Summers was told off to make him up.

His mouth tasted terrible! His tongue was thick and sticky. His knees wobbled when he walked. "Gosh, I'm weak.... I didn't have any dinner."

Summers sent out for a pail of black coffee.

Helton in a set of false Dundrearies and a loud checked suit came to him in the wings. "How's it go, Boy? Y' all right?"

"Yes, sir."

"Remember—if a line slips you, get near a door. Everybody's gonna be helpin' y'. See? We'll be right outside every exit—ready to tell y'. Understand?"

"Yes, sir."

"Get some pep in it! *Lift* it. You know?"

"Yes, sir."

The manager clapped him on the shoulder and walked away. Some one called: "Places!"

The familiarity of that—and the scared face of Pete, looking at his ex-assistant in wonder and with no little pride—steadied him somewhat. He read the first few pages of his part again—and poised himself at the door through which he must first enter.

Joyce came up and took his hand. "You look lovely," she said, and seemed very much to mean it. "That hat is *too* cute on you … And those buttons!" She squeezed his fingers. "Remember, Hek, *always*remember—in show business, eleven o'clock is bound to come."

Wasn't that sweet? Wasn't that comforting? God damn! There it was in a nutshell. *Eleven o'clock is bound to come.*

He heard his cue—and went through the door. "Eleven o'c——" steady! Then the lines came to him and he worked.

The lights were so bright. Funny, he hadn't realized just how bright before. He couldn't see the audience at all across the gutter of blazing light. There was the door. Knock. Knock. The lady opened it just as she had pretended to do at rehearsal. But this was so much easier, so much better than rehearsal, with doors and things to make the play seem real. He handed her the yellow envelope and turned with his little round hat behind him, awaiting a tip. He rolled his eyes. He felt the coin drop. He bowed, took the coin, clapped his hat on and regarded the closed door sourly. He looked at the coin—back at the door—he added fillips of his own to Helton's direction. He made his exit amid thunderous applause from his friends he thought would kid him.

In that half minute Hek's future was put in the bag. From that moment he became an actor. Some of the company were waiting for him as he left the stage. "It's *never* been played so well," said one.

"Did you see his eyes? They're worth a million dollars."

"Boy! You're a born actor. I'd swear you'd been playing the part for years."

"Where's my part?" asked Hek nervously.

When he heard his next cue he entered, read his lines, perforated the business given him and left the stage while the audience roared with laughter. To be sure, they were his friends, but their amusement was genuine. They refused to let the show go on until Hek was pushed on stage for a clumsy, flustered bow.

Well, he was making a tramp of Bob. You *didn't* have to study to be an actor; you just did it.

The company continued to praise him as he changed clothes, a little reluctantly, and took off his make-up.

Minnie was the center of a group near the musicians' card table when Hek came out of his dressing-room. Dave Sanford, "the old man", Helton and two or three others were talking. There was Florence too.

"Here he is!"

"Hello, Son," Minnie greeted. Pride in him, pride in being part of him, made her face more animated than it had been since Bob's departure. Every one was cordial. Hek took it well. That is, fairly well. The rowdy-who-has-just-won-a-foot-race tinctured the coloratura in him, although the latter was predominant.

"You did us proud," said the old man. "Bet you a dollar you couldn't do it again."

"I wouldn't want to do it again, very soon," Hek answered. "Golly, I'm tired."

Minnie pushed a lock back over his ear causing him to frown. Florence was beaming at him. "Hello, Florence; enjoy the show?" After all, she was just a small-town girl run to stalk. He could see Joyce Killfeather over Florence's shoulder, kicking the lock on her trunk.

"Excuse me," Hek said. Praise from this quarter would be sweetest. "Let me do that. You'll spoil your shoes."

"Thanks. It sticks. I have to have it fixed."

One terrific kick locked the box, for that time. Hek smiled at her and waited. "It's been broken ever so long, but on one-nighters you don't have much chance to get things fixed."

"No, I suppose not." Wasn't she going to say anything about his performance? "I—I want you to meet my mother, Miss Killfeather; she's over here."

"Mr. Knott!" Hek had to hear the hail three times before he realized he was being addressed. Joyce was getting her gloves. God, she was beautiful! Give Hek credit for discrimination here, Joyce was extraordinary. She was plump, granted, but her *hair*, her eyes, her lips—whew!—her lips. They came out, away from her face proper, as if to meet kisses. They did not pout, exactly, but they had contours, that is, topographically, in addition to their approximately horizontal outline which was also superb. They were lips one might feel one began to kiss *ahead* of time, so to speak (given the opportunity) and that one became more fascinatingly involved in kissing them as pressure against their undulant surfaces caused them to move outward at the corners and to flatten and then to continue to recede—as if one sank in a heavenly and bottomless couch; as if to this kiss there could be no end. Her hair had the color and the life of flame.

"Mr. Knott."

"Hek," said Minnie.

"Oh, *yes*, Mr. Helton."

"Your mother says you have wanted to go on the stage for some time."

"Sure I have.... Mother, this is Miss Killfeather."

"How-do-you-do?"

"How-do-you-do? Aren't you proud of him?"

"Indeed I am. Of course, I thought it was maternal preju-dice—and—and he couldn't be doing so well as he seemed to——"

"He did," Joyce assured her. "He trouped."

Hek blushed.

"Are we going to take him with us?"

Hek was himself so overcome at the suggestion—there had been a hint of it in Helton's voice—that he did not even notice Florence's countenance which, unmistakably, fell. The boy looked at Minnie's smile, at Helton's flexible jowls, grimacing in weighty consideration.

"Like to play that part—try it for a while, Knott?"

"C—could I?"

"It doesn't pay much. It's not one of the important parts."

"Oh, no; that wouldn't matter." Joyce tried to pull his coat-tail but missed it. She cleared her throat loudly and moved back of Helton a little.

"Miss Killfeather is getting you a raise," Helton said dryly, "only she isn't."

"Oh, anything you'd say, Mr. Helton. Could I—could I go, Mom?"

"Well—I guess so."

Hek suppressed a cheer mid-larynx.

"It would be a shame not to develop such talent, Mrs. Knott." Helton went on, saving a railroad fare from Chicago plus ten or more dollars a week salary. "I mean—nothing like this has ever happened in my experience. We *hear* of these things, but I never expected to see it. It isn't that the part is difficult. It's an actor-proof part. The laughs are *there*. He couldn't fail to get them; but the ease—the—the confidence—the—the—his first time on! *That's* the amazing part."

"Ye-es, I see what you mean."

"He's just a *born* actor, that's all."

"I just—hate to see him—go so soon," Minnie said slowly. "His older brother just left for camp. Just joined the army. It will leave me all alone. I—I've never been alone."

Tessie and Cedric felt their way down the crooked stairs from the stage. "Oh—this is my aunt and uncle!"

Summers, who had dressed with Hek, moved past the crowd with a groan. Wade, the leading man, joined him on the steps. "It'll take eighty-two years to take this out of him," the character man muttered. "Eighty-two and a half years!"

Wade chuckled. "Or one month on a show with you. Same thing."

"Balls!"

Both actors had to stand aside halfway up the stairs to let a bunch of boy and girl schoolmates pass. "Hyah, Hek!"

"Holy mother of Jesus," said Summers and retraced his steps to start the ascent again. Wade laughed at him. "Come on up. God, I been passin' people on steps for——"

"Careful," Summers warned.

"—for twenty-eight years—"

"Twenty-*eight*. Just a cordial, congenital, incurable, Goddamned liar.... You *been* twenty-eight that long!"

Manager Helton looked over the sea of heads. "Mrs. Knott, won't you and your son come to see me at the Brewster—a little later? I'd like to talk business."

Joyce, Hek reflected, lived at the Senate. He wouldn't be seeing her, then. But if they traveled together——

# CHAPTER FIVE
# THE BOOK OF LIFE

## 1

I N Newport News, Bob Knott was swallowed by the United States Army. He became an infinitesimal unit in an enormous machine. He disappeared beneath a smothering blanket of olive drab. He stood on a marble floor in a cold room for hours, in a line of men as nude as himself, disgust oozing from every pore. This was not necessary. He had not bargained for this impersonal brutality. He was no sheep, no steer about to be butchered. Did those doctors never smile? Were these bodies all alike to them? Were they men, at all? Was he a man?

Some of them didn't seem to mind it. What was wrong with him? Why couldn't he laugh? What had become of his sense of humor?

The injections made him sick and he had to stand in another line at midnight, waiting to vomit. And another impatient line. And another. And another. Life became a series of waiting lines. He was always standing in line. There was no privacy; he could not scratch himself without an audience. Men, men, men. How he hated them! Stupid, dull-eyed, cursing—their faces were like so many FOR RENT signs on vacant houses.

This man's war. This man's army. This man's mess.... How appropriately they had named the function of dining from tin!

There was nothing to read and no time to read it. There was endless talk of women, women, women. He could not avoid the sound of voices; men's voices booming of drunken parties, losses at poker or dice and women, women, women. Over and over and over until madness seemed the only escape. If he could only take a walk—alone. Wherever he went there were more men. Those khaki uniforms were everywhere. Millions and millions of them, all thinking about women, all leering at the calves and buttocks of every female who passed.

He was going to France to show Hek he wasn't afraid! He was standing in line listening to filthy stories to save the world for democracy.

Sick—so sick—so sick. The army, like a boundless, restless sea of a dirty olive color, eddied, swirled and closed over his head. Bob was drowned in a sea of men.

## 2

HEK would have liked a trunk. Every actor had one; but, what, Minnie asked, would he put in it? The duffel he would have run away with—including the long stockings—was packed in the brown valise and the grey canvas telescope. His costume, it was arranged, could be carried with some of the scenery. He talked Minnie out of coming to the station with him. It wasn't professional. It would look as if he was a baby.

Half the troupe saw him crossing the tracks, a leather handle in each hand. The second-business woman arched amazed brows and looked at Wade, the leading man. "We," she said, "have bought ourselves something."

Summers, with the soul of the old legit ever ready to be bruised or outraged, focused incredulously on the telescope. "Great God!" he ejaculated. "What is that thing he carries?"

"That's better-looking baggage than yours," said Wade. "Homely but practical."

Joyce Killfeather had only time to whisper: "Don't start on him the first thing!" when Hek was among them, smiling, nodding, greeting them all, his friends of the previous evening, those who had helped him to success. The quickest eye, the most sensitive spirit must have missed at first the subtle change in the collective attitude toward him. It was indefinable, inexplicable, but Joyce—that morning—was his only friend. To the rest he was a yokel, bumpkin, amateur, full of potential unpleasantness, full of certain errors and sure conceits. As Dad Summers had said the evening before, it was going to take eighty years or more to reduce Hek to normal size. Here he was, *to wit*, making an early morning jump—cheerfully; the first itinerant-thespian crime— *first* because it was the one which could be committed earliest in the day. It was a bitterly auspicious start.

"How are you?" Hek grinned at the old character-man who had helped him make-up.

"My son," an enormous silver watch appeared from the lower pocket of the tweed vest, stretched taut across a prodigious paunch, "it will be more than four hours before an exponent of the mummer's art can decently smile."

The others were used to Dad. They smiled at his stately turn and pompous withdrawal from the circle.

"Tell you what you do, Mr. Knott," said the tall, svelte creature Hek remembered as the telegram lady of the first act, "set those *things* of yours right next to Dad's keister in the stack over there. It's the ugly fiber box with the tin corners."

"Here," said Wade, taking the telescope, "I'll show you." He turned the odd box in which Dad Summers carried a miniature kitchen, as well as clean and soiled linen, on its side and set the newcomer's luggage atop it. "Don't touch that now until the train is *in*."

Joyce sighed, a little disgusted puff. "Some people never grow up," she said. "How are you?"

"I'm fine, thanks. He's funny, isn't he?"

"Wade? He's a big kid."

"Both of them."

"Dad is always the actor, on or off, and always a good one."

"Gee! I'm going to love this."

Joyce looked at him intently. "Don't let them get your goat."

"Don't you worry, they won't."

"I'll bet a *dollar* they don't," said the telegram lady, following Summers into the depot.

"What's her name?" Hek asked. "She's nice, isn't she?"

"Cora? You bet she is. Cora Davis."

"Do you like every one?" a man in *pince nez*, with a short mustache, asked unbelievingly.

"I guess I do," Hek laughed. "All of you people anyway. Everybody in show business."

"Nasty trait," said the other sourly, leaving Wade and Joyce alone with the boy.

"Who is he? I don't remember him."

"Langford, the heavy; plays Milburn?"

"Oh, yes; the fellow who really takes the money."

"My God," said Wade, "he actually knows the story!"

"Say, everybody's kidding me this morning. What's the idea?" Still he smiled.

"They're afraid you'll get a notion you're a human being," Joyce said, taking his arm and tucking it into hers. "Everybody on this show hates human beings."

"What makes you think it's kidding?" asked the leading-man. "Seriously, though, I'm glad you're coming with us. You'll be a help to me in my business. Grainger was a frost as a chasing partner."

"Carl Wade, you are *not* going to ruin this boy's morals. I won't have it." The Killfeather girl was more than half serious.

"What do you know about his morals? Maybe he'll ruin mine."

"Yours! You haven't got any."

"Oh, I say!"—but he smirked a little, turned to Hek and winked. "You and I will see that no village this opry plays is left exactly as we found it. With your looks and my brains—we'll go far ... Oh, God, here come the house dogs." Helton, the company manager, and an elderly couple, the Weymans, walked toward them along the platform. "I'm goin' t' get coffee." Wade left abruptly, nodding to the trio as he passed without slowing his pace.

Hek was not quite sure what a "chasing partner" was, nor "house dogs", but an intimacy with the leading-man seemed assured. Chasing girls, likely in each "village the opry played".

"Morning. Morning, Knott. I'm glad to see you under the wing of our spiritual guide so soon. You won't go wrong in that company." There was something malicious in Helton's expression as he patted Joyce's arm which held Hek's.

"I'm protecting him from Carl," the girl said. "He's already started planning to use him for bait."

Weyman and Helton laughed loudly. "Oh, that man!" Mrs. Weyman was shocked. "You stay away from him, Mr. Knott. He isn't fit for decent people to associate with." She seemed to be bragging. Weyman and Helton laughed again.

"Why, Mother," Weyman remonstrated, "Carl's all right. He just feels an obligation to American womanhood. With all the young fellows in the army, the country's man-hungry."

"Harry Weyman, you stop. Don't talk that way in front of Joyce."

"Well, it's true! All the healthy young men have gone to France and left their sweethearts without—er—without anybody to take care of them. Carl is just doing his duty. I don't see anything wrong in that; do you, Helton?"

"Not a thing. Somebody has to keep the girls happy."

"I wish I was young enough to do my share," Weyman went on with a heavy leer at Hek. "This is certainly a hell of a time to have your powers fail you."

"Harry Weyman, you hold your dirty tongue in front of these children! ... Come on, Joyce; come on, Mr. Knott; they're as bad as Carl Wade." The old lady hovered the two young people a few steps away as Helton followed the company baggage up the platform with Brownie, the carpenter.

"Isn't your mother here?" Joyce asked.

"No—o," said Hek, embarrassed. "I—I said good-by at home." It was peculiar that Joyce should make him feel ashamed. She and Mrs. Weyman were like neighbors, like people who lived near the Parsonage and around Trinity Corner. They weren't like show people; not like those he had known best around the Opera House. Joyce had kissed him at rehearsal and in the play. It was *business* they had together, nothing more. He was ill at ease for the thoughts those kisses had aroused. The warmth of her arm on his as the train roared up beside them added to his embarrassment. Joyce, he decided, was different. He looked at her face and let her smile still further disconcert him. *She* thought it would have been nice for Minnie to come to the train. *You're under the wing of our spiritual guide.* "Do you like Mr. Helton?" Hek asked her suddenly.

A little surprised, Joyce glanced quickly at Mrs. Weyman. "Why, certainly,"—then she signed to him with her eyes that she could not speak freely.

Wade and Dad Summers came out of the station. Jimmy, the property man, smacked his hands and rubbed them. "Got the makin's, Kid?"

Dad swelled like a frog. "What is the theatrical profession coming to when the God-damned property-man comes up to the leading-man and says: 'Have you got the makin's, *Kid?'!*"

Their laughter and the amusement of the towners, who watched this strange race of people with fascinated eyes, were cut short by the train, whistling for the crossing to the east.

Other members of the company were clustering about the "stack", the pile of hand baggage against the depot wall. The old character-man held an outraged pose, towering, mountainous over the desecration Wade had wrought. The leading-man relished his joke a few feet away, out of Dad's sight. Gingerly, as if it stank and was otherwise odious, Summers lifted Hek's telescope, turned half around and let it drop to the pavement. "In more than forty years mine • eyes have not encountered such hideous equipment for the road. These are the trappings of an immigrant." He dropped the worn, brown valise in the same ceremonious way.

Hek jumped to preserve his things. "Say! there's glass in there!"

Dad straightened, with his own worn case handle up. "And there was *soup* in here!" he glowered, then stalked toward the smoker.

Wade, chuckling gleefully, slapped Hek on the back. "*The trappings of an immigrant,*" he mocked. "There was *soup* in here!—oh, Lord!"

"Yeah—but he thinks *I* did that!" Hek objected.

"Well, didn't you? Aren't those your bags? I'm sure they aren't mine. Who else *could* have done it? You ought to be ashamed, spilling Dad's soup!"

"Don't let 'em get your goat," said Joyce, lifting her dainty leather week-end case. "That's all they're after."

"Gee whiz," said Hek.

As he followed Joyce up the steps of a day coach, Wade called: "Hey, Boy! That's the chewin' gum car."

"Come along," said the girl. "Pay no attention to him."

Then it occurred to Hek that he had no ticket. He started to mention this, but an inner sagacity stopped him. He had seen no tickets in the hands of others. He would wait.

Seated passengers regarded the newcomers curiously. "Show people," he heard some one whisper, and he raised his chin.

"Here are two together," Joyce discovered ahead of him. "Shall we turn one over?"

"Let's."

She superintended his clumsy disposition of his own bags, then hers. "There we are."

Freeport looked strange through a train window. There, of course, were all the landmarks, but oddly distorted and unfamiliar from this new perspective. He was *leaving* them. What was Minnie doing now? The kitchen of the flat was before him with his mother moving about, calling to him over cooking noises and the splash of water in the sink. She was in the flat now—all alone. Hek looked into Joyce's eyes with a perplexed frown, almost a question.

"Haven't you ever been away before?" she asked.

Hek could not understand the hurt in his breast. He was doing exactly what he wanted to do. He was a man now—an actor. He was off to see the world, to pursue a career, to become famous; yet he was miserable. He shook his head without taking his eyes from her. "No," his voice came from the tomb.

"What we'd better do," she advised him, "is go over our scenes together as soon as the train starts. You'll be in better shape for rehearsal."

It had not occurred to Hek that there would be any more rehearsals, but now that Joyce mentioned it, he saw the necessity at once. A single performance with the entire cast helping him through it scarcely made him proficient in the part.

The train was moving and he suffered a sinking, breathtaking pang. "Say!"—he cupped his chin on his hand, his elbow on the window sill—"I never thought I'd feel like this." He watched Stephenson Street go out of sight.

"I get a touch of that every time I leave home—and I've been doing it for years."

"Do you?" That, at least, made him a little less a baby. "That's the Moline Plow Company."

"Over there?" Joyce feigned interest.

"Down the tracks a ways, I'll show you where Nick Stearns was drowned last year. The Pecatonica gets somebody every year."

"Don't you want to get your part out instead? I don't like to think of people drowning."

"No," he smiled sheepishly. "Of course you don't. My part's in the telescope."

"Maybe you won't need it," Joyce hastened. That container was formidable enough in outward aspect, strapped tightly shut.... "Why did you ask about Mr. Helton—if I liked him?"

"Oh—yes.... Why, I don't know; the way he acted when he came up.... Do you?"

"He used to think he liked me—too well."

"Oh."

"See?"

"Well——"

"Until he found out that I didn't like him—*that* way, at all."

"I see. He was in love with you."

"Something like that. He wanted me to pretend to love him—for a little while, at least."

"I see—and you wouldn't."

Joyce shook her head.

"So now he's always making remarks about how *good* I am. Calls me *Saint* Joyce and 'the angel'."

Hek nodded and suddenly hated Helton. Presumptuous beast. The idea of thinking a good, pure girl like Miss Killfeather would have anything to do with him.

Wade came through the coach, his body weaving with the sway of the train. He stopped beside them and laid his hand possessively on Hek's shoulder, shaking his head at the soubrette. "You hadn't ought to do this, Joyce. Honest. This boy is just starting out in the world. He doesn't understand. He trusts you. You look at him with those big brown eyes; you wave your beautiful red curls at him—and he thinks you mean it. He thinks he stands a chance. Now, is that fair?"

Joyce flushed—and frowned seriously. "Sometimes you carry your kidding too far, Carl."

There was no friendliness in the disgusted glance with which the actor dismissed her. "Come on in the smoker, Knott. It ain't proper for a *man* to ride in the chewing-gum car. Everybody'll think you're a sissy."

"All right." Hek rose. "You'll excuse me, won't you? Then I'll come back and we'll go over the lines."

"That's all right. Go ahead. Any time."

He was displeasing her, he knew, but the bluff aggressiveness of the leading-man seemed to leave him no choice. Hek did feel a little out of place in the day-coach, the only male member of the company riding there except Weyman who sat with his wife. He started forward and heard Wade, behind him, say to Joyce: "Gosh, I have to watch you. You'd actually put a padlock on every pair o' pants in the country if you could."

That struck Hek funny and started him laughing, but he was careful to keep his face turned away from Joyce. Wade caught up to him just as he reached the end of the car and the conductor barred their way. "Tickets, please."

"Oh—well—"

"Company, company. He's with us," said Wade.

"Well, it isn't printed on his forehead!"

Hek flushed redly and crossed the vestibule into the stench of the smoker. "Let's sit down here. I want to talk to you before that goes too far.... You'll never make that, back there; it ain't to be had. She's a nice girl, pretty and all that, but everybody on the show's tried it and she just ain't puttin' out."

"No, I guess not.... I—I saw that."

"Smoke?" Wade extended Camels.

Hek hadn't been smoking. Minnie and Bob had objected—and his first few attempts had not recommended the habit highly. Now, however, it seemed the only thing to do. "Thanks."

"I just thought I'd tell you. You can waste a lot o' time on her. She gets friendly and yesses you along until it comes right down to it; then she tries to laugh you out of it.... I hate a woman like that, don't you? I could kill 'em!"

"Christ, yes," said Hek, pulling deeply at his cigarette.

"Understand, of course, it's none o' my business. If you think you're good, go ahead and play it. Maybe you're her type. I don't know; but I thought—a word to the wise—you know?"

"Sure. Thanks. But—I don't suppose they all have to do that."

"Huh?"

"I say—I don't suppose they—they *all* have to—put out."

"No—o, I suppose not. You can sit and hold hands, of course."

Hek laughed again, quickly, boyishly.

"Some of 'em think their company's enough. They lay a swell job of conversation—then 'good-night'. God, that gets me sore!"

"Gosh, yes."

"You'd think they had somethin' t' be proud of; some God-damn' jewel that was gonna disappear if the air struck it. Don't they make y' sick? ... Listen, Knott, I always tell 'em: 'It's just as much wear an' tear on *my* system as it is on yours.' That's the only way. 'Take it or leave it.' It's no damn' use to 'em unless they *use* it. Not a damn' bit."

"Not a damn' bit," Hek echoed, and he was struck by the great truth, the irrefutable logic of the older man's statements.

"If they want to save it, that's all right with me. I just don't waste time on 'em," Wade shrugged expressive shoulders.

"That's right. Me neither."

"I don't mean y' come right out an' ask 'em: 'Will you or won't you; do you or don't you?' I don't mean that. But you can tell. You can tell."

"Sure—you can tell." Hek, at the moment, thought he could tell too.

"Well, that was all I wanted. You don't know her; just joinin' the show. I thought I might save you some time. She's cold tur-key, and if you know that from the start, y' can use your own judgment."

"Well, thanks, I'm—I'm glad you told me. I'll see how I get along for a while. She—she seems to like me pretty well."

"*Like* you! Hell, yes. She likes everybody. She's a Christian Scientist. They got a rule about that. They gotta like everybody. She'll be nice to you. She'll even make love with you, maybe. But when you go just so far—*up* goes the wall, *down* come the bars— you know?"

Hek nodded. His head teemed with new concepts, new atti-tudes, new wakefulness. Wade was not a young man. Leading-men, Hek realized now that he had noted before, were not as good-looking, not as handsome, in real life as they seemed to be on stage—as they were generally supposed to be. The ease of this one's manner fired the boy's imagination, his ambition. To speak so freely to Joyce, to speak so authoritatively of women, to have so colorful a reputation with the other members of the cast, Wade must have a background rich in amorous experience, a wide acquaintance with the ways of the opposite sex. And if he, with thin, sparse hair, puffy lids and a large, loose softness about his mouth and chin, if *he* could attain so obviously high a place, how much further might Hek's features carry him; the features Ruby could not leave alone, the features which had changed the virgin status of Florence. Hek added the older man's attitudes to the self he was forming. He would remember to say these things. "What good is it to you if you don't *use* it?" and "It's just as much wear and tear on *my* system as it is on yours."

He was flattered that Wade had singled him out for these attentions, but he was wary too. They were all kidding him this morning. The actor might only be pretending to treat him as an experienced equal to draw him into some embarrassing situation, for all the men to laugh at. Probably, the less he said, the better. He'd let Wade talk, that would be enlightening.

"Yes, sir, I'm glad Helton got you to come along. All these small town dames range in pairs.... Jesus, I never could do anything with Grainger, the fellow we just fired. That damned fool just had no chasing instinct. He would do the damnedest things. I'll bet he's ruined more nookie for me this season than any other one comic has ever spoiled before in his life. Now, you know how impossible it is for two fellows to do the choosing. Y' never get anywhere. Y' gotta give the dames their head. *You* know. But that numbskull! Time after time I'd have it all set. I'd have the girls, have 'em *waiting*—then when I introduce him, he picks the one that likes *me* an' *phooey*, the evening's shot.... You can't do that."

"No—o—o—o."

"Nope. They know what they want. And it's easy enough t'see. All you have to do is watch 'em. Ain't it? One of 'em'll always make a move one way or the other. You don't have to have brains to know if a girl likes you. But not that boy! Oh, he was a dumbbell. Just as I say, he had no *feeling* for it.... I used to tell him: 'Charlie, honest t' God, I think you'd rather be layin' up in your room with a bottle o' veronal, all by yourself, than jazzin' the best lookin' dame in the world.' An' he *would*.... Well, every man to his own poison. *I* never got a kick out o' veronal."

"Hell, no," said Hek, wondering what *veronal* might be.

They rode a few moments in silence. Wade stretched. "Well, seems like I'm wastin' the best part of the morning. I should be takin' the boys down a few." He lit a fresh cigarette. "How far is this Galena?"

"Oh, Galena's only a little ways."

"Been there?"

"No, I—I've never been there. We know some people from Galena."

"Big's Freeport?"

"Oh, no! About half."

"Freeport's all right. Good town.... Ha! *I'm* tellin' *you* .... Y' know—er—Mercedes Warburg? Tall blonde?"

"Mercedes? Sure. She's a waitress at my mother's—eh—she's in the Mission Café; waits on table."

"That's her." Wade elevated his brows and watched the passing landscape while Hek assimilated the unspoken information. The information he thought he was gleaning was too intensely interesting to be passed unquestioned. Why, *he* had seen Mercedes almost every day of his life for years! It didn't seem possible that she was that kind of girl. Then the world was spread panoramically before Hek as if by magic and he saw hitherto unsuspected liaisons occurring, committed, in thousands of cities and hamlets—every night; and that had been going on for years. He was just entering this broader life. Wade had been a part of it for a long time, going from town to town, enjoying this girl and that. But *Mercedes!* In Freeport Wade's girl was Mercedes, she who stood so straight and carried so many plates at one time—and tickled him under the arms when he visited Minnie in the kitchen. "Did—did you go out with Mercedes?" Hek asked. The inference alone was not enough, he *had* to hear the words.

Wade pursed his lips and nodded. "Sure."

"I—I don't know her very well."

"Swell kid. Moves too fast for a small town.... What did you just say about your mother?"

"Oh,—my—my mother knows her too." Hek felt he had caught himself just in time. He didn't want Wade to know Minnie was a pastry cook. In view of these new revelations, he did not want it to seem that there was any connection between Mercedes and his mother. For the first time in his life it occurred to Hek that Minnie was a woman—with the capacity to love. A woman in every respect, like Ruby and Florence and Mercy, healthy, human—and a widow for a great many years. He set staring a hole through Wade.

"What's the matter, Kid? I haven't been treading on your territory have I? I didn't see any 'keep off' signs."

"Eh? .... Oh,—oh, no. Mercy? No. I—I just know her. Is—is *she*—puttin' out?"

Wade studied the boy in astonishment. "I wouldn't know," he said slowly, "after all, *you* live there."

"I don't get you."

"If you don't know, I'll never tell you. Strangers are another thing."

"What do you mean, Wade?" Leaving out the "Mister" aged Hek by ten years. "I don't understand."

The leading-man drew deeply on his cigarette and shot the smoke in a hard, straight column toward the roof of the car. "Don't get me wrong, Son. My morals won't take any blue ribbons at camp meeting. Fact, I'm pretty rotten.... But don't get me wrong. Because I talk about the featherweight—tell you she's decent—is no sign I talk about all of 'em. If I'd made her, the subject wouldn't have come up at all.... Get it?"

"Well, I get that you made Mercedes."

"Well, now," Wade laughed, "of course, if you're going to read my mind ..." He rose and laughed down the aisle to Helton's seat with the *pince nez* fellow. "How long are we on here? Shall we deal a few?"

"Don't you ever read a call?"

"Go on! I tried reading your calls the first week this turkey was on the road and all I ever got was misinformation. Twice I damn' near missed trains and once I actually found a good hotel."

"*That* was a mistake."

"We got time to play?"

"We got an hour."

"Come on, Brownie, the gamboleers foregather.... How about the kid?"

"Has he got any money?" Helton asked.

"If he hasn't you can give him some."

"No advances."

"Not even for poker?"

"No, sir; not for anything."

"This is a hell of a troupe. No advances for poker!"

"Want to play cards, Knott?"

"N—no, I think I'll go back and go over my scenes with Joyce."

"That's right," Helton called. "You do that. Rehearsal at one."

Cards appeared, and as Hek went back to find Joyce a game of quarter-limit stud engaged five of the company.

He dropped in the seat opposite the girl who put aside her magazine. *Mercedes! right under his nose had been game and he had never guessed it!* How many other girls in Freeport, girls he had known all his life, older girls, had gone out with other Wades? He had been working around the Grand for several years, working and playing, and every night that a show had been there, while he had gone straight home to Minnie and Bob with their everlasting study, the actors, the leading-men and the comedians—and others, had been going out with girls he knew, at least by sight. They had been going out and playing the game the whole way while he went to bed like a baby.

"How do you like the smoker?" Joyce asked.

"Oh, they're playing cards."

She nodded. "They're always doing that."

"Do you want to go over our lines? Mr. Helton says we rehearse at one."

"Yes, it was on the call."

"The call", Hek decided, must be investigated minutely. He knew what it was. He had seen them posted on the board at the Opera House, had read many of them, but not until now had he realized how vital a part the "call" played in the lives of all actors. It governed them. It told them when they must rise and when they might eat, when they must work and where live. But it was not apparent to Hek that the call restricted his life—exactly as school had. This was different. You got paid for this.

As they started to leave the train at Galena, Hek tried to juggle both of his bags and that of Joyce as well. "Oh, no," she laughed. "You mustn't. You have two—and it isn't done, you know."

"Oh, I can make it all right. Mine aren't heavy."

Joyce shook her head determinedly. "No, indeed. You don't understand. Go ahead, I'll tell you later."

Hek relinquished her case reluctantly. Gentlemen, in Freeport, carried things for ladies. As they walked down the street, Joyce said: " 'Toting her keister' has a definite meaning on the road, Hek. If you carry a girl's bag it means you're sketching with her."

"Sketching?"

"Living with her, practically. If you're just friends, she carries her own."

"Oh,—I'm sorry. I didn't know that." But he did recall the disparaging tone of some one he had overheard talking about a "damned grip-toter". "Thanks for telling me."

"Nothing.... Look—we're well billed here."

Window cards, half-sheets and three-sheets, advertising *Marry for Money*, were everywhere.

"Aren't you ambitious, Hek? Wouldn't you like to walk down the street and see your own picture on a three-sheet; looking down at you?——I would. I think that would be the greatest thrill on earth. I'm going to have that thrill some day."

"Me too!" Hek thought he meant it.

"If *this* were all there was to show business, I'd check out to-morrow."

"What do you mean? What's wrong with this?"

"Well, almost everything, but you don't have to stay at this level. One more season out here and I'm going to New York."

Hek had heard that song before. He fell to picturing himself walking down an imaginary Broadway, passing his portrait on the billboards. "It takes a lot o' money, I guess."

Joyce nodded. "I've been saving for it four years. You can't tackle Broadway broke. It's the one who looks and acts independent who gets the salary there, and you can't act independent on a shoestring."

Hek watched the others at the hotel desk and trembled so he could scarcely write when the pen and register were turned over to him. Accomplishing that boyish signature, with "Freeport, Ill.," after it, inflated him almost as much as had the applause from the front the evening before. These were mature activities, traveling and registering at hotels.

The bell-boy increased his importance, tipping him made Hek a complete man.

## 3

ALTHOUGH the entire afternoon was devoted to rehearsal, Hek's performance that night was poor. The dash and sparkle were gone. He walked through scene after scene, straining wretchedly to recover the pep he realized was missing. It could not be found; it could not be raised by straining. Laugh after laugh slid by, creating scarcely a ripple. Wade, in the wings, said to Heldon: "There's your actor-proof part shot to hell.... *No* part is actor-proof."

"I know it, but this is pretty close."

"He's trying too hard."

Helton smiled. "If he'd given a good performance to-night I'd have sent him home.... Don't be a nut. It's the natural nervous reaction. All second nights should be like this. It speaks well for the future."

"My second performances are just as good as my first," Wade said a little testily. "I think that's the bunk."

Helton nodded. "Well, *yours*, perhaps."

Wade, always the first one ready for the street, knocked on the door of the dressing-room Hek shared with Dad Summers. "Come," said Dad.

"My God, Three-sheet, aren't you ready yet? Step on it."

"Oh—I've—I've promised to eat with Joyce, Wade. You don't mind, do you?" Hek was still wiping cold-cream from his face.

Wade shook his head slowly, tantalizing the boy with an enigmatic expression. "No, I don't mind. It's nothing to me." He continued to look at Hek a few moments in silence. "So long. See you later."

"God, help the virgins of Galena to-night," Summers prayed. "A ravening wolf is come among them."

"It's bad luck to read the witches' lines, Dad," and Wade was gone.

Hek was uncomfortable. "You don't suppose he's sore, do you?" he asked the old man. "He thinks I'm a nut for hanging around Joyce."

Summers was wrapping cold-cream and powder cans carefully in towels, setting them in snug hollows they had occupied each night for years. Dad was an old-school trouper, as the soup in his keister may have revealed. His trunk was a flat Taylor, eighteen years old—and once "set" for the season it was never unpacked below a certain utilitarian depth, except as the changing solstices demanded heavy garments or lighter. Not even the advent of the electric iron had been acknowledged by Dad. He still creased his trousers under his mattress at night.

"There is this to be said for 'hanging around'—great God!—for *hanging around* with Joyce: it will keep you out of a sling."

"Say," said Hek enthusiastically, "that's true, isn't it?"

"Our juvenile's enthusiasm for the highly debatable pleasure of fornication with his inferiors—most of them diseased—is one of this season's greatest mysteries. I ponder it.... Another is that comedy prop you have brought among us to serve as a traveling bag. Where, in the name of God, did you find it?"

"Gosh, I don't know," Hek laughed. "It's always been around the house."

"I thought as much. *Always.* It has that look, the look of having been somewhere—always."

Joyce called from outside their door: "Are you ready, Hek?"

"Just a minute." He hurried with his dressing.

The Weymans walked with them to *a* Greek restaurant, the best eating place in Galena. The streets were almost deserted and only dimly lit. Young couples and groups passed in and out of the oasis of white light that was an ice-cream parlor. Six or seven local wise-crackers lounged here to snigger, whistle and make remarks as their neighbors, contemporaries, friends of other hours, walked their girls in or out of the establishment.

Hek was extremely self-consciously Joyce Killfeather's escort. He took her arm solicitously and led her between these louts as if he piloted a fragile craft between rocks.

"Ahum, *ahem!*" they cleared their throats.

"The very idea!" one shrilled. That was a line from the show, one that Joyce and Hek both used, a catch-line which gained humor by numerous repetitions. The girl seemed not to hear them.

"Oh, you Cherry!" said one. "Cherry" was Joyce's name in the play.

"Fresh kids," said Hek.

She smiled and with her elbow pressed his hand against her body. "You'll get used to that. They don't mean any harm." More Christian Science, he thought. She had to like everybody.——

As they ate, Helton came in with Violet de Forest and her husband, taking an adjacent table. Miss de Forest, who was really Mrs. Crane Stevens, was the leading woman. She and her husband were "New York actors", the only salaries on the show. They knew it—and acted it. They fraternized with no one and unbent but stiffly to eat their midnight supper now and then with the manager. Crane Stevens played a minor part but poorly. He complained incessantly that he was miscast. But Violet was the mainstay of the show. Secretly—but not always entirely secretly—she leaned just a little toward Wade who meticulously avoided making the slightest advance. She should have known better, and in her less bored and more sane moments did. Only his well-known and thoroughly advertised predilection for beauty and charm annoyed her. It was a little insulting of him to prefer small-town girls of no pretensions or distinction to her well-established loveliness. She was married, of course, but she knew Wade's kind too thoroughly to attribute his reticence to respect for her or for that sacred state. And Wade saw through her little devices too plainly to raise a hand. She did not like him. In fact, she disliked him. So they were always at checkmate, Violet conscious that Wade knew she was a jade but so ambitious for her beauty, so anxious for the balm of conquest that she could not refrain from a languorous smile and a meaning pressure from time to time, to establish that her charm was inescapable, so powerful that even this rounder must succumb despite his experience and his judgment.

Opportunities for this exercise which kept her in trim, at least, were limited. Crane was always by her side, save when he was on stage and she was not. The longest interval of this description occurred toward the middle of the third act. Wade was off then too, and it was in that four and a half minutes every evening that Miss de Forest disclosed that she was human. She was hiding it perfectly as she took a seat which presented her profile to Hek and afforded her a view of the entire café and all the impressed towners in it. They craned and stretched for a better view of her, and the monotony of that situation was not sufficient to rob it entirely of its savor.

Hek looked around for Wade when Langford and Cora Davis came in. Only he and Dad were missing and Dad would be eating some lunch of his own devising in his hotel room. Jim and Brownie, the crew, would be hauling. "Every one's here but Mr. Wade," Hek volunteered.

Weyman began chuckling. "He's probably in somebody's kitchen by this time."

"He'll come waltzing in here with a couple little floozies on his arm any minute," said Mrs. Weyman. "He's utterly shameless."

"Well, wait till he does before you begin kicking. If he does, I'll tell you this much: one of *them* will pay the check."

"Oh, let's talk about something else," said Joyce. "Mr. Wade's exploits are a little uncouth, it seems to me."

Weyman made a face and Mrs. Weyman said: "Vulgar!"

As they were finishing their coffee, Helton leaned back in his chair. "You were a little tight to-night, Knott. You'll have to loosen up a lot." He made no attempt to be confidential. Hek blushed.

"I guess I was trying too hard to remember my lines. I'm sorry, Mr. Helton."

"Oh, that's all right. We'll work on it at rehearsal tomorrow. You were all screwed up, you know."

"Yes, sir."

Joyce put her cup emphatically down in her saucer. "Let's go," she said very low.

"And, Knott," Helton went on.

"Yes, sir."

"For the love of God don't write *Freeport* on hotel registers. Put Chicago or New York or something. Freeport looks awful, like it was a home-talent offering."

"Yes, sir."

Helton resumed his conversation with Violet and Crane.

At the cashier's desk, Hek fingered his money in flustered embarrassment. It seemed so odd to allow a lady to pay her own check. Yet, he saw that she must, if they were to eat together often—and he hoped they would, often.

The town boys had gone home. Only half a dozen lights punctuated the darkness of the street.

"I guess I was pretty punk to-night," Hek grieved aloud. "I was all screwed up."

"He needn't have told you about it in front of every one," Joyce sympathized. "That was just a dig at me."

"At you?"

"Oh, he didn't mean anything, Joyce. It was just thoughtless." Mrs. Weyman often found it difficult, but never impossible, to be on both sides of a fence at once.

"Oh, I had it coming, all right. I was scared stiff. I was more scared to-night than last night."

"You'll loosen up," Weyman encouraged. "You're going to be all right."

"Of course he is," said Joyce.

They got their keys at the hotel desk. "Shall we play rummy for a while?" Mrs. Weyman suggested. "We don't have to get up."

"I will," Joyce agreed.

"Sure," said Hek.

They carried extra chairs to the Weymans' room and dealt an old pack of greasy cards. The game had hardly begun, with banter and friendly sallies, when Wade knocked at the door.

"What's the matter with you?" Weyman demanded. "Have they taken in the streets?"

Wade grinned. "They're just starting ... Playing cards?"

"We *thought* we would," said Joyce.

Wade nodded, acknowledging the barb by squinting at the Killfeather girl and winking at Weyman. "Rummy's good three-handed," he said.

"You ought to be shot," Mrs. Weyman sniffed.

Wade turned to Hek. "I've just met a couple old friends of mine, Knott. I didn't know they lived here. They're just crazy to meet you. Like to come down and say hello?"

"Well, I don't know," but he arose. "We were going to play——"

"Just for a minute. These people think you're good."

"Gosh! After to-night?"

"They don't know the difference. My God, they been raised on *Mutt and Jeff* shows."

"Well, just for a minute."

"The train leaves at nine forty-seven," said Joyce. "Same station."

"You folks don't mind, do you?" Hek was pointlessly formal.

"No, no," Weyman urged him on. "Go ahead."

"I wouldn't want to break up the game, and I'll be right back."

"Sure, run along."

"Good-night," said Joyce coldly.

"Good-night."

"These two aren't much to look at," Wade warned the boy, as they hurried downstairs, "but they're sure fire.... The short one is mine. The other one wants you."

"Yeah? Gee! How old are they?" Hek foresaw that his own youth might prove embarrassing in this adventure which he had always regarded as strictly for adults.

"Old enough.... When they're big enough, they're old enough; and when they're old enough, they're big enough .... I hope they waited. I had a hard time finding you."

Two girls, just that and nothing more, hugged the darkened front of a store.

"He was hiding," Wade greeted them. "I found him under the bed."

The girls tittered.

"Miss Smith and Miss Jones," the leading-man made a mock of introduction, "this is Mr. Smith."

"Mr. *Smith!?* Isn't he killing?"

"His name wasn't Smith on the program," said the taller girl. "It was something else."

They moved down the street, pairing off. "That was a misprint," Wade insisted. "His name's Smith."

"If we believe that you'll tell us another."

Hek and his girl took the lead, turning off the business thoroughfare into a tree-lined street of residences.

"Did you enjoy the show?" Hek asked.

"Ye-es, I should say so. Gee, you were swell."

"Really? Gosh, I—I didn't think I was very good tonight."

"Oh, you *were*. You all were, just swell. You took your part off to a T."

"You really think so?" There was no sound behind and Hek turned to see if the other couple followed. They were wrapped in each other's arms, their heads forming a single unit in the shadow. "Look at *them!*" Hek blurted, and caught the arm of Miss Smith or Miss Jones. She had expected nothing less, it seemed, but their noses collided clumsily several times before a thoroughly satisfactory angle of incidence was arrived at, whereupon Hek gave himself over to an exhibition of his kissing prowess. He became conscious of her breasts pressing against him, and as he continued his attempts to excite her, she answered by suddenly throwing her hips forward and up. They rocked thus a moment until the others came upon them. "Those two must be in love," said Wade, then to Hek: "Selfleperalflate. Talflaker dowfloun another streelfleet!"

"What did he say?" Both girls were giggling again.

"Where are we going?" Wade asked suddenly. "You girls going to show us the town?"

Neither young lady seemed to know.

"Well, gosh, you must have some parks or sompn. Old battle-fields or cemeteries."

"Yeah," said Hek, "show us the places of interest."

"Is *he a* fast worker!?"

When the girls' laughter had subsided so they could talk, they held a consultation. "Can we go to your house, May?" "Sure. Want to?"

"Absolutely," said Wade.

They moved again down the dark street, stopping occasionally to renew that thrill of bodily contact.

A side door of May's house admitted them to an unlighted sleeping porch. They sat like four nigger-babies in a row on a hard, narrow bed. Conversation languished and they held hands in communal reticence. In the minds of the four was only one thought, but there were too many people present. Finally May whispered to Carl Wade: "If you want to, you and I can go inside."

"Let's."

Hek drew his girl slowly backward until they lay side by side on the bed. This was familiar ground. From this point they were playing the hammock game. Hek started in the time-honored fashion by attempting to raise the girl's skirts, to introduce his hand beneath them. He proceeded slowly, almost casually, as if this would deceive her as to his purpose. There was no remonstrance. A kiss continued without interruption. At length, after several inches of nude thigh had Hek thoroughly aroused, the young lady, who could not—at the moment—speak, managed: "Huh-nh," definitely a negative sound, and one of her hands caught his and held it rigidly in its place. She moved her head. "Don't get the wrong idea about me," she warned him. "Just because your friend met us kind of funny, don't get the idea I'm a streetwalker."

"Of course not!" Hek assured her. "Gee whiz, I never thought anything like that."

"Well, I don't know. He just came up and started talking to us. I don't want you to think I'm a street-walker just because I let you kiss me and—and do like that." She spoke in a hoarse whisper.

"No! Gee! I don't think that. I *like* you."

"I like you too, but not that well. I—I've never done that with a boy in my life."

"No? Gee—you don't know what you've missed." He suited his tone to hers.

"Well, then I don't miss it. A girl has to be careful in a little town like this. If she gets a bad name she can't ever live it down."

"But you can't get a bad name with *me*. I'm going away to-morrow. Nobody'll know."

"*She'll* know."

"May? Say, she's doin' the same thing herself."

"Oh, no!"

"May?"

"She wouldn't."

"I'll bet they *are*, right this minute."

"Oh, no; not May."

"Well, how's she gonna know anyway? We'll be quiet. For all she can tell we're doin' it right now. She don't know what we're doing."

"That's all right."

"Does she?"

"Sh-h-h. Listen."

There was a muffled creaking from the next room, no other sound.

"They *are*," Hek insisted.

"No, they're not. Anyway, I'm not a street-walker."

There had never been so much talk in the hammock game before. The shame of the "street-walker" had never before in his experience been invoked. "I *know* you're not. Even if we did do that, I'd know it was all right. I wouldn't think you were that."

She started kissing him again, and Hek thought he had convinced her. By turning his wrist ever so slightly, he escaped her hand and the march was resumed. Carefully he explored. His encounter with Florence had skipped this. It sent ecstatic shivers all over his body and his companion relaxed suddenly. Involuntarily she cringed. "No, no; you're hurting me."

Hek took her hand. "This wouldn't hurt you."

"I know—but I won't.… But I'll do *this*, if you'll stop."

"You want me to *stop?*"

She sighed in quick relief as he obeyed her. "Listen!" she commanded again.

From the next room they heard May's voice: "Is that man really her husband, or is it just that way on the stage?"

"You don't *need* to do that, unless you want to," Hek said. "Tired?"

"No. I'll do it. I'd like to do the other, but I'm afraid."

"What are you afraid of? There's nothing to be afraid of."

"Oh,—I think there is."

"What?"

"Suppose I should have a baby."

"Nah. You *wouldn't*."

"I might."

Voices were raised next door again: "Come on, honey," May was heard to say. "I'm ready."

And Wade, evidently exasperated with himself answered: "Ready! What in hell have *you* got to get ready?"

## 4

HELTON'S transom showed light as the chasers sought their rooms. "They're dealing a few," Wade said, tossing his head toward the door. "Play?"

"Well—"

"Come on. We'll see who's winning anyway."

"I was going to play with the Weymans and Miss Kill—"

"They've gone to bed hours ago! The house dogs and the angel don't stay up after twelve. Get next to yourself."

"O. K."

Langford, Cora, Brownie—the carpenter, Helton and two fat men Hek had never before seen, sat around a twenty-four-inch stand over which a blanket from the bed had been folded. "This is a business conference," Helton said, shuffling, "go wash your hands if you want to play."

"The little boy doesn't play *cards;* does he?" Cora asked maliciously.

"The 'little boy' plays more games than one," Wade defended him. "Show 'em your handkerchief, Hek."

"Aw, no." He was blushing furiously.

"Go ahead." Wade was taking off his coat.

"Ahm gonna shave if that towel dries soft," one fat man laughed.

"This is Fessenden, Henry Fessenden who used to own the theater, and his brother Alf. He used to own a shoe store down the street but I'm gonna own both of 'em in just one more half hour," Helton introduced the strangers. "Mr. Wade, our juvenile, and Hector Knott, still more juvenile. They've been out playing hide-the-wienie with some of your local buds."

"I need a pair of shoes," said Wade. "Move over, Brownie."

The withered little man looked up at Wade from under the brim of a soft black hat. "Sit on my lap," he said and sat, if possible, still more solidly in his place.

"I don't think I'll play," Hek decided. "There isn't room. I guess I'll go study."

"You don't get out of here without showing us your handkerchief," Cora asserted.

"Come on, produce."

Wade tried to jerk it from Hek's pocket, but the boy ran laughing to the door.

Langford removed his glasses and massaged the bridge of his nose. "Think of carrying a thing like that about with you!"

"What would *you* do with it? Throw it under the bed so her mother'd find it next morning?" Wade asked.

"Good-night," Hek called and stepped quickly into the corridor. Between him and his own door, Joyce's stood ajar, releasing a rectangular patch of light. He meant to pass, but she stood in a dressing-robe, brushing her hair, facing the door. She tried to look at him sadly, tried to make her eyes speak of an inner hurt. The effort was wasted. No eyes, no possible expression, could compete with the attention-value of that flaming halo. Hek had been ashamed to face her. He had been dreading breakfast and the train. He felt shabbily sinful, as if even her scorn was to be obtained under false pretenses. But the startling glory of her hair, then the wistfulness of her face which he finally detected, together with her dishabille and the knowledge that she had waited to accost him, drove the shame for his makeshift pleasure of the evening out of his mind. He stepped into her room and closed the door softly behind him.

Joyce smiled at him then, smiled at the impulse which had closed the door. "Please leave it open, Hek. I was worried about you." The hair brush continued its sweeps through that magic gold. Instead of opening the door, he dropped his cap on a chair and crossed the room to her in three masterful strides. He stopped her brushing and laid the implement on the dresser. "You are the most beautiful thing I have ever seen in my life," he said all in one breath. "Kiss me, Joyce." As he spoke, he seemed to be standing beside himself watching this scene develop. He applauded the young actor who had just taken the girl in his arms. She made no move to stop him, nor pulled away, nor pressed close, but stood with her head thrown back a little, watching him yearn for her lips.

"Would you—really? *Would* you kiss me—now?"

Her body, despite its pose of indifference, seared his at all points of contact. Not even Ruby had affected him more. But—would he kiss her—*now?* His arms dropped from her shoulders to his sides. He looked at her eyes, at her lips, at the place he had been standing watching himself, then back again at her. Strangely, his audience seemed to be gone and it was really Hek who said: "I would kiss you any time you would let me," in a very low voice. He handed back her brush and walked to the door, very low, his entire body *hanging*, like an old coat on a peg. That slow cross, the lethargy and dejection of his spirit, called back the spectator--—-Hek—and he smiled a little sadly at this picture of himself slowly and deliberately turning the knob and passing into the hall. And the Hek who watched, turned with elevated brows and a genuine surprise to study the woman in this play who was *not* calling him back. The author, it seemed, had played his audience false, had cheated his characters.

Down the hall and into his room, Hek continued to perform for his own delectation. He gripped both edges of the dresser top and sighed at his comeliness in the glass. A cad! Joyce was right to reject his advances. Yet—and he smiled at his reflection first with only the left side of his face, then with the right alone—she would have liked him if he had been less rotten. Hek was pridefully sorry for this rotten man, so evil that a good girl shrank from his touch. He lowered his right brow and raised the left. A rake, a roué! Well—nobody but Miss Jones (or Miss Smith) and he knew what had happened. And—at least—a girl *had* been involved. That was some advancement, at his age, his first night away from home. He ran water in the bowl and dropped the handkerchief into it. Hot water at the turn of a faucet! There was something cosmopolitan about that. Hek counted the four clean towels on the rack. It was thus real people lived in the wide world, luxuriously. He passed the mirror slowly again and then sat in a studiedly graceful position, before giving himself over to channeled thought.

Joyce had stayed up late to know what time he came in. She had left her door open to intercept him. Perhaps her half-clothed state had been calculated too, to woo him from Wade's company and their traffic with easy women. And—he remembered that it was still possible—he might be her type. Every woman would succumb, by Wade's theory, to the right man for her, to her "type".

Well, even a rounder had to sleep some time. He undressed slowly, following his movements in the mirror and imagining Joyce in his bed, watching him, waiting for him. In Hek's critical but perhaps somewhat biased judgment, his body was nearly perfect, his muscles large, yet lithe and smooth, his skin clear and white, his shoulders broad and his hips tapering. He rubbed his chin on which not even down had yet appeared. He would, of course, have to begin to shave soon.

## 5

TUESDAY they played Clinton; Wednesday, Cedar Rapids; Thursday, Oskaloosa; Friday, Ottumwa; Saturday, Des Moines.

The death-trail, Summers called it, and business was not too good. The following Saturday they were booked in Dubuque, only a few miles up the river from Galena. Hek bought a small atlas, Tuesday, and brought it to the theater. "Wouldn't you think they'd play these towns kind of in rotation?" he asked Dad. "It seems to me they'd save a lot of railroad fare."

"Where did you get that?"

"I bought it."

"Bought it? Bought it? Bought an atlas instead of a suitcase?"

"Oh, let up on my keister. I'll get a good one in Des Moines."

"One like white folks use," Dad insisted.

"Why didn't we play Dubuque to-day instead of coming clear down here to Clinton?"

"Well, Son, I'll tell you…. You know how a show is routed, don't you?"

"No," Hek grinned expectantly, "you tell me."

"Very well, it is done in this manner. A large map of the State to be played is spread on a pool table and the balls are racked. The producer of the show breaks them—hard—and the spots covered by the balls when they stop rolling are played in the sequence that the balls are numbered, one first, two second, and so on. Or, another system is to have a little, blindfolded girl draw the names out of a hat."

"It looks like it," Hek agreed. "We have to go all the way back through Ottumwa to get to Des Moines."

"As if once in Ottumwa were not enough."

They were waiting to rehearse. Joyce came in, breezily, smiling, lighting—Hek thought—one whole half of the stage. He handed the atlas to Dad and followed her to her dressing-room.

"Will I have time to unpack before they get here?" she asked, quite as if nothing had happened the night before, quite as if he had not avoided her at breakfast and ridden in the smoker all the way on the train.

"It's called for two," he said, leaning against the doorjamb. She jingled her keys. "Let me." In opening the trunk, their bodies collided and Hek turned quickly, catching her about the waist. "Joyce," he pleaded, "I'm sorry about last night. I don't know what was wrong with me. Won't you forgive me?"

Her hands rested lightly on his shoulder and her head was drawn back in that alert position Hek knew could frustrate any attempt to kiss her.

"There's nothing to forgive, Hek. You don't owe me anything. I'm nothing to you."

"You *are*, Joyce; I'm crazy about you. You know that."

She shook her head. "No, you're not. You just think I'm pretty. You don't care for me—really."

Never before in his life had Hek so much desired any one thing as he did her lips. "I *do!*" He leaned slowly toward her, begging, reaching. "Please—" he whispered. Joyce did not move until Hek's mouth was almost upon hers.

"Have you washed that other away—lots?" she asked, her warm breath touching his chin.

"Lots!"—and they kissed. They kissed in such fashion that Hek did not remember to move his hands, up or down or any way at all, did not remember to protrude his tongue nor adjust his body, but clung only to her lips with his, waiting for the first pain of gratification to abate, waiting for the end of that dizzy descent. It did not come. She seemed to have a thousand mouths, each different, one supplanting another in quick succession without intermission. By mutual, unsignified consent their heads were separated. "I love you, Joyce. Oh, God, how I love you!"

As she breathed deeply, catching her breath in a miniature sob, her belly palpitated against his diaphragm and Hek buried his face in the curve of her neck. She pressed her head tightly against his, and held him. Hek was not conscious of thought, sensation or emotion. Only to stand thus, without moving, without blinking, without interruption—forever, seemed the end-all of his desire, the utmost reach of his most selfish imagining.

If Joyce tired sooner than he, it was probably because she *had* wanted to get unpacked. It were the veriest falsehood to say she was unmoved. "This isn't good for us," she phrased it. "Don't you know that?"

"It's beautiful," Hek murmured without moving his head. "I've never felt like this before in my life."

"Not even last night?"

"Never!"

"Come!" She pushed him half away. "You're sleeping. We have to rehearse."

"Rehearse? Oh, God!" He reached for her lips again.

"No! No, no, no. Come, Hek. Come, darling. Pull yourself together. The others will notice."

"Joyce."

"All right now?"

He dropped in a chair and stared at her. She caressed him across the dirty dressing-room with her eyes, then, with a quick, birdlike quirk of her head the incident was closed. She turned and ran a finger over the make-up shelf. "Oooo! dirty!"

"Joyce.... I'm not going out with Wade any more. Would that make any difference to you?"

"Don't you want to ask Props for some old newspapers like a good boy? This shelf is filthy."

Hek's blood was cooling. "Would it?" He arose. "Would you like me better?"

"I think it's bad for you to—run around—with just anybody. Come; papers?"

"Kiss me!"

"Nope."

"Joyce—"

"No, Hek. That's all."

He grinned at her. "I'll get some."

Most of the company had assembled, but they did not seem to notice that he came from her dressing-room. The stage-hands were bolting the knock-down interior together under Brownie's direction. The wizened carpenter looked at Hek askance. "I'll be glad when you learn your verses, young sprout, so I can have the stage of an afternoon."

"Brownie," Hek answered with a swagger, "when they see me troupe to-night there won't *be* any more rehearsals."

"All right. I'll watch you. I'll tell Helton if you'll do."

Summers had been pacing the ground-cloth. "My dear Mr. Knott, is it necessary for you to fraternize with the stage-hands? Have you no feeling for the dignity of your position?"

Brownie made a very inelegant noise with his mouth, and Hek said, "Why, Dad, *I'm* a stage-hand. I carry a card."

"*Good God! Quiet*, man! ... Don't ever say that again. You dress with *me!*"

Every one within earshot laughed, and Dad resumed his pacing, well pleased.

All that day Hek kept Joyce in sight. He walked back to the hotel with her after rehearsal, he lay across her bed and talked as she mended a rent costume. Wade, he ignored, but a girl behind the hotel desk was not so easily banished. She not only smiled at him with superfluous cordiality, but she touched his hand deliberately when she gave him his key. As he escorted Joyce downstairs to dinner, the same girl passed them in a second-floor parlor, displaying her teeth again and twinkling her eyes. Hek noted covertly which door she entered, as he helped his companion negotiate a fairly simple turn in the stairs.

As they left the dining-room, Hek excused himself long enough to gain Wade's ear. "Find out who lives in the room at the top of the stairs, marked 'B'," he said. "I'll tell you about it later."

"Hey. Don't rush off. Get into your clothes to-night and we'll save time. What's in 'B'?"

"I gotta go now; Joyce's waiting. Just find out who lives there."

"Get dressed. Y'hear me?"

"I hear you." He ran back to Joyce's side. "I told him I wouldn't go, Joyce. Now do you love me?"

"Suppose I said 'yes'; then what would you ask?"

"Uh-huh. I would."

"And then I'd say 'no'!"

"Then I'd ask again."

"And that would get so boresome that I just won't start it."

"Do you love me—a *little?*"

"It was very cloudy as we came in. See if it's raining."

He stayed so long in her dressing-room that he scarcely had time to make it. He panted to his first entrance, still buttoning his uniform coat. Wade passed him during Dad Summers' big scene near the end of the first act. "The proprietor lives there, Dope, with his wife and kid. It's four rooms along the whole side of the house."

"Yeah? Well, either his wife gave me a big tumble or his 'kid' is full grown. I can't go with you to-night. Me for that."

"Well, there's no rule about me doing all the fixing. Ask her if she's got a friend."

"You're *on.*"

Wade entered the set. "*It's no use, father. Just as I told you, she's going to marry that ostrich.*" The show went on.

Joyce and Hek ate alone. At her door, down the hall from the suite marked "B", she took his hand. "You can come in, Hek.... Be good."

"I will."

She closed the door herself.

The proprietor's wife, or daughter, had not been in evidence.

"Did I tell you you gave a splendid performance to-night? Better than your first one."

"Why not? I meant every word of our scenes to-night. I'll do it better every day."

"Silly."

"I'm not silly, Joyce. I love you." He clasped his hands around her waist and she swung there, balancing her weight on her heels.

"Hek," she said seriously, "you're just a child for all your experience and your ability. I know you hate that, but I had to say it.

"My mother used to tell me, before I went into this business, that no man had a right to tell a girl he loved her until he was ready to marry her. 'I love you', according to her old-fashioned way of thinking, was equivalent to a proposal. Of course, in show business I've heard that a good many times when the man had nothing like marriage in mind. You get used to it. But you're too nice, you're too sweet to go around telling girls you love them— unless you mean it. Do you see what I mean? It cheapens you. It cheapens them. It cheapens love.... There, now," she kissed his forehead with a little smack, "that's all of the sermon. I just want you to understand how it makes me feel to hear you say that all the time. I'm pretty and you are attracted. Your lips are as much fun as a good ripe peach fresh off the ice, but we're not in love, Hek, and I don't want you to think we are, either one of us. See? You don't want to marry me. You don't want to marry any one— at your age. I can't marry either. I think too much of my work.

Now, then. You sit over there in that big chair while I wash a pair of stockings."

Hek bent and sat as she pushed him backward. Newness, the complete and utter newness of the thoughts she expressed and of those aroused in him, stunned him. He had nothing to say. His brows wrinkled in perplexity and his eyes followed her quick steps to and fro and around him. "I don't ever intend to marry," his voice articulated numbly and without inflection, as if it were something he had thought to say before and did say now although the time for it and the excuse for it had both passed.

Joyce stopped before him. "Then don't you think it is a little unfair to me to talk about love? Don't you see that it is rather insulting?"

"I do *now*, Joyce, but I didn't think of it before. I didn't mean it that way. You know I didn't."

Sometimes Minnie smiled like that. "I know you didn't, lamb. But—you see—I have to keep a pretty good opinion of Mrs. Killfeather's little girl, Joyce. I want every one I like to share it. I wouldn't care much what you thought of me, if I didn't like you."

"I want you to like me—so much."

She winked at him. "I *do*."

Why did this girl remind him so much of Minnie? He had thought of it before, several times. He must write to his mother. He had promised to do that often. Joyce really did like him. His lips were—what? Something about peaches. Gosh, he would marry a girl like her. She would be worth it, almost. If one of his professors in the diner-lunch-counter academy had not impressed him so thoroughly with the adage that *it is cheaper to buy milk than to keep a cow*. It was the excruciating cleverness of the statement that had won him rather than any faith in its accuracy. By Wade's method, "milk" was free. Wade stayed away from girls who smiled at you as your mother did and talked about "cheapening love". Why! the *world* was waiting for him. The girl in room "B" was probably down in the café waiting for him to come in. That had been a tumble, unmistakably. Joyce was too goody-good. If only she didn't kiss so divinely, she would be easy to forget. If he could be sure that her resolution to remain—but *was* she still a virgin?

Joyce returned from the bath, pulling the wet hose into shape. She made a sour face. "You look so forlorn. What's the matter?"

"I don't know."

"I do."

"Yes? What?"

"You've been hoping I'd play—real hard …. Haven't you?"

… "Yes."

She pinned the stockings on the lace curtain and sat on the foot of the bed facing him, her chin on the back of her hands clasping the bed-post. "I won't, Hek. I'll tell you that now so you needn't stay—now, or any other time, with me. That's frank; isn't it? I hate to think of you growing up to be a shoddy heart-breaker like Wade, three-sheeting on every street corner. I hate to see you chasing the riffraff of every town we play. You're too big to do it. You have too fine a future to do it. It tears you down."

"Is that the only reason you've paid any attention to me? Just trying to keep me a mamma's boy—because you're a—a Christian Scientist?"

Two tiny vertical lines came between Joyce's brows. She bit her lower lip and rose stiffly. "Perhaps."

"I thought so," he pouted, sullen.

She moved behind his chair where he could not see her and stood looking down at his head. Where had that nastiness come from? What had injected that note when she had thought they were getting on so well? "You'd better go now, Hek. I don't know quite what to say to you. We seem to be getting further apart instead of closer."

"Just as you say," he jerked out of the chair. "I gotta write home anyway."

"Oh, *will* you?" Her round face shone with pleasure. "Do that, Hek.... And let's be friends."

"Oh, sure."

"Good-night."

"Good-night."

"Tell your mother you put on a perfectly *grand* performance, and give her my love."

"All right. Good-night."

Joyce wanted to kiss that pout away, but he did not look at her.

Hek walked toward his own room only until he heard her key turn, then he went back to the parlor. A wild elation pounded his ribs within. She was reading a magazine under a standing lamp in one corner. It was easy to hide his joy. He put on a tired smile and sat beside her. How would Wade begin this? "Are you enjoying that story?" There was the taste of brass in his voice. His energy itself was bitter, acrid. In short, he didn't care particularly whether he made this or not. *She* had started it, smiling at him, trying to hold his hand, even before she'd seen the show.... Anyway, all women made him sick and none of them should either save him or break him. He'd do just as he damn pleased.

"No," the girl said with utter finality, turning a bright, quizzical expression on him to see how he would start again.

"Then what are you reading it for?" She was twenty or a little more, Hek estimated, dark with an animal cast of features emphasized by brows which almost met.

"To kill time until you came in." Which could be disconcerting candor or the baldest sarcasm. Her eyes neither added nor detracted a jot from her words. Hek took them at face value. His misunderstanding with Joyce lent him a precocity in this play, a false competence that frightened even him. On any other night, without the stimulation of anger and this urge to *hurt* somebody, the girl was more than his match. Under ordinary circumstances he could not have held his own a moment before her direct frontal attack, and—failing—she would have lost interest at once.

"I've been in the hotel an hour."

"I know it."

Every time she spoke a fresh start was necessary. What is more utterly conclusive, more strictural to any conversation than the blunt lie: "I know it."

"What's your name?" Hek tried, without thinking that a monosyllable could answer that.

She was generous. "Fortuna Allardyce Larned. What's yours?"

"Hek." Now it was her turn.

"Are you swearing?"

That broke the ice and they both laughed. "Sh-h-h," she switched out the light, "be quiet. No one *ever* comes in here, but if we kick up a row, some one might."

"Does your husband own this hotel?" Hek demanded.

"My husband! No. My husband's in France. How did you know I was married."

"I didn't."

They both held their hands over their mouths until their amusement had passed.

"Oh, where have you been all my life?" asked Fortuna Allardyce.

"Say—" Hek was skeptical, "you're not a Clinton girl."

"Well, maybe not. I *thought* I was."

"No, sir. I'll bet you're from some place else."

"From What Cheer maybe."

"What cheer?"

"That's a town—in Iowa."

"No!"

"Sure it is,"

"I'll be darned. But, look, did you really sit out here waiting for me?"

"Wouldn't you like to know?"

"Of course I would."

"You aren't trying very hard to find out."

Now, what did she mean by that? "I can't see you well enough to know how to take that."

"If I say 'Boo!' real hard will you run away?"

"I'll be damned if I will." He seized her chin and turned it firmly toward him. The sharp contrast between her thin lips and their sinuous reaction to his kiss and the full deep opulence of Joyce's was so startling he drew his head quickly back.

"My God," said the girl, "did I sting you?"

Hek laughed aloud before he could stifle it.

"Now, you'll have to quit that or Fortuna will have to go home."

"It's your fault; you make me laugh."

"Poor boy!"

"I'll tell you what. Come on in my room. Then it won't matter if we laugh a little. No one will know who's there."

"You make it sound very enticing, but a man got me in his room once and almost immediately made a very improper suggestion."

"I'll bet it wasn't half as improper as one I can make."

"You have the very same thing in mind; I can tell it."

"How can you tell it?"

"By the expression on the front of your lap."

Hek doubled up, choking with laughter. Several people came up the stairs and turned down the corridor without a glance into the darkened parlor.

"This is so comfy here. Let's stay."

"It's much nicer in my room. There's a bed in there,"

"To tell you the truth, I'm not sleepy,"

"We needn't sleep."

She did not answer at once and Hek ventured another kiss. "Aren't you afraid I'll sting you again?"

Hek felt himself quite the connoisseur of kisses as he noted the idiosyncrasies of Fortuna's embrace, and contributed something on his own side for her to think about. "You've gone to night-school somewhere," she accused him. "*That* was never learned in daylight."

"Come on, Fortuna, let's walk down the hall to number six."

"No, let's stay here."

More than kisses, the Knott boy assumed, were going to be required to bring about the desired effect. He began a series of excursions to excite her desire, soft devices he had imagined might some day be performed on his own anatomy by an inventive and passionate female, a combination of many suggestions gleaned by listening back-stage, around the depot, at the Third Ward Fire Station and at the Academy. *This* was selected by advice of a veterinarian who had attended a sick horse near Aunt Tessie's; *this* was culled from a bawdy story. Another movement came from those far-off hammock days, so dimly remembered now. *That* was a bold imitation of something Ruby had done to him—and this he had made up himself. The girl suffered the mauling for fifteen or twenty minutes without complaint. Some of it was pleasant. From time to time he interrupted the performance to whisper again that greater freedom, more complete enjoyment and the most esoteric revelations awaited her in his room.

She was adamant—until Hek, still bruised from Joyce's words, still smarting, lost patience and desisted. His own desire was keen, blood can scarcely become hotter, but his pride was beginning to suffer. "Well, look, sweetheart," he said, without making it sound very endearing, "*I'm* going to my room. I'll leave the door unlocked because nobody is going to steal my baggage. You think it over for a while, and if you *want* to come in, I'll be there."

They parried a moment, and thrust, but his mind was made up. After all, she had started it. He had met her more than half-way. "Good-night," he said. "Do you want this magazine?"

"No. Take it along."

"Thank you." And they separated.

Hek undressed rapidly, throwing his garments viciously from him to every corner of the room. Life's stock had hit a new low. Hek was undecided which was the greater nuisance, to be good or to be bad; both entailed entirely too much effort, too much thought, chicane, diplomacy and maneuvering. *Damn* women! He flung himself into bed clad only in his undershirt, and began turning the pages of Fortuna's magazine. He would look at all the pictures; then he'd turn out the light and go to sleep. He wouldn't wait for any of them! He wouldn't run for shelf paper nor open trunks nor even kiss them any more. If they wanted his kisses let *them* do the active work, let them seek him. To hell with 'em!

It was, in very fact, Hek's first major engagement. That he was assisted in winning it by the scruples of the now slumbering Joyce is neither here nor there. It taught Hek much. It gave him a manner. It taught him the value of independence, the swaying power of scorn. He was no more than halfway through the pages of the periodical when his knob was turned from without and Fortuna slipped quickly in. He looked at her calmly over the edge of the book as she twisted the key behind her. She had undressed, donned a nightgown and a kimono, unpinned her hair.

"You devil," she whispered. "How did you know I'd come?"

"I didn't.... But I *thought* you would." He turned another page.

"Well——"

"Well?"

"Aren't you going to ask me to sit down?"

"You didn't come in here to sit down." He smiled at her friendlily to take the bite out of his words, and turned the covers back without revealing her surprise. "Come on, Fortuna, I'd have died if you hadn't come."

She switched off the light at the wall and in a moment Hek felt her long legs stretching coolly the length of his own. Possessed at last of all man strives for, Hek tried to maintain his calm. He tried to acquit himself with honor—and, in some measure, succeeded. Fortuna did not leave for several hours.

### 6

HEK was a little lofty next morning. Wade's jowls seemed to hang lower and the pouches under his eyes were more puffy. The thinning paths which ran back over each eye were more noticeable. Probably he had been a good enough man in his day, but it was also probable that the finer points of chasing had escaped him, even in his prime. Hek didn't want to talk to him. There was a quality about this morning's memory which demanded solitary musing for its full enjoyment. He turned away—and bumped into Joyce.

"Good-morning," she smiled, as if the new day cancelled all differences between them. "Did you write to your mother?"

Hek tried to make his manner more matter-of-fact than patronizing, but that was a failure. "No," he admitted, and what was she going to do about it? "I met an old friend of mine. I didn't know they lived here." His feet were braced, a little too far apart. For all his height, he reminded Joyce of a bantam cock, crowing.

"Oh, I see." She went on past him and into the depot.

Over his shoulder, he watched her go, without turning his head. So that was going to be her attitude. It was none of her business and she wasn't interested. O. K. She was right, by God.

He was rotten. Too rotten for her to wipe her feet on. Rotten with a vengeance this time. No makeshifts! No half-measures! He'd made a woman older than he come to him!

Violet and her husband turned the corner of the building, taking their constitutional. They'd always done this *on deck*, she sometimes explained, every morning when crossing.

"Got a cigarette, Crane?"

The New Yorker was too dumbfounded to deny it. "Uh—certainly. Fatima?"

Hek took one from the proffered pack, smiling at Violet. "How are you?"—assured, he was, a full man in his own sphere.

Miss de Forest nodded, seeing this Knott boy for probably the first time in her life. "Very well, thank you."

"Thanks,"—for the cigarette. He stepped aside that they might resume their "turn around the deck".

Crane and Violet looked at each other. "Astounding?" he asked, almost chuckling.

" 'Crane'—too! Did you hear him?"

They looked back. Hek, lonely, on his eminence, had struck an attitude, leaning gracefully against the corner of the building, his head tilted back, his eyes searching the morning sky.

"Will you get that pose?"

"My God! he hates himself."

"But isn't he a good-looking dog?"

"In a way."

"In a *way*? He's the prettiest child I've seen in years.

"'Got a cigarette, Crane?'—wasn't that priceless?"

"He'll be calling me 'Vi' to-morrow!"

"My God! he's cocky."

"He does play the part awfully well."

"I don't know why not? There's nothing to it. He's a perfect type. I'd be surprised if he couldn't."

"Look! He's asked some one else for a match! I'll bet it makes him sick."

Hek left his baggage in the smoker and walked the length of the train—to see the heads turn, to hear the whispers, to be pointed out as an actor.

The rest of the troupe saw nothing more of Hek until he assisted a town girl to alight from the train in Cedar Rapids. Helton shook his head. "Hardonicus Perpetualis works night and day," he pointed the boy out to Wade. "He doesn't miss anything."

Hek helped his new acquaintance into a big Packard marked FOR HIRE and fumed inwardly when its driver tried to hawk the remaining seats before driving away. Wade got in—and Crane, Violet and Helton. Hek introduced them all. "This is Miss Charpentier," he informed them, "a French girl. She's been having a lot of trouble with German spies."

"Not really," Violet disbelieved.

"She's been telling me all about it on the train. They make her life miserable."

"German spies," Helton said sympathetically, turning around in the front seat to look at the girl.

Mlle. Charpentier was a little flustered, a little diffident in the presence of so many new faces.

"Tell them about it," Hek encouraged. "Tell them how your house has been watched and your phone cut off."

"Because I'm French," she managed. "I'm followed everywhere."

The taxi took a corner faster than necessary.

"German spies in Cedar Rapids?" Wade asked, looking down at the girl beside him who seemed undernourished and a little stary.

"They're *everywhere*," she assured him. "They never sleep."

A peculiar sound came from the driver's seat, but when the actors looked at the chauffeur his face was blank, his eyes seeing nothing but the road ahead.

Mlle. Charpentier was dropped before they reached the hotel. As she sought a coin in her purse Hek waved her away. "Never mind that. *I'll* take care of it. Good-by. I'll see you to-night."

"Oh, thank you so much. *Au revoir, Monsieur* Hek."

He waved his hand as the car jerked away.

"What's the idea payin' her taxi fare?" Wade demanded. "Didn't I tell you about spending money on 'em? My good God, boy, you're crazy."

"I won't take his money," said the driver. "That's Sadie Carpenter. She's out of her head."

"*I* thought so," Helton exulted. "I thought so. It's in her eye."

"Hallucinations," said Crane.

"Oh, what do they call that, dear? Dementia præcox?"

Wade shook his head sorrowfully at Hek. "Pickin' on halfwits!"

"Everybody knows Sadie," the driver explained. "She's just simple; wouldn't harm anybody."

Hek had nothing to say. Now that he thought it over, he had been suspicious of the girl all along. She had acted very peculiarly.

Helton began by chuckling, then allowed his amusement to crescendo into a loud laugh. "Oh, boy! That's rich. And Three-sheet's got a date with her! Oh—oh—oh—God!"

"Whadayamean, 'Three-sheet'?" Hek grumbled.

"Ain't there enough healthy women in the world without you pickin' on somebody out of a home?"

Violet watched Hek's discomfiture with an amused smile which scalded.

"I knew she was crazy," the boy protested. "Don't you think I could tell?" His agony was relieved by arrival at the hotel. The chauffeur detained Wade by holding up his change purposely.

"Don't let your friend meet her to-night, Pardner. The boys kind of look out for her—you know?"

"Oh, I see."

"She lives with her aunt; just the two of 'em. She ain't responsible for what she does. We—the boys—kind of keep an eye on her, see?"

"I'll tell him. It'll be all right. Don't worry."

The taxi man handed him his change. "One guy had to leave town in such a hurry he couldn't even wait for a train—account the boys caught him fooling around her. She ain't responsible."

"O. K.... O. K.... He won't meet her."

"O. K."

As the clerk assigned their rooms, Hek noticed that his was next to Joyce's. In another car, she had arrived before them.

"Listen, old Son," said Wade, directly outside Joyce's door, "lay off that moll to-night. Don't keep that date. The taxi man just told me—they ride 'em out of town on a rail for messing with her. It's poison."

"He told you that?"

"Yeah.... Say! You didn't intend to go, did you; after you found out she was nuts?"

"Listen, Wade," it was Hek's toughest manner, "that guy is stringin' you. If I'm not there, *he* will be. Don't fall for that."

The leading man studied his precocious disciple intently. "By God, you'd use a snake if you could get somebody to hold it. You're the rattiest little bastard I *ever* met."

"Mind your own God-damn' business," said Hek—and he slammed his door. He sought his greatest admirer, over the dresser, and spoke directly to him. "Can you imagine that? That old, worn-out——hound calling *me* a rat! After all the dirty things he's done in *his* life! ... Look at the fun she'd have! Jesus, I'd be doin' her a favor. Maybe that's why she's nuts; nobody'll have anything to do with her." He took his brush and comb from the valise and fussed with his hair, drawing the waves toward his ears and setting them. Satisfied, he watched his eyes a moment, as they must have looked the previous evening. The vision of his own beauty was so appealing that he backed away from the glass and sat high on the bed, propping the pillows at his back. Three trips from dresser to bed were necessary to achieve the desired picture and relaxation. With his hands clasped behind his head, Hek reviewed—ever so slowly—the major events of his life, beginning with his discovery of the charm of a swelling breast.

There had been three little girls in school, each contributing something, all called "horny" by the boys. Their structure had differed; the structure of all his women differed; there were no two alike. Louise had breasts, Hek thought of them as "titties", which came to very sharp points. Mabel's were big and round and firm; Helen's were only starting—one decidedly larger than the other, a phenomenon he had also noted regarding Florence. Minutely, he recalled the intimacies these little girls had permitted. With consciously lascivious intent, Hek rehearsed every touch, every squeeze, every pressure. Louise, Mabel, Helen— then Ruby, Florence and Joyce. He dwelt upon Ruby's kisses, and wondered where she was now. *Babes in Starland* had come over the "death trail" through Iowa too. He might run into her. If he did—ah! if he only would. That ague would not seize him now, after so much experience. He would not tremble like a bird, like a frightened child, in her arms. Hek left off remembering to picture his next meeting with Ruby, watching his facial expression as he recognized her, greeted her, drew her close—all the way, all the way. Then—even though it shamed him a little (a little less each time he played this psycho-sexual solitaire)—he went on to the evening with Miss Jones-Smith and finished with his flourishing conquest of Fortuna.

Hek scrutinized the record and was pleased. He smiled kindly, proudly, at his reflection, and stretched. What a man! God! he was rotten. Taking them all, knocking them over, leaving them where they fell. And he was still only a kid. Wait until he really hit his stride! Just wait.… And to-night it would be Miss Charpentier. Different lips, different breasts, different reactions. They couldn't scare him. He was doing her a favor. It cut no ice if she wasn't quite right in the head; she was probably all right elsewhere.

Joyce was locking her door as he went out. Hek hesitated— and if the affront had not been too bald, would have gone back into his room. Then, expansively, he greeted her, smiling. She was cool, reserved. She was the kind of girl men married. Some men; not his kind. But, he'd walk with her. There was no use being unfriendly.

"Going to the theatre?"

"Yes. I have mail here."

They had only half a block to walk, but it seemed a long way, since neither spoke. Hek was punctilious in deportment, changing sides when they crossed the street, pointing out a rough gravel spot and apologizing when he brushed her arm. He held the heavy stage door open for her and repeated the ritualistic "Where's the mail box?" to save Joyce the trouble.

Their scenery was being unpacked. The local master of properties wheeled trunks to the dressing-rooms. "Well, you can have your God-damn' stage to yourself to-day, Brownie. There's no rehearsal."

The carpenter did not look around. "There'll be one tomorrow. You'll go up to-night."

"Never!"

"Here's a letter for you," Joyce said, bringing it to him.

"For *me!*" Who on earth would be writing to him? Oh, Minnie, of course. "Thanks."

"From your mother?"

"Yes." Hek dropped into the electrician's chair and opened the fat envelope.

April 12, 1917.

My Dear Son:

Now that you are gone, I cannot for my life see how I came to permit it. I live in constant dread of the consequences. If Robert had been here, I am sure he would have vetoed the very suggestion.

Sure he would have! That mutt. What did he know? Hek would have liked to see *his* face—if a girl flirted with *him.*

How do you spend your time? You aren't traveling or playing your part every minute. What do you do between times? How do you get clean clothes?

Poor mother. She didn't know much about the world after all. She'd never been out of Freeport but once in her life. One measly trip to Chicago. She didn't know what went on. Wouldn't she be shocked to meet a man like Wade? Wouldn't she die if she knew about Wade and Mercedes?

> You must write often and tell me everything you do. I feel like a criminal, sending you away from home like this without any instruction, without any warning about the thousand and one things that can happen to you. You and Robert have always been so different. Your opportunities have not been the same. His studies had prepared him to face life, but you and I have never talked those long, serious talks we should have.
>
> I hardly know where to begin. What are those people like? The people you work with? Do you like them? Are they clean and honest? How are they all related? Are there any other married couples besides the Weymans? Any brothers and sisters? Do you make friends in the towns you visit?
>
> A great deal depends on the kind of people around you, Harper. There are so many vile characters in the world. Do you understand mother? Choose your friends carefully. Ask yourself if you would be ashamed for me to see you with this person or that. Stay away from the drinkers and the kind who make slighting remarks about women. I do not mean to preach, but your future and my peace of mind are entirely in your hands. I am asking you to be strong for both of us, to attempt to correct what I feel has been my mistake. If anything should happen to you, I would feel entirely responsible—and I am asking you to be doubly careful to spare me the bite of conscience.
>
> I *can* depend on you; can't I, Son? Watch your health. Eat food that is good for you. You know what

I mean. See that your bowels move regularly, and if they do not, take Pluto water. Get plenty of sleep and drink lots of water. Do not be afraid or ashamed to ask me any questions you want to about your daily problems. That is what mothers are for. Do not pick up too many chance acquaintances. Try to spend as much time as you can with Mr. Helton—without annoying him. He is an older, more experienced man. He is your employer and from what I saw of him he seems to be a competent business man. Try to learn from him. If you are going to make the theater your future, you cannot begin too soon to learn all about it that you can.

I have been very well. Florence spent the night here, Monday night. I was so lonesome with both of you boys gone. I had a letter from Bob yesterday. The first one from France. He is very cheerful but I know he hates that life.

I wish you could have had a long talk with him before you went away. It is difficult for me to say the necessary things. Hek, my darling, stealing and drinking are not the only bad things a boy can do. He can get mixed up with the wrong kind of women. All women and girls are not like mother and Florence, Son.

Oh, boy! *That* was a hot one. Poor, poor Minnie. She was like a child, floundering, trying to advise some one who knew twice as much as she did. When he wrote he would let her know how well he could take care of himself. He would tell her about Joyce—so pure they all called her "the angel". He wouldn't hurt Minnie. She *meant* well. That much was true, anyway. All girls were *not* like Florence.

There are dreadful consequences attached to loose associations with the wrong sort of women. I need not tell you about the possibility of you becoming a father. You know that. But there are other possibilities—the most horrible of diseases, of the body and of the mind. Girls who give you their favors easily, women you meet on the street are almost all infected with one or another of these diseases. Many of them do not even know it and there is no way for you to tell. The only safe way, the only manly way, is to avoid such women. Buy yourself a good book and go to your room and read after your work is done at night. Do this not alone for me—but for yourself and for the girl you are going to meet and love and marry. Every boy owes that one good girl a debt, Harper. You owe it to your future wife. Keep yourself clean and wholesome and strong.

Oh, God! Fol-de-rol-de-rol! Get a good book and go home and read! Wasn't that just like her? Wow! What a family! She and Bob would turn into a book if they weren't careful. Read a book! Be careful of women! Hek supposed mothers had to be like that. They had to give just so much advice. The girl he married! He'd like to see her. He'd like to see a girl he'd marry.

"She wrote a long one," said Joyce.

Hek nodded. "Yeah."

"I'll bet she misses you."

"Oh, sure." Hek folded the bundle of sheets and put them back in the envelope.

"I'm going to take a walk," said the girl. "Come along?"

… "Sure. If you want me."

She took his hand and they entered the alley, swinging their arms in unison like children.

They left the business district, walking slowly, enjoying a sun which held a suggestion of spring warmth. "You remind me so much of my mother," Hek said. "Gosh, you're just alike."

"It's sweet of you to say that, Hek. I don't know what prettier compliment you could possibly pay a girl.... I think it's lovely."

The rounder was taken aback. He hadn't meant to be sweet. Of all the things he never in the world wanted to be, "sweet" stood first.

"Well, I mean—you're both so set on everybody being *good*. Neither one of you wants a fellow to have any fun at all. You don't want to let a man *be* a man."

"There are lots of ways of being a man, Hek. Just being a male isn't being a man."

"I don't know how you're going to be a man unless you're a male."

"But you needn't devote all your time to demonstrating how male you are. There are lots of other things in life besides sex."

"Yeah, *books!* I know. I been waiting for you to tell me that. Why don't I go home after the show and read a good book? God, that makes me mad."

"Don't you like to read?"

"*No!* Gosh all Friday, that's all anybody ever does around my house. My brother's read ten thousand books and he still wants to go to college.... Not for *me*. I'm going to live!"

Joyce said nothing. This *living* was so complicated. It was often difficult enough to keep oneself on the track. What right had she to meddle, after all?

"Haven't you ever felt like letting go? Don't you ever get lonesome, Joyce?"

"Often; but not lonesome enough to be a fool."

"You think I'm a fool, don't you?"

"I think you're going to take an awfully hard bump some day, Hek, a bump that is going to hurt for days and days." "Well, all right. I don't care. I guess I can stand it."

"Every time we talk I seem to have less and less to say to you. Let's not talk about us. Let's talk about—oh, about—well, let's talk shop. Unless business gets better, the notice is going up."

"You mean the show might close?"

Joyce nodded. "Freeport was about the only date that's been good enough in a month. Helton is banking on Des Moines."

"Is that so?" The thought of losing his job appalled Hek. That would mean returning to Freeport, becoming a *boy* again. Being out of work was meaningless, but being deprived of the opportunity to "live", losing his part, having his chasing interrupted!—the prospect sickened him. "Gee, what will you do—if it does?"

"Oh—get a Summer stock. There'll be lots of those—beginning about now."

"Ye-es? In Chicago, eh?"

"That'd be the best thing in the world for you."

"How do you mean?"

"The experience! You'd play a different part every week. You need that. It gives you ease, stage presence. You need that. There's nothing like stock—if you intend to stay in the business."

"Oh, sure, I'm going to stay in the business."

"You'd need some wardrobe, of course. I don't know what you'd do about that."

"Wardrobe?"

"Costumes. Suits and hats and things. A tuxedo and a Stetson and a cane or two. Shoes."

"Gee, I'd like to carry a cane."

Joyce shook her head at him. "You're not a day over six. I don't know why on earth I listen to you when you talk about 'living'; I ought to take you across my knee and paddle you."

"What all do I need in my wardrobe? Will you help me make a list?"

"Of course, if I can. I don't know; playing your line of parts.... The most important things would be plain suits, like that. You'd need four or five of those to start. Flannels, a tux, evening slippers—you know—dancing pumps and sport shoes."

"Let's go back to the hotel and make a list; will you? Write it down."

"Sure."

His enthusiasm was infectious. Joyce found herself thinking kindly of a Summer of unremitting labor, actually regarding the long nights of study with a thrill of pleasure. In her room, she humored Hek, nurtured this new ambition. He was not, she had convinced herself, essentially a bad boy. His talent was marked and unmistakable. If he could be made deeply interested in his work, his first adolescent spell of sex-madness would pass.

"I'd need a couple trunks to hold all this stuff," he beamed up at Joyce. "At least two."

"Uh-huh. I've got four at home, just jammed. Of course, a woman's things take up more room, and they need more stuff than a man does."

"It'll cost a lot of money, won't it?" His face fell.

"Not so much. You won't need everything at once. You can buy lots of that as you go along."

"I suppose.... Say! Wouldn't it be great if we could get a job in a Summer stock together?"

"Would it?" she asked dryly.

Hek could not miss the rebuke. "*I* think so.... Oh, Joyce, if you'd only be reasonable, I'd give up every one else. I'd never go out with another girl."

"Why did you have to start that? We were having so much fun."

"I'm sorry. But, gosh, Joyce, I'm only human. I can't look at you without wanting to kiss you. You know that."

"That's no compliment. You can't look at any girl without wanting to kiss her. You want them all."

"But I want you most." He stood quickly beside her and held her arms. "Doesn't that mean anything to you?"

Apparently it did, for they were kissing, and they got on the bed, somehow, but there it stopped. Callous as the boy was, the antics of other encounters were not even attempted here. He held one silk-clad knee, its plumpness filling his hand and sending a thousand suggestions mindward, but he did not move his fingers.

"We've got to stop, Hek. This isn't good for us." She had said that before. It wasn't good for them. He flung himself off the bed and across the room to the window. She stood behind him in a moment, holding his shoulder, allowing her body to touch his.

"I can't stand it, Joyce. I can't." He turned. "If—if you won't have me, I'll just have to stay away from you. It's killing me."

"Do you think I find it so easy?"

"Then why——?"

She answered him with a gesture.

Their partings were becoming monotonous. They met, talked, perhaps kissed, then separated as if the gallows shadowed them. "Thanks for helping me with this list, Cherry. I'm going to begin picking that stuff up right away. Maybe—if we work together long enough—maybe you'll change your mind."

## 7

THE performance dragged that night, but it was not Hek's fault. The house was only half full and Langford was pretty drunk. Cora was angry—probably because he had been drinking without her—and that showed in her work.

Once, between scenes, as Dad Summers and Wade stood talking together quietly, Hek came up. "Did you see what the boy found on the train this morning?" Wade asked. "A dippy little girl—comes about his shoulder. Cuckoo, you know? She thought he was an actor."

Dad squinted at Hek's make-up. "Behold that mask," he said in his most profoundly Hamlet voice. "Hidden from the world by that cherubic countenance is the blackest heart, the dirtiest soul I think I have ever seen."

Hek dug the old man in the ribs. "You're just bragging because you know me," he said.

"A potential murderer."

"Maybe a character-man," said Wade.

The boy was dressed and packed before the house lights had been extinguished. The French girl had promised to be at the corner of the alley, and in view of the opposition to his meeting her, he felt she should not be kept waiting.

At the dressing-room door, Hek paused. He remembered something. "Say, Dad; why does every one call me 'Three-sheet'?"

"I have never called you Three-sheet."

"No, but others do, and I want to know why."

"Well, you know what a Three-sheet is; don't you?"

"It's a piece of paper."

"A *stand* of paper."

"Well?"

"You don't see the resemblance?"

"I'll be damned if I do."

"Take a good look at the next one you pass. Get the pose. The chin line, the bent knee, the elevated brows. You're puncture-proof, but if you study it, it'll sink in."

"Oh, go to hell."

The French girl was at the appointed corner, but behaving strangely. Before Hek reached her side, she said: "Go out the other end of the alley and wait. I'm being watched." Hek's heart raced. Probably she *was* being watched, if what Wade had said were true. He stopped short in his tracks and turned, still in the shadow. Miss Charpentier walked away.

She joined him a block from the theater. "We better get off the street," Hek said. "Which way do you live?"

"We must hurry." She clutched his arm and dragged him along after her, in the direction she had come. Hek wondered if the espionage the local boys were said to exercise in this girl's behalf was not responsible for her idea that she was pursued by German spies. Perhaps she had been crazy in the first place, but they were just making her worse. Arc lamps drew a sulphurous gleam from her dancing eyes. Their pace, her excitement and the necessity to watch behind them at every step, stimulated the boy, raised his pulse and peopled his fancy with a thousand phantoms.

They turned a dozen corners, scarcely speaking beyond a breathless: "What's *that?*" when a shadow moved. In the back yard of a poor two-story house they paused. "Do you live here?"

"Upstairs," she whispered. "Come in here. Don't make a sound." They sat on the enclosed steps. Hek welcomed the need for silence. He preferred no talk at times like this. When the girl would have whispered, he stopped her. He learned, then, that not even an acrobat can achieve the impossible. The stairs themselves were impossible; but, the matter had progressed considerably beyond a stage that could be called preparatory, in a standing position, when heavy steps were heard in the yard. Her sharp little teeth stopped gnawing his lips. "They've found us," she whispered. Hek groaned—and desisted. "You go up here, right through the house and out the front door. Hurry!"

The little French girl stepped into the yard. Four big men were there. They surrounded her. "Where's that actor?" One of them looked up the stairs. "There goes the son-of-a-bitch!" Their ward was knocked down by their zeal.

Hek traversed four rooms in as many seconds—unlocked a door and descended the front steps. On the walk, a lookout tried to grab him, but the boy was too quick, and the chase was in the open. Down the street he sped and around a corner, the five heavy-footed men pounding after him grim-lipped, silent. In three blocks' run he had distanced them, but they were scattered between him and his hotel, and Hek was thoroughly lost. He made a grand detour hiding while autos passed, stepping behind shrubbery or the boles of large trees for every passer-by, working gradually around the city, to come upon the hotel from the side.

He proved a poor woodsman, or the hotel had been moved. He was in a manufacturing district, between almost blank brick walls. He walked another half hour, and found himself on the main street, a long way from the hotel. Cautiously, he approached, peering ahead until he saw three of his pursuers, waiting. He began another circuit. At three o'clock in the morning, he gave up. The hotel was thoroughly guarded. Entry was impossible.

By four Hek had found a straw bed in an empty box-car near the depot. The train left before seven that day.

Joyce had as little sleep as he. She had waited up for him until three-thirty, then slept in fitful cat-naps until dawn. When the clerk called her she was dressed. She knocked on Hek's door.

Then she asked if his key was in the rack. It was. She called Wade. "Do you know where Hek is?"

"I do not."

"He didn't come in last night."

"Am I my brother's keeper?"

"I'm worried, Carl."

" … So am I, now."

"What do you mean?"

"Nothing. I'll tell you later." He hung up and flew into his clothes. A conference with Helton brought forth a plan. The manager paid the boy's bill and claimed his baggage. "Somebody else will have to carry it, though. I'll be damned if I'll do that."

They found him, moving nervously around the freight station. "Stay out of sight until the train is in and half the stuff is loaded. We'll act as if nothing was wrong. Then you make a run for it. Probably they won't be around, but even if they are—you get on that train."

"Yes, sir," said Hek. "I'll make it."

He skulked between rows of gondolas, waiting, unable to see surely whether any of the people on the platform resembled the vigilantes.

The show was more than half loaded when Hek made ready for the run. It was fifty yards to the nearest coach, most of the distance an open stretch of packed cinders. He would walk until the train started, or until he should see a threatening movement on the platform, then he'd make a dash for it.

The story had circulated rapidly in the company. Every one knew what was happening—and why. Joyce, watching the towners suspiciously from her seat, saw two big fellows nudge each other and move close to the train. "Oooh—" she moaned aloud.

Helton and Brownie were standing on the platform of the smoker.

"A-a-all aboard!"

Hek ran.

They caught him from the bottom step and tore his fingers from the handles. A stone fist smashed his face, his ear. A boot caught his bottom, then his middle. The train was moving. Helton and Brownie left it, confusing the two men by attacking them from the rear. "Jump on, Knott! *Jump!*"

Hek clambered up—and sprawled on his face in the vestibule. Brownie flipped easily on a step—and Helton ducked just in time to miss a flying fist and ran down the track as the wheels clicked faster and faster.

From puffed and bleeding lips, Hek tried to thank them. They did not even smile. "You're one o' my actors. I had to get you out of town. I need you; but don't ever speak to me again, like a white man. I don't know you."

Brownie had not waited to hear the speech finished. He yawned his way to a double seat and curled up to sleep.

The manager's attitude was a complete surprise to Hek. He looked for his bags with a puzzled expression, dabbing at his lacerations with a handkerchief. He decided to try Wade. "Thanks for getting my stuff down, Carl. They had me sewed up."

"Yeah! It's a God-damn' pity they didn't kill you."

"Why, what the hell's the matter with you? You've told me a hundred times——is——if it's hung on a cow."

"And so it is—but it ain't fair game for a man to take it away from a simple-minded kid."

"She wasn't so God-damn' simple-minded. She knew what she wanted."

"Maybe.... Maybe it's all right, but I just can't take it. It gags me."

Others, strangers, were looking and listening. Hek took the brown valise to the wash-room and tried to repair his damaged face. The bastards! Turning on him! He got beat up first, then his friends turned on him, after he'd walked all night long—and hadn't actually accomplished the act they all pretended to detest. How did they know she was simple-minded? Maybe the Germans *were* after her. There was stuff like that in the papers every day. Were the papers simple-minded, too? She'd acted pretty much like the other girls he'd been out with. They were *all* nuts.

Made as presentable as possible, he went back to where Joyce was expecting him, and sat beside her. "I suppose you're through with me, too," he said. "Those birds act like I'd killed somebody."

"Did they hurt you?"

"Who?"

"Those two men."

"You can see what they did."

"Yes, I see."

"Are you going to hate me, now—worse than ever?"

"No, Hek."

"Every one else does. You will too when you hear the story the way they tell it."

"Wade, too?"

He nodded. "All of them. They won't speak to me."

"Well, that's a revelation."

"What?"

"I didn't know there was anything a man could do bad enough to disgust Carl Wade and Helton."

"Oh, I'm rotten," Hek whispered. "Rotten clear through. God, how I hate myself!"

"I don't think you are, Hek. I think you're fooling yourself."

"Oh, I don't know *why* I do it. Why am I this way? Why do I want every girl I see? What's wrong with me, Joyce?"

"I don't think there's anything wrong with you. You just haven't learned to control yourself. Liberty has swept you off your feet. You've been watched pretty closely at home."

"Not very."

"But you didn't run around, wild like this, in Freeport."

"Yes, I did—some."

"Didn't your folks teach you to—control yourself? Didn't your mother tell you how you'd be tempted? Is your brother like that?"

"Oh, those two were always trying to teach me something. They know it all! I think with my emotions. They got started too late. My judgments are superficial …. Like *me?* Bob? Hawph!"

"Didn't you and your brother get along?"

Hek's scorn for Robert Ingersoll shot from his eyes. "We got along all right as long as I did what they told me."

"They never told you anything that was bad for you, Hek. They tried to make you grow up the right sort of man, honest and respectable."

"Oh, who wants to be honest and respectable? If they do, let them." He snapped to his feet and lunged out of the car.

By God, he never *would* be respectable now. This was the last straw. He'd never do another clean thing. He was a rat, born. From this day on he'd *be* a rat. Dad Summers was right; his cherubic countenance hid a heart blacker than any other in the world.

Langford, looking for another poker player, passed through the vestibule. "Got a cigarette, Langford?"

The heavy-man appeared surprised that this creature should address him. "Buy your own," he answered and passed by.

## 8

It is, perhaps, not uncommon for Eighteen to tilt the world. It is not uncommon for Eighteen to be bitter. But Hek entered the lists uncommonly well prepared to carry out his rather simple threats. It isn't difficult to be bad, even *very bad*. In fact, it's comparatively easy.

He began, that afternoon, with a chambermaid who helped him on his career more than he realized until about five days later.

She was buxom, willing and cheerful. She really laughed *too* much. And, just as Minnie had said in her letter, a man could never tell who was diseased and who was not. There was nothing in this girl's easy laugh to arouse the least suspicion.

In Des Moines the notice went up. The show would close in Dubuque the following Saturday. In Des Moines Hek bought a suit of clothes and a "white man's" Gladstone.

There was a vaudeville house in Des Moines, and on the bill were three songbirds. They lived at Hek's hotel and the shrillest of them was in the writing-room when he went there to answer Minnie's letter.

Hek smiled and she smiled and he sat at the desk facing her. "You're at the Orpheum, aren't you?"

"Yes. You with the dramatic show?"

"Yeah. How's your business?"

"Why, I don't even know you!"

"No, I didn't mean that. I mean at the Orpheum."

"Oh, excuse me. I was quite taken aback.… It seems to be all right."

"Not so good for us."

"No? That's too bad."

"We're closing Saturday."

"Lots of shows are, productions. Where was it, just the other day—? We had a change and there was a musical show laying over there. *Babes in Starland*. They were closing too."

"Oh, yes?" Hek grinned as if that were good news. "I know a girl in that show. I know them all, for that matter. Did you meet a girl named Ruby?"

"Ruby? What's her last name?"

Hek grunted. "Huh. That's funny. I don't know.... Gee, isn't that funny?"

"Oh, it happens. Didn't you even take off your hat?"

"It didn't go that far. Her boy friend caught us."

"Is that where you got cut up? Lord! look at that ear."

"No. He didn't do that."

"Her husband was *supposed* to be out of town. Oh, you legits slay me."

"Say, what's that you're writing there?"

"I've got to address one more envelope."

"Go ahead—and then come on upstairs. I want to show you some pictures."

The songbird let that pass, and addressed the envelope. Nobody had shown her any pictures since Lincoln, Nebraska, where a black-face had taken her fancy. That had been two weeks before. "O. K., Mister. Vot is the name, please?"

"Knott, Hek Knott. What's yours?"

"Geraldine—but not Farrar."

Two soldiers rode up in the elevator with them and got out at the same floor. The girl and boy watched them amble suspiciously down the hall, studying the numbers. "What do you suppose they're up to?" she asked.

"I'll make a guess .... Here. I'm in here."

"Oh! We're right across the hall. The three of us get a room with two beds."

Hek unlocked his door. The soldiers had turned a corner out of sight. Geraldine dropped into the one large chair. "Where's the pictures?"

"What pictures?"

"*What* pictures! Help, help, help. I've been enticed under false pretenses. Help! a man's got me in his room!"

Outside—at another door—a timid knocking was heard. "Shhhh. It's those soldiers."

"Where are they?"

"I think they're across the hall."

"At *our* door?!"

"Listen."

A muffled feminine voice was raised to inquire who was there.

"That's Estelle."

"Sh."

"*This is Sam—and Jo.*"

"*Sam and Jo who? What do you want?*"

"*Listen, girlie; do you want to do something for your country?*"

Geraldine screamed—then clapped her hand tightly over her mouth and rolled on the bed. "Oh, God! Oh, God! Oh, God! Did you ever hear anything funnier? 'Do you want to do something for your country?' Estelle ought to take them up on that. She's patriotic."

Hek joined the girl on the bed. She looked at him archly, and kissed him. "Where are my pictures?" she whispered. "You don't get off that easy."

"I haven't got any pictures. Sorry. Let's undress and be comfortable."

She nodded, and kicked off her shoes. Hek drew the shades down.

"Turn on the light," Geraldine suggested, "and pull the dresser over here. If you won't show me any pictures, I'll show you some."

Hek reflected that some such valuable bits of knowledge could be picked up almost every day if a lad were really earnest and sincerely wished to learn.

"What if your husband comes home?" he whispered in her ear.

"Where I come from, Mister, husbands only come home once."

"Where's that?"

"San Antonio, Texas. Down there they don't bother with fists."

"Now, wait a minute," said Hek. "Maybe I'd better go."

"Fool!"

"I wouldn't want to get shot."

"Then don't run out on me *now*. 'Cause I've got a cannon in my trunk across the hall that's just wastin' away for exercise."

"You scare me, Lady. You scare me."

So Hek proceeded, and all unwittingly, thus contributed to the spreading of a great social pestilence. The downward path looked up.

On Tuesday evening, nine days out of Freeport, Hek felt the first strangeness. Next morning the evidence was unmistakable. "Well, I'll be God-damned!"

Since the morning in Cedar Rapids, he had been an exile, an outcast, a pariah in the company. He had traveled entirely alone. All ragging had stopped, all jokes and banter. Groups dispersed when he came near, although he had no intention of joining them. Joyce alone acknowledged his existence by speaking. The others would not even nod.

So—his resolution had been given no chance to waver. It was always uppermost in his mind. His own bestiality, that enormous lust within him, partaking of both pride and shame, was ever in his consciousness from waking to exhausted sleep. The ostracism struck what iron there was in Hek. He sneered at them. It was becoming. That little twist at one corner of his mouth added mystery and some age to his handsome features. Heads turned as he passed with even greater regularity than before. Hek did not mind being ignored by the other members of the company. He needed none of them. This show was closing. In another, the people would not have heard of the incident.

But *now* he needed advice. He had never taken notes at the Academy. All the cures and courses of treatment discussed by those professors had been without bearing on his life. He had listened without learning because he had been innocent. Even to the oft-repeated saw, *You're not a man until you've had it*, Hek had said to himself: "Then I hope I'm never a man." It was the utter inadequacy of *hope* as a prophylactic that had put him down.

Now he needed advice. Wade could have helped him, of course, if things had been different. Wade would know all about this; what to get and how to use it. Fear of the law made him put doctors out of his mind. Since the sex act outside of matrimony was illegal and this disease could be acquired only in its commission, a doctor might hand him over to the police forthwith. "Here! This boy has been doing wrong." No telling what would come of that. So Wednesday slipped away, while he tried to decide what to do. Thursday, too.

By that time he was waiting for Chicago. Freeport was out of the question. A Chicago doctor's address was on those little tin signs in so many theaters and depots. *He* wouldn't be likely to turn patients over to the law after advertising to get them.... The while the thing advanced, flourished, took root.

Saturday night in Dubuque, Helton came to his dressing-room and counted out his salary, then his railroad fare *to*

*Freeport.* The others got tickets to Chicago. Hek was in almost constant pain. He could not sit or stand still. His hands and feet moved in spite of him. There was no rest in any position. He cleared his throat nervously every few moments and his teeth clenched without his sanction. In the next dressing-room Wade sang, to the tune of *Belgian Rose:*

> *"Those early morning jumps;*
> *Oh, we played all the dumps.*
> *For every hour of sleep that we had*
> *We drank ten coffees and they were all bad,*
> *They caused us lots of pain.*
> *Next year well play them again.*
> *The hotels take all your money from you;*
> *Those cheap beanery steaks a man scarcely can chew;*
> *Some day we'll find repose,*
> *Playing nothing but two-dollar shows."*

"All right," Hek said sharply when the money had been counted, "thanks." His signature on the salary list was hardly recognizable, it skated sidewise and went off with a crazy lift at the end.

"What's the matter, Knott? You're sick."

"No, I'm all right."

"You better go home to your mother and settle down. You may be an actor but you're not a trouper; there's a hell of a lot of difference."

It was not the time to say that. Hek smashed his ugly nose without a word of explanation.

## 9

MABRY FOR MONEY had been out thirty-one weeks. The actors were anxious to get back to Chicago for a rest, to see some shows, to see faces other than those of their own troupe. Thirty-one solid weeks of one-night stands—brought to an abrupt conclusion on "the death trail" through Iowa. Hek had been treated to only a taste of it. His initiation had been light. The jumps had been easy those last two weeks, with no lay-overs in the middle of the night, very few calls for four or five in the morning. In the others was the memory of two hundred seventeen different versions of coffee, the same number of different beds. They had taken it all with the trouper's growl that but thinly hid a laugh. They cursed this life—but loved it. Now, however, with no more performances ahead of them and with the final salary list signed, no known means of locomotion was swift enough to take them to a room they need not check out of in the cold dawn, a bed in which they might loll until noon. No train, no plane could put them near food of uniform quality, near a laundry, quick enough to suit their taste.

Dad Summers, Joyce and the New Yorkers had saved money. Cora and the Weymans had put a little by. The rest had let their salaries slip through their fingers—with nothing to show for it.

There was an all-Pullman train out of Dubuque about two. The troupe took it in a body—with the exception of Hek. For him it would have been too costly. He would have to pay for his hotel room in Dubuque whether he slept in it or not, plus a berth, plus the fare from Freeport to Chicago. Some fifteen dollars or more, all together, out of his capital of forty-two; with a doctor—who was certain to be a cash-and-carry doctor—a strange, big city and no job at the other end of the jump. By this time, too, he had learned that part of the actors' creed which says, "Never look down-at-the-heel. If you've got only a quarter, get a shine."

After the commotion he had started by striking the manager had subsided, Hek knocked at Joyce's door. "Decent?"

"Yes."

His lips were drawn grimly against the urgency within him, drawn to withstand the nasty, gnawing burn.

"You're ill, Hek."

"Yes, I feel punk."

"What's the matter?"

"Oh, a bad headache. I don't know. It'll pass off. You going to-night?"

"Yes. You?"

The boy shook his head. "*I* can't afford it."

Neither had smiled. It was as if they stood on opposite sides of an open grave in which the remains of a still-born and illegitimate love were to be deposited, as if they stood waiting for the interment, talking across the black hole.

Joyce covered her hair with her hat, and pulled it. It was probably the last time, Hek thought, the last time he would see that hair. "You ought to go back——"

"Joyce!"

She turned around, astonished.

"Don't tell me I ought to go home. I *won't* go home. I'm *never* going home. I took me long enough to get away."

"Do you want to kick that lock for me? It hasn't been fixed yet." She was ready to go.

Hek locked her trunk. "You can have it fixed in Chicago."

"Going to eat?"

On the cleared stage a crap game was in progress. The last week's salaries and the season's savings of almost the entire company were in the process of changing hands. Little Brownie had the dice and he breathed on them tenderly before sending them across the baiz, saying: "*First* love!"— which meant that he wanted a nine. Hek said good-by to Jim Coffee, the local stage manager and read the signs over the switchboard once more, in case he never saw anything like that again. *Don't send out your laundry till we've seen your act* and *Where's the mail box?*

Joyce and Hek had chop suey—down the main street—swallowing their real thoughts with their rice and speaking as jerkily as the soy sauce came from the shaker-top bottle. Joyce's suspicions about Hek's condition were confirmed when he had to excuse himself in the middle of the meal. She sought Divine Love, for his healing, in her plate as she waited for him. Why was he such a little fool? Why was she? Was the responsibility she felt for him a manifestation of Christ within her or did she, unaccountably, unreasonably—even stupidly—love him? Joyce had not decided before his eyes, burning with pain, were again across the table from her. She had not decided—a full week later—when they met in Johnstone's office at Randolph and Dearborn, that corner of the Loop which strove so desperately to be a Rialto. Hek was waiting to interview a manager.

Her heart recognized his back and rose to confuse her speech as he turned. An intangibility—a current—an energy, an essence some future science will bottle and purvey, denied the Christ-within hypothesis by shooting forth and back across the office, from pole to pole, and thence to nerve centers in her body which throbbed with a more than religious throbbing.

Hek cupped one of her hands in both of his and held it to his breast. "Well, ruhlly," said a waiting leading-woman, turning her head away. Embarrassed, he let go, and Joyce touched her nose quickly once or twice with a tiny handkerchief. "You're looking better," she said.

"I *feel* better."

"Where are you living?"

"At the Paul House."

Utter despair drowned her joy at their meeting. The Paul House! The plague spot of Mid-Western show business. The walls themselves were cankerous. Joyce had thought the growth of the city northward had torn the building down. Apparently not, since he had found it. Joyce knew the place only at second-hand.

"The old Paul House," character-men said with rheumy eyes, dreaming of their potent youths, their voices lingering on the o-o-old, as if they meant shortly to sing. Probably it *still* stands. Probably human hands cannot demolish that building. It has, likely, an Equity contract, providing for its destruction *only* by "an act of God". The walls and floors crawled with vermin in 1917. The air was heavy with bed-bug poison, corruptions, abortions, nasty and meager little harlotries—and sewer-gas.

Here Hek had gone. Here he was living. Poor Joyce; her tormented spirit stamped its foot in futile denial of a physical law. Water, in spite of her, found its own level.

"Oh, Hek; why did you go there? It's a terrible place."

"It's not so bad. Everybody stops there. Wade and Dad are there too."

"Wade and Dad! … Dad goes there because he remembers when it was a good hotel, when stars lived in it, and it's cheap. And *Wade—!*"

"Well, you needn't worry about me. *I'm* not doing anything wrong."

"Will you come out to my house for dinner? Mother's a grand cook."

*Mother.* That frightened Hek. Mothers talked morals and goodness and sweetness and light. "Gee—I'd like to—but—I've—I've got to see so many people——"

Joyce drew him out into the hall. "I wish I were a man, Hek Knott. If I were, I'd just punch you and punch you until you woke up. *You're drifting along in your sleep!* What's the matter with you? Why do you fight everything decent as if it were going to kill you? You make me *so* angry."

Hek smiled crookedly, with less affectation than usual, and looked at her steadily as his head wagged from side to side. "I don't know," he said slowly. "I didn't know I did."

"You *do*. You repel the slightest suggestion of anything wholesome. You turn yourself wrong-side-out at the thought of being good. What do you want to be that way for?"

"Oh, I don't know. I didn't know it was as bad as all that. I'm just tired of it, I guess. At home that's all I heard. My grandmother was giving me that stuff morning, noon and night. Gosh! Then she died and my mother and brother started singing about 'the light of pure reason' and the darnedest string of stuff. Everybody worries about that junk too much. Gee, what's the difference? I don't care what's gonna become o' me when I die. I think they're all crazy."

"I'm not talking about dying, Hek. I'm talking about living. Don't you know you could have avoided this trouble you've got—if you'd been sensible?"

"Oh—that." He moved uneasily.

"Yes, *that*; every bit of it. Just your own foolishness."

It was obvious that she knew what was wrong with him. He blushed and swallowed hard. "Mm, they say're not a man t'll y've had that," he mumbled.

"They! Who are 'they'?"

"Everybody."

"Riff-raff like Carl Wade. And you listen to them instead of doing what you know is right. You *take* suggestions from them in preference to what your mother tells you—and others who love you."

Hek's eyes opened wider and his smile was boyish and pleased. "I begged you to say that once, Joyce. You wouldn't."

The girl frowned a little. The suggestion was that she could have prevented him from coming to harm if she had chosen.

"I *could* love you, Hek, if you showed me you were worth it. Right now, the dirtiest little trollop in town wouldn't have anything to do with you."

And it had always been thus between them. His anger rose in a surge of uncontrollable desire to hurt, to best, to beat down what was before him. "You don't need to rub it in," he snapped. "I know I'm rotten."

"You *want* to be rotten. You glory in it."

"Well, just let me alone, then. I'm not worth a minute of your lily-white time. You go ahead and be good and let me go to hell in my own way."

"I don't know why I *don't!*" and Hek was standing in the hall alone.

## 10

THE *dirtiest little trollop in town wouldn't have anything to do with you.* Hek caressed the plump upper arm of Olive—Olive Dorland, of the chorus—who lived on the floor below. "I wish I wasn't sick," he said.

"Huh! Don't I?"

"Do you?"

"Sweetness!" She rolled over on the soiled counterpane and kissed him.... "You know—I just thought of something."

"What?"

"Oh—well—never mind. I'm just crazy."

"What was it? What did you think of?"

"No." Olive shook her head with provocative determination. "No. Not you. I won't mention it."

"What *is* it? Come on——"

"Well——"

"Go on."

"Well, I'll tell you what I *thought* of; but you understand—it has no connection with you. I wouldn't even breathe it—that way."

"All right, what was it?"

She told him.

"Can you imagine that? ... Well—I'll try anything once.... You'll have to teach me, though."

"I'll teach you," said Olive.

# 11

OH, Ruby, Fortuna and Olive and Kate—the things you taught to Hek! Was it chance that tossed him so? What made him lecherous? What made him vain? Not Grandma nor Minnie nor Wade. Not you, perhaps. Not I. Not circumstance, I trow.

Shall we blame it on the stars?

Oh, Ruby and Helen and Mary and Jane—see what you've done to him! But I'm not blaming you. Surely no one's responsible for his bruised knuckles and barked knees, no one but Hek, if he chooses to clamber up and over jagged rocks and nettle-patches just to feel your flesh. No one's at fault but Hek.

Just to feel your flesh. What focused his life on that? The theatre? You know better! Florence, Fortuna and Ellen and May—you've never faced an audience in your lives. It wasn't the theatre.

It seems too bad we can't place the guilt. It's a human life's been played with. Maybe I'm silly to be so upset about a single life. Hek's hadn't even been taken, and over in France—as this chase was going on—they were killing each other in swarms. Over there, where Bob finally landed, men were being tried by fire. Over there, they went to grips with Death; do you see what I mean? They saw hell yawning, a pit all right, filled with half-men, the other half maggots. Trial by fire—that was.

Over here, Hek was at grips with Life. What kind of a trial shall we call that? No trial at all? since millions have withstood it? Millions have looked into this other pit, this fringed pit, and walked away unimpressed. Hek couldn't leave. He hung around the edges, looking down at your bodies there, luscious, pulsing, emitting musks and unguents, rolling and lolling and rubbing together. Oh, I think that's *some* kind of trial. Not a trial by fire; we won't steal the other fellow's heroics, but—let's give it a name. Let's give it a name—if not to alibi Hek, then at least to give those who endure it scatheless full credit for their feat.

What shall we call it, Ruby? What kind of a medal shall we give a boy you kiss like that—if he never comes back for more? Come on, girls, it's a game! You know your power; you know your strength; you spend your whole time at this business. What kind of a crown shall we put on the heads of those men who watch you dressing to excite them, stretching to incite them, talking to flatter them—and then laugh at you? On the heads of those who have lain in your arms when you really *tried*—and then turned celibate, or even monogamist? Don't all vote for ass's ears; it isn't kind.

Well, maybe *I'm* wrong. Maybe war is harder on men than women are. Maybe Death is a tougher antagonist than Life. One thing is sure, he's cleaner. He doesn't kiss in the clinches and stroke you with false tenderness when he has you down. His obscenities are sooner done.

It would have been most interesting, most illuminating, if the testing of these brothers could have been reversed. Suppose Hek had taken the trial by fire, and Bob the trial by——. Without detracting from the man he was, without disparaging Bob's fiber or the value of his study, I submit that Hek would have cut the prettier figure. Hek would have been a good soldier and if Bob had kept his head it would have been by Divine Intervention.

Then it *was* circumstance. Oh, let's give up. I don't know what it was and I don't think you care. Hek couldn't take it, that's that. He got a Summer-stock, in Indianapolis; went down there for juveniles and some leads. The agents laughed at him when he told them he'd been doing comedy. "With that head and those shoulders? Comedy!"

Joyce went to Montreal.

# CHAPTER SIX
# THE BOOK OF PAIN

## 1

W HAT a capacity for misery these Elling-Knotts developed! It's almost unbelievable. How wretched they made themselves! And *why?* What did it get them? … Minnie had to admit that half the twists and wrenches her heart had endured were self-inflicted. No one had meant her ill. Oliver and Tessie escaped it. Her brother and her sister lived their vegetable existences— placidly and without question—as man must have been meant to do, as their mother and father had.

In what particular, pray, was her existence superior to theirs, however cabbagelike? In the particular that she *knew* she was more than ninety per cent water and resented it? That was all. Just in the matter of thought. And where their thoughts differed, hers were a torment.

Minnie's family, and what friends she had kept, blamed Ted for making her different. She knew they were wrong. It had started before she knew Ted, when she was a little girl. At about fourteen, and the memory was still sharp and clear as she turned doughnuts in the bubbling grease, she had played with the two children of the preacher before Reverend Harper. In looking back on their youth, they talked of Santa Claus and Minnie settled to a nicety the day— almost the minute—that childish faith had left her.

"We *never* believed in Santa Claus," the boy announced astonishingly. "Our parents don't believe it is right to lie to children, even about things like that."

"Oh, but *that's* not a lie! Your mother and father *are* Santa Claus."

"Father says it's a lie."

"Oh, I think it's nice for the children, when they're *that* age, to believe in him," Minnie thought.

But the minister's son and daughter had never been lied to. That was impressive to Fourteen. Within a week, she sucked a lump of sugar, pilfered, and offered two somewhat grubby ones to them.

"Oh—*lump* sugar?! Do you eat that?"

"Mm—hm.... Why not?"

"Why, it's blood and bones, ground up."

It was blood and bones—ground up!

"It isn't."

"It is."

"It isn't."

"Is!"

"It's *sugar*."

"Lump sugar is blood and bones ground up and Daddy says so! He *showed* us! He took a piece and *burned* it with a match and it turned into big red drops—like blood!"

That too was impressive to Fourteen—and Minnie pondered it long. It was a lie. The *minister* had told a lie. He wouldn't lie about Santa Claus, something that his poor children would enjoy, but he'd lied about lump sugar—so they couldn't enjoy that either. Not that alone, perhaps, but such-like incidents had taught Minnie she was a cabbage.

Then her marriage to Ted and the strife between family and love. Fun to outsiders. They made mother-in-law jokes about that situation, but it had been horribly in earnest between them, all trying to get along under one Parsonage roof.

Then the struggle between Darwin and Moses, between Spencer and Saint Paul, Robert Ingersoll and Jesus Christ. Why had they chosen her breast for battle field, her head for dueling place? Strife, strife, strife—constant and unremitting. With a child to bear and a life to live, she must be honest with herself. *Three times* she had been forced over that same ground. Three separate times Minnie had neatly to arrange her love and respect for her mother and this new and dangerous faith in Logic. She had hardly done with the concession-making for her own peace of mind—when Bob had asked the questions we have heard. They two had only halfway got this straight, on some sort of working basis, when Hek had demanded to know.

Toss all this off with a shrug to-day. Vats of blood and gin have gone over the dam since Minnie took it seriously, since she let it knot her vitals with its seeming importance. Toss it off; what the hell?

And a box had been buried—with a caress on its hideous side. And a mother had been hurried off because she took so long to die.

Decisions! All these years Minnie had been called upon to make decisions. How cruelly she'd punished herself! Two-thirds of them could have been avoided. Why hadn't she avoided them? She pretended to admire expediency. Why hadn't she been expedient? Now the little doughnut-hole eater was in Prance, defending the flag he had refused to salute—and that other one didn't write. That other one had gone off with a swagger—several months before. There had been *one* two-page note.

Minnie looked in her mail-box hopefully, made a disappointed mouth, and carried her steak up the stairs to broil it for herself alone. A calling card had been slipped under the door. REV. ARTHUR L. HARPER, D.D. It was funny that she had been thinking of him, just that afternoon. What could he want? To urge her to attend Sunday services, likely.

What a capacity for pain she had! Minnie scanned the casualty list, short and easy to read in Freeport, before she lit the gas. She recognized three of the names. How soon would it be? Why were they putting it off?

She practically ate from the pan. It seemed such a waste of time to set the dining-room table just for her.

Her knitting, so much in evidence in its basket there beside her, afforded the opening topic of conversation when Reverend Harper, Mrs. Schorke and Elmer Trautle called later in the evening. "I'm assured, on excellent authority, that the things we make and send them are sometimes actually delivered!"

The three callers smiled because Minnie did. It had seemed to them an entirely pointless thing to say. Several other conversational fuses sputtered out in similar fashion before their real errand was broached mid-cough and behind a hand. It was her mother's pledge. Only a few of the pledges remained uncollected. Embury had been finished some time, but—of course—it was not paid for.

It took all three callers to get it said, so thoroughly had Minnie's views become known. Stripped of all sham, deprived of all cloaking, brought to light from beneath the blankets of self-hypnotism, the motive of the call was merely to heckle. The churchmen had reverted for the nonce to the ape. None of them knew it. Minnie did not know it. They were but picking a cosmic scab.

Minnie said that she had entirely forgotten the pledge. It had been something her mother had wanted to do. She herself was not a member of the church.... She was so gentle about it, so leisurely in coming to the negative point, that Elmer Trautle, Treasurer of the Building Committee, took heart, took heart and mentioned Memorial Windows. For five hundred dollars, Elmer pointed out, that second, side window she must have seen in passing, could have a leaded pane put in at the bottom, a leaded pane: *Sacred to the Memory of Letitia Elling*—with the dates of her birth and of her death.

That saved Minnie's whole day. The sardonic ebullience which rose so close to her palate restored some of her self-esteem. Pertinently, that solitary, secret, inward smile which none could possibly share was worth a good deal. Oliver and Tessie, for instance, were denied such moments.

## 2

A POSITIVE genius for suffering was in these people. The men around Bob cursed the rain and the command and the chow; cursed and relieved themselves by cursing, while the parenthetical cuts around his mouth deepened and deepened, while his desperate need to be for a moment alone, out of sight of them, away from the sound of their voices, drove him to cow barns and roofless sheds—where he was sometimes discovered.

"His Nibs", they called him. *His Nibs* had been sent down around the cow's bedroom again! Oh—yeah? "Me—I never could get her to stand still."

It wasn't funny to Bob. If he had ever possessed the sense of humor Minnie had told his teacher about, the A.E.F. took it out of him. He was brevetted adjutant (made a paper flunky) to a captain of engineers. The captain was sorry for him. The captain was a rich man in New York, a partner in a firm of builders. "Are you ill, Knott?"

"No, sir."

"You look ghastly."

Bob looked at the man and considered what he should say next. The remarks were so obviously meant for kindness. What should he say? How many sentences could be exchanged with a *captain* before the man's stupidity would be revealed? *One* did for all the privates Bob had met. Two disposed of the brightest looey. To a single sergeant he had talked, off and on, for three days before learning that he was a Mormon.

Captains?

"It's kind of you to notice it. My health's all right. Thank you."

"Your *health's* all right, eh? Company bore you?"

"Not yours, sir."

Captain McAllister laughed. "I call that a God-damned clever answer—delivered in exactly the proper tone. Where you from, Knott?"

"Freeport, Illinois."

"Sounds almost as bad as the army. Where is it?"

"A hundred miles west of Chicago."

"That so? You get into Chicago, do you?"

"No, sir. I've never been there …. Except on my way East to Norfolk."

"College?"

"No, sir, but I've read a lot. I mean to go."

"How old are you?" McAllister did not attempt to conceal his surprise.

"Twenty-four, twenty-five; what year is this?"

"Truly?"

"I look much older."

"My God!—forgive me—I should say you do. I thought you must be nearly forty."

"No, sir."

"What have you read?"

"A little of everything," Bob's eyes showed more animation than they had since his last evening in Freeport. He was actually going to be permitted to pronounce a few well-loved names—if no more. The question had been asked. He could go right ahead and say them, right now, and some of them would be recognized. *This* soldier was no ignoramus. "The classics, mysticism, metaphysics, drama; mostly mathematics, of course; Balzac, the Russians, Spencer and Huxley and Kant. My father had a large library."

"What was his business?"

"He was a—printer, sort of; an editor too, I guess. He wrote a little."

"And you inherited his love for books?"

"Yes, sir."

"Miss 'em here? Me too."

Bob smiled. "Just talking about them a moment has been a relief. Thank you, sir."

"I wish we could get together some way. It's damn' near impossible."

"I understand that. Yes, sir."

"Nobody at my mess ever heard of Gogol."

"And Turgenev!"

"You know *The Red Laugh*, I guess?"

"And *Sanine*."

"Get out of here—I've got work to do!"

"Yes, sir," Bob saluted. "And Baudelaire and Verlaine, too." He did a right-about face and walked to the door in cadence with the officer's chuckle.

"Heine!" said McAllister to the private's back.

"*Faust*," said Bob, and closed the door behind him.

But a captain is a captain. It was a week before that many words could be exchanged again. Their headquarters had been moved three times in those seven days, and this last move had left them exposed to almost constant shelling. A bridge at this point—capable of sustaining tanks—would win one small part of the war.

In the ninety seconds they talked, McAllister offered Bob a job with his firm, when and if. He put it that way, *when and if.*

"I'll have leave coming when we throw this span across the creek. I'll take you to Paris. Like that?"

"Yes, sir," said Bob, beaming.

A Heinie gunner must have heard them, for a shell drowned their voices with its detonation and both men were buried for an hour. Robert Ingersoll survived; survived to return to that low, dispirited level from which McAllister had raised him.

Demons for punishment.... It was uncanny. Bob grew sardonic too. Out of the whole damned army, that shell had to fall on the only man on the Western Front who could quote whole pages of Montaigne.

Sardonic Knotts! McAllister had been gone two days when a bag of mail came through. It was the first mail they had seen in thirty-eight days. Bob stood on the outskirts of the gang as a top-kick, mounted on a wobbly table, bawled out names and threw packages and letters this way and that. Somebody got some cookies—and when the mêlée quieted he held the string.

"Knott!"

He hadn't expected it.

"Robert Knott!"

"Over here!"

It was in Florence's hand. Bob started his futile search for a deserted, an unpopulous, an ungarrulous spot in which to read his letter. He finally sat down in what had once been the middle of a street.

Dearest Bob:

Since I am the closest to you of any one here, this duty falls on me. Bob, dear, your mother—

Had he stopped reading—or had his eyes quit seeing? There was paper before him with words on it. It was a letter from Florence in Freeport. Other letters, cheerful, encouraging, loving letters had been burned, torpedoed, lost. But *this* one had come through. This one had found him!

"Look at His Nibs!"

"Hi! That ain't the can."

Your mother has been in a terrible accident. She was out riding with Mr. Schraeder in his car and something went wrong with the steering gear. They were going out Adams Street, near the high bridge—and witnesses say he tried to swing it into the ditch before they hit the wooden rail. He couldn't do it, and they ran over the bridge and fell to the railroad tracks. Both of them were killed instantly.

I don't know what to say to comfort you. I know how much you two loved each other. The funeral was Saturday. It rained all day. You know the old saying, Blessed are the dead that the rain falls on.

I did all I could to locate Hek but he seems to have dropped out of sight entirely. I found a letter from him to your mother with an Indianapolis address, but my telegram there was returned. I didn't know what more to do. Your Aunt Tessie had not heard from him and did not know how to go about finding him. Maybe you can tell us. It seems so terrible for him to be going on somewhere for so long thinking she is all right. It will be a dreadful shock to him when he learns about it.

I wish I had some good news for you, Bob. The only comfort I know is that your mother didn't suffer and linger like your grandma did. She was killed *instantly*, the doctor said.

They buried your mother on Saturday and Mr. Schraeder on Sunday, so people who knew both of them could attend both services. Your mother was buried from the funeral parlor and Reverend Kroch of the German Reform Church officiated.

Reverend Harper was asked first, of course, but he told Cedric and me that he knew your mother would prefer to have some one else. It seems that he had called on her only two days before, about your grandma's pledge for the new church. He said he understood from her that she had left the Methodist Church because of some disagreement with its doctrine, but that if we couldn't get any one else, he would say a prayer at the chapel and a few words at the cemetery. He was really nice about it, but he said he knew your mother would not want to be buried from Embury and she did not like him.

Oh, Bob, dear, I wish this horrible war was over and you were back here. If you had been here this terrible thing would never have happened.

She looked lovely laid out and there were a lot of flowers. Your Uncle Oliver from Rockford had a broken wheel made up out of carnations and …

## 3

HEK had been fired from his job at the English at the end of his third week, and *not* for making love to the manager's wife. They told him his wardrobe was insufficient, that was the excuse, but the real reason was his instant popularity. The leading lady couldn't stand it. Stock leading women are like that, most of them. Draw a sigh from their following and they'll have your heart's blood. This one delivered her ultimatum to the manager—who was also her husband—and Hek was sent back to Chicago.

He had been in the company long enough, however, to add his tithe to the Knott tradition. From an actor who had been a Professor of Urology at the old Academy, Hek learned that the treatment he was using would take years to dry it up. "Throw that stuff away and get yourself some permanganate of potash. Get the crystals and mix it yourself. That's the only way to stop that."

It stopped. All the way back to Chicago Hek was congratulating himself on his cure. There wasn't a sign. He waited all the next day to make sure, ignoring—in so far as he was able—an increasing tenderness and soreness in his right side. By six that evening he was convinced. He was *well!*

Remembering Joyce's remarks about the Paul House—and smelling, in memory, the sewer gas—Hek had gone several steps higher in theatrical hostelries and engaged a room at the Walter. At six, after treating himself with the new medicine an extra time for luck, he ventured out of his room to see the town. He wouldn't really *look* for anything, but—since his health was restored—he wouldn't throw anything over his shoulder. He walked toward the Loop on North Clark Street, comparing the bustle and rattle of evening here with the quiet of Stephenson Street, Little's silent tower of white plates next to the Brewster at home. A tired smile of sophistication did for Freeport. The screaming newsboys mispronouncing Ypres and Przemysl at their loudest, told Hek that a war continued—somewhere. He'd been enthusiastic about that once. His smile grew still more tired. Just a child, he'd been. Crazy wild for the opportunity to be shot at. Imagine him trying to enlist now! What a chump Bob had been to let himself be talked into it. He should write to Minnie.

You know ... They should make actors exempt in the draft. They were needed here at home to keep people cheerful, to make the widows forget their troubles. This was a noble profession which engaged him, or *had* engaged him until his wardrobe had proved insufficient. He should write to Minnie and make clear to her why he had left Indianapolis. Perhaps she would send him enough money to buy an adequate wardrobe. It wouldn't cost much.

From the back of bunting-draped trucks, pretty girls in Salvation Army uniforms of military cut sang *Over There* and *Tipperary* and belabored the passers-by to "give till it hurts!" Posters suggested that he "tell *that* to the Marines!"

That hypersensitive spot he had been trying to ignore began a methodical throbbing as he walked through the Loop. At the corner of State and Van Buren, a drunk stumbled and held Hek's arm for support. "Thanks, Pardner, thanks t' you."

"——all right."

"Say! 'N' I know you? 'N' you Knott 'm Freeport?"

"Yes.... Oh! hello. Paul Gherke! How are you?" Paul was a fireman on the Illinois Central.

"Eh——phhh." The fellow blinked and shook his fuddled head. "Got 'n early start.... Too early." He smashed his spread hand down the length of his face, snorting. "Got sober up."

"You aren't so drunk."

"C'mon. Black coffee. Got *go* West Side. G'date 't a cat house."

They entered a Greek restaurant. Gherke drank three glasses of water and, after scanning the menu without seeing it for nearly five minutes, ordered ham and eggs.

"Oh—yeah," as his mind cleared ever so little. "'At's too bad…. I wanted to tell you. I'm very sorry 'bout that."

"Oh, that's all right," said Hek, "don't mention it."

"No. I guess not. No use mention' it. No use. No help things like that. All get it."

"Sure," said Hek.

"Too bad."

Minnie's younger son thought this was a great deal too much fuss to make over an accidental collision. He changed the subject—which Paul assumed to be a self-protective measure, an attempt to avoid the pain of thought.

"Atta boy," said Paul, clapping Hek's shoulder. "Don' dwell on 't. Come on along 'th me 'n' have a helluva time."

"O. K."

"Atta boy!" the railroader repeated. "Here t' day 'n' gone t'morra; ain't it?"

"That's right."

"Say! You ain't had a drink!"

On the foundation of ham and eggs, they laid a second one of bourbon before boarding the street car. It was Hek's first spirit. Beer, he had had, but never before any whisky. He had been far too busy to waste time drinking with men. The first swallow closed his windpipe. "Got it down the wrong way," he coughed after strangling a minute—and when he tilted the bottle again he was careful to exhale *over* the liquid as it went down.

At Halsted, Gherke led the way out of the car and into an unlocked stairway to apartments over the stores. "What's goin' on up here?" Hek asked as they climbed.

"——'," said Paul. "Plain, old-fashioned——'."

"Is it a whore house?"

" 'S it look like a roundhouse?"

"Y' mean y' gonna *pay* for it?"

Paul stopped. "Y' think it's free?"

"It is to me," Hek bragged. "I never paid for a piece in my life."

"It ain't much. Y' got five or ten bucks, aincha? A few rounds o' drinks. They're good-lookin' women."

The booze made Hek more elegant than ever. He struck a pose. "But *I'm* an *actor!* Actors don't pay for it." It had so far escaped Hek that upkeep was also an item.

Paul made a sound of dismissal. "Pay for it honest, once. Here, have another drink."

A door opened at the head of the stairs as the whisky gurgled into Hek's mouth.

"C'mon up out of those stairs," said a gruff-voiced female. "Do your drinkin' inside."

"Hullo, Mary!" Paul yelled. "Howza baby?"

"Oh, *you*," said Mary in welcome.

"This's m' pal. He's 'n *actor.*"

"Hello," the woman said to Hek, taking his hand and smiling. "We can't have so much noise outside. There's a couple sailors here."

"The girls doin' their bit?" Hek grinned, remembering Geraldine, the soldiers and Des Moines.

"That ain't nothin'! There's eight hundred dollars worth o' Liberty Bonds in this house and I didn't make them buy 'em."

The straight bourbon had clouded Hek's eyes. He did not see the tall, bleached blonde very clearly. He did not see the gray edges of her wrapper, the deep coarse wrinkles nor the straying hanks of hair. In the glow of his condition, Madame Mary appeared desirable. Hek tried to kiss her. One strong arm pushed him gruffly away. "Save that for the next one," she said—and Hek, through the increasing cloudiness of mind, felt an instant revulsion. Commerce and Love were poles apart to him, and to be tough about a kiss, to treat lightly the ministrations of *his* lips, was the insult supreme.

A tin piano operated by nickels ground out *Minnie Shake Your Shimmy for Me* while two couples jiggled up and down in the middle of the parlor. One man was a sailor. On a couch, a third couple revealed a callousness to onlookers such as Hek had never dreamed possible. Mary spoke sharply to them and Paul laughed as they turned sex- and gin-bleared eyes toward her voice. A toss of her head drove them from the room, arms around each other.

"Everybody's busy," Mary told Paul Gherke, "but Myrtle ought to be right down.... What does the kid like?"

"Whatdayasay, Knott? ... Howdya take it?"

Hek's lips encircled the whisky bottle. "Anything," he said agreeably. "Anything at all."

Finally he was alone with a hard-mouthed, wiry female who called him *dearie* with every breath. Mechanically, he performed a ritual, made interminable through the numbing effect of the liquor. In a coma, he walked away from the place with Gherke who swore dully and ceaselessly until they both slept, fully clothed, on Hek's bed in the Walter.

Perhaps they were cursed, these Knotts; these Elling-Knotts. Surely it is not common for an ordinary carouse, a single bottle of whisky and an innocuous visit to a house of that kind to result in such consequences as Hek suffered. The head, pass by, but that pain! that copious and abundant return of the evidence of disease! that intelligence which hovered on the tip of Paul Gherke's tongue for only a scant ten minutes after they awoke. These things are typically, distinctively Knottean.

"Whahrrruff," Paul greeted the one P.M. dawn.

"Is aspirin liable to hurt a guy in my condition?" "Huh?"

"Aspirin."

"Hurt what?"

"Hurt *what!*"

"F' Chris' sake. And you went t' Mary's with *me?*"

"Why not? I was well yesterday."

"Well!"

"Sure I was."

Gherke prescribed hot water. "Put a lot o' soda in it, then it won't hurt you so much. Jeez you got a nerve. Now I can't go back there no more."

Hek tried to understand that. "I told you I didn't want to go. You were so drunk you wouldn't listen."

"I was crocked, all right. Boy! I remember cryin' on your shoulder about your mother."

"Yeah? I don't remember."

"Sure. Early. I couldn't think o' nothin' else. Jesus, I felt so sorry for you."

They laughed at how sorry Paul had felt, then, vaguely Hek recalled the fellow's tenacious apologies. Phrases repeated themselves. "What about my mother?" Hek asked, lifting himself painfully from the bed. "What about her?"

## 4

Dear Florence:

How are you? I am pretty well except for some trouble I have been having for some time. Nothing to worry about.

I met Paul Gherke last night and he told me about my mother and Mr. Schraeder. Isn't it terrible? I can never forgive myself for going away and leaving her alone. Did you write to Bob? I am sorry you did not have my address so I could come home for the funeral. I guess there's nothing to do about it now. Who is taking care of the house? Will they just let it sit until Bob comes home or is Aunt Tessie taking care of that? Is there anything I can do? All those books are Bob's, of course, I guess somebody will take care of them for him. I don't want anything. Traveling the way I am all the time I don't need a home and I don't want one. I suppose you and Bob will get married now, when he gets back. You have my blessing. Will you think of me sometimes—*after* you are married—and remember that one night? I think of it very often and no matter how many other girls I have I can't forget you. But I'm not the marrying kind. Bob is. There's too much fun in the world for me to settle down for good and all with any one woman. You know, statistics show there's three times as many women in the world as men and if I'd marry you or anybody else the other two would be cheated of their share. Ha—ha.

Well, I have to study my verses now. I have twelve sides to learn by Monday when I open in a vaudeville act in St. Louis. It's a war act and very dramatic. A sketch. The lady in it is Miss Alice Leigh who was Robert Mantell's leading lady for nine years in Shakespearean rep. She is a marvelous actress and there are two other men in the act besides me. They are all New York actors and that is a swell thing for me as Broadway is the only place to get anywhere in show business. Chicago is just a village in comparison and the producers here are all hams. I am taking a very small salary, only $40 a week, because the experience with people like these will be so much good to me when I go East. That may sound like a lot to you, Florence, because it's more than Bob ever made, but don't mention it to any of the boys around the Grand— the crew I mean—because they couldn't understand a union man taking less than scale just to play parts. They wouldn't understand. They'll understand when they see my name in lights on Broadway!

Well, I guess I'll close now. We have twenty-six weeks of play or pay contracts over the Western Time. I'll send you route the next time I write. You can write to me, at *St. Louis*, Orpheum Theatre, or Springfield, Illinois.

If there is anything I can do about mother, let me know, but I guess it is too late for anybody to do anything now.

Think of me once in a while, Florence, even if I'm not worth it. I always think of you when I'm alone, and remember how sweet you were—that one time.

I'll close now,

Very truly yours,

HEK.

5

LOUIS DELANO, who had once aspired, in Italian and without avail, to the honors of Chaliapin, was Alice Leigh's husband. The other man in the act was Chot Gibbs, a second-business man who had appeared in *The Girl of the Golden West* with Wm. S. Hart.

Hek hobbled to rehearse with them, but hid his pain in their presence; when the part said "run", he *ran*. Fresh, callow, rude and conceited, Hek felt their calm. *Names* fell from their tongues without pretension and they assumed that he shared their contempt for this miserable three-a-day grind. When they mentioned the theatre or their work, in a public place, they lowered their voices. From them he learned of "Equity" and a proposed agreement which "the managers" must recognize.

He kept to his bed between rehearsals. The short part was easy to learn. He turned from it often to muse on this third world he had discovered.

They ignored the letter "r", these people from Broadway and protested that they should have starved to death in Chicago if it were not for the De Jonges and Vogelsangs. Hek, for the first time in his life, was aware of discrimination and taste. The presence and bearing, the dress of these people, inspired emulation and Hek dropped an "r" or two of his own. He made up his mind to get well, to let the women alone, to save his money, to see Times Square for himself.

St. Louis, Springfield, Champaign, Terre Haute, Fort Wayne, South Bend—then the Butterfield Time. From Chicago to Battle Creek, Hek had been good. Through a score of cities in Illinois and Indiana, his debility and his new ambition kept him from acknowledging street smiles, bed willingness and bald overtures he could not avoid seeing. In Battle Creek, the depravity of some one before him worked insidiously to prevent any Knott from escaping his full measure of pain. He could walk almost normally by that time.

At the edge of a thin panel of a door connecting his hotel room with a bath in use by a couple next door, a lascivious penknife had cut a peep-hole. Jack and Jill, the comedy team next-to-closing, lived there—and Jill was more than pretty. Jill was tall and proportioned at a Sultan's command. Through the first three-quarters of their act she was clothed, but as the finale neared, she lost her dress and achieved encore after encore in black opera-lengths; opera-lengths for one of the longer operas—and the broader.

In the theater, Hek had turned resolutely from the sight of those overweening thighs. He had looked another way when her large eyes had smiled at him and her soft, roving lips had released a provocative naughtiness. But he was no match for a peep-hole to her bath! Hek was no match for that! He lay in his bed like a little gentleman, reading a book, by God! (*Tarzan of the Apes*) until he thought he was sleepy. He killed the light—and that slit shone, a pencil line of yellow in the blackness of the room.

Our Pasha's favorite scratched herself in voluptuous leisure, and, discovering a tiny pimple, squeezed it. She donned a bathing cap and walked beyond the slit's range to start the shower pouring. Hek—

What *is* the use? It was like that every way he turned. A soft fuzz, not unlike the down of a peach began to grow on his brain. Kalamazoo, Lansing, Saginaw, Jackson, Bay City, Hek left his mark in each. They crossed to the Upper Peninsula and went from the copper country through Wisconsin, to Minneapolis, St. Paul, Duluth and Rochester in Minnesota.

In Rochester, Hek flirted with the girl who checked hats in a café. They talked quite frankly, but she was married and was not inclined to cheat. He did not press her. He was sick and weary and dull. There was scarcely room for a clean shirt in his bag, so full had he packed it with bottles, and pills and appliances for his relief.

In the hotel elevator, an exquisitely garbed woman smiled. Hek left the car at her floor. "I saw your show to-night," she said. "That's an extremely good act."

"Isn't it? An Englishman did it. Many critics prefer it to Nazimova's *War Brides*."

"I haven't seen that.... Won't you come in a moment? I'm dying of loneliness."

"I'd love to."

Hek went in for a moment—and stayed all night. The next evening he took her to dinner where the hat-check girl was married. There was no particular reason for taking her there, save, perhaps, to show the checker that all the good-looking women in Rochester were not married, or—if they were—that they didn't all work at it.

The girl was excited, upset, when she gave Hek his hat. "It's none of my business, Mr. Knott, but—I've got to ask you—have you been out with that woman? Have you kissed her?"

The girl's manner told Hek not to kid. "Well? If I have—?"

"If you have you better get to a doctor right away. You know what she's here for? She's eaten alive with syphilis."

Hek looked behind him to see if the woman were close enough to hear and then voiced a rejoinder that is classic. "Oh,— yeah?" he said.

## 6

THE False Armistice found them in Milwaukee, the real one in Chicago. The mad crowds which jammed the theater at every performance rang bells and blew horns for applause, stamped and yelled and whistled. The act, which had to do with the glories of war, ran fifty minutes that day instead of the usual twenty. Each dramatic line was greeted with that cacophonic roar and the actors had to stand awkwardly speechless for minutes on end before they could again be heard.

The act worked another month, then Hek went to Freeport for Christmas. So long had his condition remained apparently unchanged that he seldom thought of himself as sick. Pain that had once seemed excruciating had become such a constant companion that he scarcely noticed it. Treatment which had at first been so great a nuisance and bother had come to be as much a part of his toilet as washing his face and cleaning his nails. He never called his bag a "keister" or a "suit-case" or by any proper name, but invariably referred to it as "the drug store". It would have clinked when he walked if there had been space enough for a single bottle to move. The weeks and months of medication, the changes from doctor to doctor, from Professor to Professor, his willingness to try any and all suggested remedies had ruined his digestion. For Christmas dinner he had a bowl of milk and graham crackers, served by Mercedes in the Mission Café.

He had arrived only that morning and had not yet called on Florence. He had taken a room at the Brewster—as if Freeport were just another town on the itinerary. That's all it was, now, he reflected, just another town. It hadn't changed a lick. Same old sleepy streets. Same old faces.

It astonished Hek at first to have familiars pass him without speaking, without recognition. My God! had he changed that much? What a homecoming! What a Christmas! He jabbed half a floating cracker with his spoon.

"You been all over, I guess," Mercy suggested.

"All over."

"You see a lot of country, traveling that way, all the time."

"Yeah, you sure do."

She was called to another table.... "Do you remember how ticklish you used to be?"

They both laughed. "I'm not that way any more. You could tickle me till the cows come home."

"I'll have to try that out."

"Is that a threat or a promise?"

"You tell me," she said coyly. "What do you think?"

"I'll let you—but not here."

"Well, hardly."

"Where? What are you doing to-night?"

"Oh, I'm going home to-night. I've got a tree for the kid."

"*What* kid?"

"My sister. Didn't you know I had a baby sister?"

"No! Y' know, I don't even know where you live. I was just a kid myself when I left here."

Mercedes grimaced. "And now you're an old man I suppose, like John D. Rockefeller, living on crackers and milk. Honest, is that all you're gonna eat?"

His head nodded in resignation. "I been havin' a lot o' trouble with my stomach."

"Y' oughta see a doctor."

"Yeah," Hek sniggered, "I guess maybe I should."

"What are you laughin' at?"

"Nothin'.... Say, how about me takin' you home and seein' the tree? I ain't got any place to go."

"Hmph! Is that the only reason you'd come? Jus' because y' haven't got anything better to do?"

"Aw, no! Don't be that way. I got lots o' places to go. I go to visit all my old friends, see my aunt and—lots o' things. I *want* to take you home."

"All right," she smiled. "That's a go. I'll be a little late to-night on account of Christmas."

"That's all right," Hek leered slightly, "I don't mind waiting— for you."

She squeezed his hand and left the table to supply the unreasonable demands of other diners.

The tree was not a large one, but "the kid" was. Hek appraised the little flat, its worn furnishings, the scantily trimmed sapling

and the meager array of presents. "Gee—it's pretty." He was looking at the younger girl.

"Mercy always has a tree for me," the child said, "even if I am
getting too big for it."

"I think it's swell," said Hek. "Gee, if I'd known I was coming, I'd have got you a handkerchief."

"Oh, she's got one," said Mercedes, moving chairs, picking
up ribbons and strings and brushing tinsel from the somewhat
threadbare rug. "Will your stomach take some elderberry wine?
Sit down, for heaven's sake."

"Oh, yes! I can drink wine all right. It's just meat and stuff
that upsets me."

"You'll live a long time!"

"Isn't she great?" asked Sister, pulling her legs, which belied
her fifteen years, up under her on the sofa.

"I'll tell the world," said Hek.

"Oh, be still," Mercy disparaged herself, going for the wine.

"Hurry up and sit down, Mers. You been on your feet all day."

"Well, we can't let our guest be thirsty," the waitress called
from the kitchen. "We have to show our Southern hospitality."

Hek laughed, louder than was necessary. "Do you know that
one too?" he called.

Mercedes, with jug and glasses, scowled and winked. "Soft
pedal," she warned.

Hek nodded understandingly and raised his brows in deference to Sister's virtue.

"Don't I get any?" the girl pouted. "Not even a sip on
Christmas?"

Mercy took it under advisement.

"Go ahead," Hek said, "give her a little for Christmas. It won't
hurt her."

"Well——"

Half a glass was handed to her. A telephone rang. Mercy's features stiffened, her eyes grew hard.

"Shall I answer it?" Hek watched the quick legs appear from beneath the child.

"Let it ring.... I know who it is."

Sister subsided, ill at ease. Conversation was impossible while the telephone continued its imperative, insistent, nerve-trying jangle. At its sixth or seventh metallic outburst, the younger girl said quietly: "He'll be awfully sore, Mers."

A deep shadow was in her eyes. "I know it," she said. "That's just it."

"Shall I tell him you're not home yet?"

"And make him still sorer?" She jerked her body out of the chair. "I'll answer it."

"Hello! ... ... I was in the bath ... ... She didn't know it.... Well, what's the difference, I've answered now? ... ... Oh, there is *not*.... Absolutely not.... I won't answer that; you know better."

"So you used to live in Freeport," Sister's embarrassment was profound.

"Yes, I was born here."

"That's funny, isn't it, that we never knew about each other?"

"Well, you went to Lincoln and I went to Third Ward."

... But they could not drown out Mercy's voice. "I told you I was going to stay home with her to-night. I told you that weeks ago.... Well, that's *your* fault; I told you .... Oh! is that so? ... Oh, is *that* so? ... I'll do nothing of the kind! ... I'll do *nothing* of the kind.... I won't. Oh, George, be reasonable; it's Christmas——I——know, but I've always stayed with her on Christmas.... What? ... What did you say? ... No, I mean after that——Oh—ooh—well, I didn't mean it that way—— *Yes!* I'm *sure* you do.... Yes, you act like it——All right; all right;

all right. I'll come. I'll come for a little while.... Oh, right away. But you'll have to let me come home early. I can't stay late.

She stayed *too* late. She stayed so late that Hek, appalled—at last—at his own enormity, took an early morning train to Chicago without letting Florence know he had been in town.

Good God! what had he done now? Where in all the world was there a swine so low? Pretty little soft and tender Sister—sweet and innocent and white and pink. He ought to kill himself. He wasn't fit to live. And the worst part of it was, that it was *done*. He could do nothing about it. This was not something in his head; something he was just making up; something he could stop by looking in another direction. It was too late. It was like Minnie's death. She couldn't decide not to take that auto ride now. She couldn't change her mind,—nor he his.

In Freeport, too. Right there at home where everybody knew him. Oh, God; oh, God; oh, *God!* It was a good thing Minnie was dead. What a hell of a son he'd turned out to be. What a rat!

But Hek didn't kill himself. Not all in one day. He took the more roundabout method, always highly regarded by rakes and scoundrels. He started to drink himself to death.

# PART III

# CHAPTER SEVEN
# THE BOOK OF PEACE

## 1

THERE was no Silver Cornet Band and no parade in Freeport when old tried-by-fire Knott stepped off the train with his kit-bag, in lieu of a shield, in his hand. It was a Tuesday in June.

There were no heavy-handed back slaps, no Methodist arm-pumping. Several people spoke, cordially. Bob grinned and nodded his way up Galena Street to the flat. He filled his uniform. His temples had grayed. His hands had grown brawny and brown.

The butcher who owned the building gave him a key. "Everything's just as she left it. I didn't know if you'd be wanting to move.... What's a couple months' rent, one way or the other?"

"That's fine."

"You do just as you want. I wouldn't fight about a few dollars. Life's too short."

"I don't imagine I'll want to move."

"There's a woman, a widow-woman, name of Schneider; she'd like to clean it up for you. She'd do a good job. She needs the work."

"Tell her."

"All right."

Bob walked through the dim, close rooms, putting up the shades and opening windows. In the front room he ran his hands lovingly over the backs of one shelf of books, and patted them. Life was going to be strange for a while. He'd get used to it.

He'd pretty much decided to forget college, at his age. It would be a joke to call on Florence that evening, and to tell her he already had a job. He looked into his clothes-closet and brushed some suits with his palm. Civies—or as he stood? The moths seemed to have left the coats unharmed, at least. But he wore his uniform. It would be a retort to those who had made fun of him before he enlisted.

Stover's needed him. Yes, indeed. When did he want to start? Once that point was settled, the War came definitely to an end. Then he changed his clothing. Hek, of course, could have told him to keep the khaki on until Florence had seen him, if he cared anything about the girl. Hek himself would have borrowed some medals for the occasion. Robert Ingersoll wouldn't think about things like that. The bare prospect of greeting Florence was chilling his blood.

He waited for her on the corner of Spring Street and Chicago Avenue, a few blocks from Raleigh's, in an old brown hat and a dark suit that pressing would have improved. It did not occur to Bob that waiting thus and meeting her in the same old place, at the usual time, held certain essentials of drama. It was just that she was pretty certain to pass that way going home.

He saw her long, lithe body between two other girls, striding toward him with almost masculine strength. He was choking before there was any necessity for speech. But when their eyes met and she gripped the arm of one companion fiercely before running three steps toward him; when she stopped there, ten feet away, Bob knew what to do.

The girls who had walked with Florence, dabbed their wet eyes and held each other. "Ain't that—*sweet?*" one asked.

The principals were crying too. Neither had uttered a word. If Florence missed the uniform and medals, she did not mention it. She was glad enough to see that he still had two arms and two legs. She turned half around, holding a pinch of his coat sleeve, but her throat was not ready for speech. Her eyes brimmed full again and she gulped at her sister label-stickers. One hand made a fluttery, uncertain gesture. The weeping of the three girls became furiously audible and Bob shifted his weight in abject embarrassment. "Hey!" he said.

"Bob."

"Hey. Don't cry."

"Oh, Bob."

"Look; you got your friends cryin' too."

Florence smiled. "They—started me."

The other girls turned off at the corner, planning a shower—a linen-shower—at the earliest opportunity. "Ain't she the lucky one?"

## 2

"I DON'T want to see any one else, Florence. Let's hide—and talk."

"All right, Bob."

"How about your dad?"

"I'll leave a note. Where'll we go?"

"The flat? It'll be *our* flat—soon."

She squeezed his hand. It was all right now. Everything was all right now. Bob was home—and Bob was the boss. Whatever he said was all right. Her life was his whatever he said——

The widow-woman had not yet appeared. Everything was dusty. Florence looked at Bob quickly, to see if memory were causing him pain. His smile reassured her. "Funny?"

She nodded.

"Life's funny."

Her fingers closed around his forearm. "It's going to be all right."

"Oh, sure. I didn't mean anything." He embraced her, studying her face. Her eyes were frank and open and honest. She touched his hair at the temples. "We're going to be happy, Bob."

"Of course we are. Wait and see."

"*I'm* happy *now.*"

"*Are* you?" He pressed her close and their mouths touched in mutual assurance. "I'm going to work Monday."

"Already? At Stover's?"

"Sure. I went over this afternoon."

"How about—college?"

"I'd rather have you."

They kissed again, and he nuzzled her chin and cheek, and ended on her eyes. "You *do* love me," she said.

"Of course, I do."

"Of course?"

"Of course."

Florence smiled her forgiveness.

"I suppose I'm not very romantic. It took me a long time to tell you; but I've felt it—always. Haven't you? Really?"

"I thought I knew it—years ago."

"Let's sit down."

"This place certainly needs a good cleaning. I'll have to get in here with my sleeves up."

Bob pictured her cleaning his home for him. "We'll have a woman do that. It's time you had a rest." He dropped on the couch beside her. "When shall we do it? To-morrow?"

"To-morrow?" A Wednesday! No veils, no ruffled tots, no carriages. Well, she hadn't actually *expected* them. It was just a kind of dream. Most girls went without them. She *was* getting

Bob. No other girl could have him, even with the most gorgeous church wedding.

"Too soon?"

"Not for *me*, Bob."

And so it was arranged. Reverend Harper could marry them in the new parsonage. Florence would have some of her friends take the afternoon off to stand up for them. It seemed extraordinary that Bob should have no friends in his birthplace. They tried to think of some one for a "best-man".

When that was all arranged and it was settled that Florence should not go back to Raleigh's at all, in spite of the dust all over everything, they lay beside each other on the couch and celebrated their nuptials, some fourteen hours ahead of time. That was all right. It was a perfectly holy union. Their spirits had been wed for years. Nor did Hek come to mind. No. Neither of them thought of him. Bob, of course, couldn't be expected to, and there was so little in this act to remind Florence that anything remotely resembling it had ever occurred to her before, that she just didn't. This was, in all truth, a wedding night. It was so nearly perfect, so ideal, in every particular save its date, that your long-time observer of human actions and their consequences will anticipate untoward results. There were none.

### 3

THE shower came off too, a week later, attended by young people from the medicine factory and the foundry. Old Man Mitchell was there, and Tessie and Cedric, and—somehow—Pete, from the Grand Opera House. The chief topic was the miracle of miracles—*Freeport* was going dry! It had taken a World War and a Constitutional Amendment to effect it; Congress had been forced to send all the young German bucks of voting age back to the Old Country to shoot at their ancestors' ghosts—to bring it about. But it was happening. The wettest spot in Illinois outside of Cook County was going dry in a week. Several cases of good B & o were part of the shower.

Old Man Mitchell had brought Florence a letter when he came. He handed it to her quite openly, with Bob's eyes full on them. It didn't matter. Her guilty start, the momentary panic about her heart, were useless, uncalled for. Florence recognized Hek's hand but her husband did not. He attached no importance whatever to the incident. Asked—ten minutes later—what her father had handed his bride, Robert Ingersoll would have guessed either napkins or pillow-slips.

Florence tucked the missive in her bosom at the first opportunity, and proceeded with her duties as hostess, passing a plate of some comestible whenever the coming of Prohibition seemed to have lost its power to inspire any one further. She did not think of the letter again until Pete, having learned nothing from Bob, asked of her after his former assistant's health and fortune.

"Don't he ever *write*, even?"

Florence touched her breast to see if it still crackled. "Why should he write to *me*?" They had been pretty thick, this Pete and that Hek. Florence must be excused a slight nervousness.

"Oh, I don't know. I thought one of you ought to hear from him. He never writes me." It seemed sadder than it could possibly be, for just a moment, that Hek never wrote to Pete.

"He was in St. Louis, the last I heard," Florence said. "That was a long, long time ago."

"He was a great kid." Pete flattened his lips like a Billiken and chirruped as if urging a horse.

"Indeed he was.... Excuse me, won't you?" She shoved sandwiches under a nose or two. The guests were opening their own beer. She knew Bob didn't approve. He moved stiffly around the rooms, a set smile advertising his pleasure. Groups formed about him and dispersed. Sometimes he talked to a lone man; from time to time he was the center of a group of girls. No matter who was with him or what was being said, his eyes were slightly dazed, his mask with its painted lip-corners never entirely concealed his bewilderment.

Through the early part of the evening he declined drinks steadily, constantly. Later he hit upon the device of carrying a glass half full of beer around with him wherever he went to show to the bibulous who insisted. They began going home at eleven.

Pete's departure again reminded Florence of the letter in her dress. "If you hear from that kid, I wisht you'd let *me* know. If I had his address I'd write to him."

"We will," Bob agreed. "Be glad to."

The letter began to glow and to warm her throat. Florence was ashamed—painfully ashamed of herself. In the very first week of their married life, she had started deceiving him, having secrets, hiding things. She wanted, before God, to open that letter in front of him, to read it to him, hand it to him for his own perusal. She dared not. How did she know what Hek might say?

She would read the letter first, then—if there were no reference to "that night"—she could pretend it had just come or that she had forgotten to tell him about it. She had no desire to correspond with Robert's brother surreptitiously. All the happiness, all the security she had longed for through the years seemed to be made of straw and to be resting on stilts in very muddy water— like an Igorot dwelling.

"Did you have a good time?" Bob asked.

"Oh, a *grand* time; didn't you?"

"It surely was—thoughtful of them."

"Don't you like Piney—and Edith?"

"If you do."

"Monkey! Let's look at all the pretty things.... Who is that scarf from?"

Bob looked just beyond the scarf to where a book lay with a wet glass surmounting its cloth front. "What idiot did that? Well, I'll be damned! Just look, Florence! on my Volney."

"Oh, Bob——"

"Wouldn't you think they'd have better sense?" He was tenderly blotting the ring of beer from the binding.

"Oh, Bob; it's only a *book*——"

His fingers stopped wiping. His eyes searched hers. He nodded. He had nothing to say. Perhaps that side of Florence would have borne closer scrutiny—before. Bob had pretty much assumed she understood about books.

"It won't really hurt it; will it?"

He laid it aside. "No; I guess not."

"It's just the cover."

"The binding—yes. Oh, it doesn't matter. Let's forget it. It was an accident."

"Oh, I'm sure they didn't mean to—"

"Of course not." They didn't *mean* to! What sort of people were they who went about doing things they didn't mean to? Just ordinary, everyday people, of course. It had probably been Aunt Tessie. One's only consolation lay in that one need not associate with that sort as a steady thing. Oh—needn't one? Did he expect Florence to forget she was an human being—because he had nothing in common with his neighbors? But he could fix that. *She* should be taught to love books too.

As Bob undressed, Florence read her letter in the bath.

DEAR FLORENCE—

How are you? I am fine. I haven't had an ache or a pain since way last fall. And guess what? I'm married now. I was married last December just before I went through Freeport. I was sorry I didn't have time to stay over. I would like to see you and everybody very much and put some flowers on Mother's grave. Is Bob home yet or when will he be home? The last letter I had from him was so long ago. I can't remember. I answered right away, while I was with the vaudeville act, but lots of letters went astray going "Over There." Tell him not to feel bad if he didn't get it. I'll write him another one some day. Ha—ha!

Well, what's new in Freeport? I suppose you hear all kinds of scandal about me—don't believe all you hear. Believe me, it takes two to make a bargain. *You* know what I mean. Anyway, it doesn't matter—now that I'm married.

I've got a cold that's hung on all Spring. "Denver, last half," as we say in show business. My wife is an actress too and we work together. If you answered right away, Jefferson Theatre, Louisville, Ky., I might get it. I wish you would write as I am anxious to hear from you.

With much love, very truly yours,

HEK.

There was at least this much truth in that letter; he had a cold, a chest cold that kept him coughing, off and on, all the time.

## 4

IT was no sense of guilt, no "agenbite of inwit" which kept that letter secret. It was sheer intuition. Florence sensed the true nature of the note without the slightest knowledge of what it veiled. There was something. That was all she knew, all she could divine. Hek wanted to know something. He thought she could tell him. But what?

He had been in Freeport! Florence gave up trying to see through it. She didn't believe he was married. *There was probably lots of scandal about him?* What *was* he driving at? She had heard nothing. Before tearing the letter up and flushing it out of her life, she memorized the name of the Louisville theatre. Next day she wrote him there, guardedly trying to warn him that any more letters from him must be suitable for Bob's eyes as well as hers. She dared not say it openly. Committing such thoughts to paper would reveal her guilt. Such a letter would be a terrible weapon in any man's hands.

Hek read her note, with a bitter smile for the laden spaces between the lines. Florence was afraid of him! Afraid of what he could do to her. One word—and Bob would kick her out.

She had a right to be afraid of him. So had they all. Spawn of Satan he was, probably the lowest creature in the world. Women had a right to be afraid of him. They'd ruined his life—the good ones and the bad. From his grandmother to this shop-lifter hooker he pretended was his wife, women had brought him nothing but bad luck and disease. No matter what he did to them now, they had it coming for what they'd done to him. He'd make them *all* suffer. Pots of corruption! Cesspools of filth and evil! What a refutation of religion they were. What a denial of munificence in nature.

Oh, there were a few good ones; damn' few. Minnie and Joyce and a few preachy ones like that. Lord God, what was the *use of* living if the greatest of all pleasures carried such penalties as he had suffered? For that matter—what did he *know* about Joyce and Minnie? Both of them might have been loose as ashes so far as he knew. Maybe they just put on their wings and halos around him. Lots of girls and women who denied him nothing were models of virtue in other company. You couldn't trust *any* of them.

Well, they couldn't fool with him. He was poison now—and he took 'em all, six to sixty, saving only a scant half dozen for pall-bearers.

Just before he went in the hotel to join Gloria, he tore Florence's letter to bits and dropped them in a trash can on the corner. Florence could have been explicit, for Gloria was a shrew.

## 5

AFTER the shower, Bob assumed they would be much alone. They would read together. He would read aloud to her, starting with amusing, short things to make Florence laugh, so that literature should not frighten her. The mere ability to close his own door on the world and to turn around in a silent room without seeing a face was heavenly. Her face he wanted to see.

Florence, on the other hand, had been alone too much. Mistress of her own home, now, she wanted it known. There had been catty remarks. She wanted to feed those cats at her own table, to impress them. Bob's erudition and his quiet manner were so effective, such a contrast to the bawling self-consciousness of the new-husband *genre* she had observed. She had some friends in for dinner and they stayed the boring evening. Bob made a gallant effort to be unselfish.

Between fixing up the house and visiting and "entertaining", it was another week before a really free evening occurred.

He brought up the reading business. Florence's enthusiasm seemed genuine. He chose an one-act play by Andreyev, *Love of Thy Neighbor*, and told her to get ready to laugh. She did—and sat perfectly still for twenty minutes, all ready. Bob's own chuckles got weaker and weaker and finally stopped entirely. He read on in dogged disbelief for another five minutes before he gave up. When he stopped he did it graciously and with a smile.

"I'm afraid you aren't enjoying this. Perhaps it's the wrong mood for to-night."

"Oh, I think it's wonderful. Please go on. They get him down soon, don't they?—and go on with the story?"

"Eh——"

"But *you* aren't enjoying it. You've read it before."

"*I?* Yes, I've read it several times—but I'm afraid they don't get him down. You see, *that's* the idea. That's the author's device for creating the humor."

"Oh, I see."

"My throat is tired. You don't mind, do you?"

"Oh, I'm so sorry, Bob. Of course not. Stop, by all means."

She made him a cup of cocoa and they went to bed.

Bob only tried it one other time, taking an entirely different angle. He started Kenneth Grahame's *Wind in the Willows*. He only started it.

Then he tried settling at his desk for an hour after the movies or after folks had gone home, reading to himself. Florence wooed him with undress and honeyed tongue.

At the end of two months he was crawling nightly from her side without waking her, and sitting until dawn, in robe and slippers. But Florence discovered the deception and put a stop to it. Did he want to ruin his health?

# CHAPTER EIGHT
# THE BOOK OF CRIME

## 1

G LORIA had no right to the name, she stole that as she stole everything else she could lay her hands on. "The poor blind lady," she would say, to Hek, of her new hats, "the poor old blind lady wasn't looking." That happened every few days. She stole perfume and stockings and trinkets every day. In cities as large as Louisville, she took jewelry—and there it was she got her fur coat.

Hek objected at first, on moral grounds, until she laughed him out of such baby notions, then in defense of their safety, but later he got used to it. From toleration he slid by easy stages into pride for her skill and finally became more greedy than she. He railed at her when she failed to get the particular muffler he had picked out. Gloria railed right back. She split no hairs and minced never a word. She told him what he was as no one else ever had. Hek knocked her down with a quick right to the ear.

Until then Gloria had not realized that she loved him. It took that belt to show her. For he went all to pieces when his aching hand told him how hard he had struck—and he followed her to the floor to plead tearfully for her forgiveness, to cry in her hair and to kiss her ear, tenderly at first, then—at her unspoken suggestion—wantonly. Thus ears were added to Hek's repertoire. He had her to thank for "snow" also. Oh, Gloria helped. And because of his many afflictions Gloria insisted that a drug sundry be always on hand for emergencies of this kind.

Yes, the first time he ever socked her, he was contrite and frightened. Later, he beat her rather more thoroughly; and oftener than not walked out and left her groggy on the floor. There was that in Gloria which demanded these attentions and she used purposely to incite him, waiting for the first stinging blow with voluptuous expectation. Hek grew to enjoy the bouts too, but he couldn't keep it up. The exercise made him cough—and once he started it was hard to stop. Sometimes he spit up blood.

They were the scandal of the show, with their eccentricities and their lewdness. Once a local constable came to the depot with a search warrant because lingerie had been missed just after Gloria left a store. He found nothing and went away with his tail tucked. As he turned from the last trunk Gloria had said in front of troupers and towners—two dozen—"and now, Mr. Policeman, would you like to kiss my——?"

Only Hek had laughed.

Another time, she had become so excited, so overheated in the very middle of a drubbing that she had run into the hotel corridor clad only in a silk shirt. The manager had complained about that to Hek.

Hotels were forever asking them to move. Whenever the management actually insisted, and they had to pack in the middle of the night and look for another place, Gloria smilingly took a razor blade and slit the under side of the mattress eight or ten times, neatly clipped the little points off every electric light globe within reach and—if they had a private bath—opened the tank of the stool and bent the thin brass rods or punctured the floating ball.

Even to the day he left her, saw her taken off between two cops to serve ninety days in the women's side of the jail while he did his stretch in the men's, Hek had tried to prevent that vandalism. "It doesn't *get*you anything," he objected. That was the old Parsonage frugality coming out, an almost atavistic respect for plumbing and electrical fixtures and chattels. But when Gloria had been insulted—and being asked to move for screaming foul words at Hek in the small hours of the morning was an insult to this high-strung young lady—she was deaf. Hek quit objecting only after his arguments had once driven her to commit a nuisance in a dresser drawer. After that he had nothing to say about cutting up mattresses.

What a team they made! The rest of the troupe despised them and repeatedly urged the manager to supplant them with decent people. It was only Hek's fire on stage which kept them on. It was only the brilliance of Hek's performance—he was usually high on coke—which sustained the very poor show.

Then—everything happened at once. The leading-lady missed her wrist watch and needed only one guess to settle her own mind regarding the guilty party—and two plainclothes men stopped Gloria and Hek in the post office. This was in a sizable Southern city which shall be nameless.

"Mailin' a package, girlie?"

It would have been impossible to deny it. The damned thing was in her hand, stamped and addressed.

"What's it to you?"

"Don't be tough. Let's see it."

Hek considered flight as the parcel changed hands.

"Going to Gloria Fairfax, eh? Monroe, Louisiana. Well—is—is Gloria a relative of yours?"

The girl answered only with the venomous hatred in her eyes.

"What's *your* name, girlie?"

"Aw, cut the comedy. You ain't funny."

"You ain't Gloria Fairfax, are you? You ain't gonna play Monroe with this show in a couple days; are you? And maybe receive a package?"

Hek eyed the door once more and measured the chance for escape.

"I'll say you ain't," the cop declared. "You're comin' with us."

The show did not go on that night because the manager had not thought to look for them in jail until it was too late. When he did find them, the leading-lady who accompanied him identified her wrist watch, part of the contents of the package. The show closed.

## 2

NINETY days! ... That doesn't seem like such a long time. The judge thought he was lenient. Gloria was all set to take it. In court she could have got Hek off with a third of that if she had wanted to. Let him stick around too, until she was out. It wouldn't hurt him—much.

It might have done him good—if they had let him have his drug store.

"I'm a sick man," he pleaded with the turnkey. "I've got to have my suitcase."

"What's wrong with you?"

Hek looked at the Irish knob before him and decided to let it go. *What was wrong with him?!* Where should he start? What was *wrong* with him! "Never mind."

He stuck it out four days without a prophylactic, a sniff, a pill, dose or shot of anything. Then he collapsed and they put him in the prison hospital.

Gaunt; on his frame which stood so nearly six feet when it *could* stand there was only sufficient flesh to make his weight one hundred twenty-four pounds. His pallid face was the front of a skull; worms crawled back of his eyes. They gave him a shot in the arm and that night he slept.

A new doctor was on in the morning, a doctor with pronounced inclinations which he prided himself on hiding. He took Hek's "history and physical"—and saw a little hope. "Do you *want* to get well?" he asked.

Hek spotted him at once, but wisely did not reveal his recognition. That was a funny question. Did he *want* to get well?"

"Sure."

Doctor Belmont tapped the history. "You haven't acted like it. This reads like the story of a man committing suicide—in the slowest and most painful way possible. Have you been trying to kill yourself?"

Hek was embarrassed. "No, sir." Then he was exasperated. Why had he said "sir" to this damned fairy?

The doctor smiled. "If you'll give a fellow a hand, I'll get you well. Will you try?"

"Sure, I'll try."

But it was not so simple a job as it seemed. With such a variety of pathology from which to choose, it was difficult to know where to begin. Hek's resistance was shattered, his spirit broken, there was no fight in him—and never had been. But treatment was begun. Belmont concentrated on the ulcers, and tried to work out a schedule of injections which should not conflict. The three months got him nowhere. Hek was cleaner in that time; he did not crave the hop—but his ankles had begun to swell and he smoked cigarettes interminably—"so there'd be something there to cough."

In those three months, Belmont had fallen in love with the boy, foolishly, pointlessly, passionately. What this cursed but reputable and admirable man had found in that shell to arouse him is beyond discovery. Was it the occasional flashes of boyishness? The *kid* showing through the shell? Was it his helplessness? Was it a grudging sort of compulsory admiration for a figure who had crucified himself on his own lust?

Whatever its cause, it made Doctor Belmont wholly miserable, and when his sentence was over, Hek was moved to the fellow's home.

It took Gloria a week to find him. God only knows what *she* wanted with him either. Just looking for more black eyes, I guess.

"Jesus, ain't you sweet? All pure and sanitary. Gettin' well for papa? Gonna wear knickers when he takes you out?"

"Close your hole!"

"Nuts to you."

"You bring me a suit o' clothes and a shirt and I'll show you."

"Willya, honey? Honest?"

"You think I'm stayin' here because I like it. Y' think I'm gonna be any God-damn' faggot's *boy*? I'm a *man*."

"Don't *I* know that?"

"You get me some clothes and come back at the same time to-morrow. I can walk all right."

"Who's the character-woman?"

"His mother."

"Will she let me in—again?"

"Sure. She's stupid. Socks too."

"Give us a kiss!"

"Christ almighty, you taste of Lysol."

# 3

HEK had said he could walk, but he couldn't. The cab driver and Gloria practically carried him down the stairs and into the waiting car. The doctor's mother fluttered like a white-haired and broody hen around them, almost tripping them on the steps. "Get the hell out of the way," said the cabby, suiting the action, as it were, to the words.

When the old lady told her son about it, she called the day's work a "kidnaping"—and almost convinced the doctor that Hek had wanted to stay.

For a month he remained in hiding, sleeping with his head out of a window and eating milk and eggs Gloria provided through prostitution. They lived in a poor place, cracked and worn. The bath was on the floor below. Gloria perching on the edge of the lavatory annoyed Hek. "That's the way those things all get pulled off the wall," he complained. "You can always tell where one o' you tarts has been living."

He exercised a little each day and finally was able to walk a few blocks unaided. By the end of the first month the situation had palled on them both. Hek was not strong enough to fight with her or to use her body, and Chuck, the cab driver who did most of her heavy procuring, kept drumming it into her head that she'd get T. B. if not something worse, living around Hek like that.

One night she'd promoted some snow and they had a real party, almost like old times. The following evening Gloria was out and Hek went for a short walk. When he returned, she was plying her trade in his bed—and he resented that. The man assumed this newcomer was her husband and fled. Hek beat her—weakly, tentatively, and walked out. It was still early. He had a few dollars in his pocket. He headed for the center of town. Hek Knott had never lacked a bed! He didn't need her support. He was still good; could still slay 'em. They couldn't take that away from him. It was something in his eye. He made several half-hearted sallies toward passing women. They ignored him.

A shooting gallery where a tab show played was just emptying. He studied the photos in the frames. Carl Wade! It was a small world after all. He nosed around to the stage entrance, finding it by instinct and without asking. Bygones must be bygones by this time.

It was Hek's first theatre in over four months. The odors and sounds beckoned him in and the ranging scenery welcomed him. He went down steps and listened to the jabber of the chorus through the thin partitions. A face was slapped and there was a momentary silence before that fight began in earnest.

"Wade!" Hek called. "Wade."

"Here.... Number four."

Same old voice. *He* couldn't sing! What was he doing with a tab show. Hek went through the door marked "4".

Wade sat at the make-up shelf, removing cold cream; on the far side of the dressing-room a woman was bent over a trunk, exposing to Hek, although it was covered, something else which he thought he had seen before.

"Well, f' God's sake—Three-Sheet! … Hello, Scurvy, how are you?" The leading man half rose and extended a greasy hand. The woman turned and straightened. It was Ruby.

She did not recognize him, but nodded. Hek smiled. This was a funny one; one for the book!

"Fine," he croaked. "You?"

At the sound of his voice, Ruby frowned and looked at him more closely.

"Great! Meet the woman; Three-Sheet, Mrs. Wade."

"Mrs. Wade," Hek repeated, stumbling closer to her. "You don't remember me, do you?" He tried to put all he had back of it. He was working for an audience; he was *trouping*.

"N-no—can't say I *do*—but—yes——"

"You two *know* each other?"

Hek looked her over slowly, from the hair henna had made, over the pretty features and the chemise-clad body to the knees and delightful ankles. It had been a long time since Hek had rated so much as the sight of a woman of these proportions. Gloria was so stringy. "I don't know yet," Hek said. "I remember *her* all right. Ruby, isn't it?"

"Ye-es," she said.

"He's got you down, kid. 'Fess up," Wade struggled into his trousers.

"You—you ain't the prop kid—from Freeport?"

"Ho!" Wade bellowed. "That ought to hold you! 'Prop kid!' Let *that* sink in …. You've called him, Honey. That's exactly what he is."

Ruby took Hek's hand. "I remember you now; of course I do, but, Holy Christ, what have they done to you?"

"I just got out o' the hospital."

"No!"

Hek nodded.

"A little more o' the same?" Wade asked.

"No, nothin' like that. I got ulcers in my stomach."

"Haw! That's a 'wrong belief'! Remember the angel? The Christian Scientist. Everything was a 'wrong belief'! She *died* of the 'wrong belief' of pneumonia—you hear about that? Up in Montreal."

Hek clenched Ruby's fingers. "No! Is it true?" He squatted suddenly in a chair.

"Sure. Rich, ain't it? After all her preachin'?"

"So Joyce is dead." He still held Ruby's fingers desperately.

"You were nuts about her, weren't you? I forgot that."

Ruby turned to Wade. "He's awfully sick, Carl. Look."

Through his shock and the scarcely fathomable sense of loss, Hek felt Wade's scorn for a man who was "nuts" about any woman, and it shamed him as Wade's scorn always had. "Oh, I liked her—pretty well," he said. Why did he feel so desolate at this news? Minnie's death had not caused any comparable disturbance. Limping from a long-forgotten cell in his memory, came a wasted phantom of a dream; a picture of Joyce and him, living happily together, perhaps as man and wife. Where had that picture come from? When had he ever thought it? Why had he not attempted to realize it in fact—if he desired it so? ... It was too late now.

Joyce was dead. Minnie was dead. Bob and Florence were married. Now, here he'd met Ruby again. He had always felt he would, somehow. He'd pictured that too, but not like this.

Wade tied his tie. "Get into your clothes, Rubby," he said. "What are you waiting for?"

Rubby! What a pig the man was. How had they come to be sketching? Hek was sure they were not married. Anyway, Rubby was *Ms* girl, by rights. She withdrew her hand and made a sad face.

It would be fun to take her away from Wade! Old Wade, the grand-past-master of chasing. Wouldn't that be sport? Just to show the old reprobate that he was the better man, sick as he was. "I used to be nuts about *you*," Hek told Ruby boldly.

"You remember—do you?" She was drawing a dress over her head.

"Yes. I remember. I'll never forget."

"Say; what the hell *is* this?" asked Wade. He received no answer, but the eyes of the other two were locked.

Hek looked at himself in Wade's mirror. He was frightful, he had to admit—hideous even to himself. "I've got one foot in the grave," he muttered. "Can I use this powder?"

"Sure.... Hek! Will you ever forget the Kane sisters—where was that? Their old man worked for the railroad, remember? The chocolate cake! Those were the days."

"Those were the days," said Hek.

As they drank coffee together, Hek was seized with a coughing spell. He hadn't wanted that to happen. He *looked* badly enough to scare her off, the cough would probably finish any vestige of chance which remained.

"Where are you living?" Ruby asked, suspicious with a woman's suspicion.

"Down the street a ways. Why?"

"The Brunswick?"

"No-o——"

"My God, is the dive so bad *you're* ashamed of it?" Wade demanded. "It must be something awful."

"Well, if you must know—I haven't got any place to stay. I just got out of the hospital and I'm broke."

"Well—you can check *in* a hotel. You can get a few bucks from home before you have to check out," Wade suggested.

But Hek had thought of that. Money was not now his only consideration. "I haven't got any baggage. You can't check in anywhere—where there's a café in connection—without at least one bag." ... As Wade took out his cigarettes: "Let's have one of those, willya?"

"He could sleep on that couch," Ruby suggested, "until then—for a little while."

"*What* couch?" Wade pretended.

"Oh—I'm not going to bother you folks," Hek interposed. "Don't you worry about me. I wouldn't think of it."

"You can see for yourself how sick he is," Ruby told her alleged husband.

"What is it, Hek? Your stomach, eh?" Wade was playing the part of doctor for a moment. His manner was extremely, ludicrously professional.

"Yeah. Ulcers.... And I've had this damn' cold for a year. Can't shake it."

"Well, we got a couch. We're in an apartment—little place. You're welcome to that until you can hear from your mother. Y' really ought to go home."

"Walkin's bad. My mother's dead."

"No!"

"Auto accident."

"Jesus, that's too bad."

And to Hek's memory came another incident that would have interested Wade; the most shameful incident in Hek's life. He would have liked to hint at it. He might say—perhaps later— "Did you know Mercedes had a kid sister?" But that story would turn Wade against him again. The couch would be withdrawn— and that would deprive him of the opportunity of pitting his skill at seduction against the older man's power to hold this woman.

Ruby placed her hand over the scrawny back of the boy. "You've had some lousy luck, haven't you?"

"Sometimes they run like that," Hek quoted from poker, "and then they get worse."

All three shook their heads.

Hek went to the dingy and shoddy little apartment with them, buying a tooth brush on the way so he would have *some* baggage. They had to help him up the steps, and doing so impressed them both with the seriousness of his condition. They felt death through the ill-fitting sleeves of his coat; they heard the sound of it in his lungs and its fetid odor came to them on his breath.

They made him a bed on the couch and withdrew to talk of these things.

"His brother's name is Bob. We ought to write."

"*Write!* You better wire. God Almighty, we can't let him die here."

"You think it's as bad as that?"

"Didn't you see his ankles? They're as big as your hips."

"What does that mean, Carl?"

"It's the last stages of T. B."

"Jesus! Watch him so he don't spit anywhere."

"Maybe we ought to call a doctor."

"Who'd pay him?"

"Oh—his brother'd make it good. Hell, we can't let him die."

"He ain't gonna die *to-night*. That stuff kills 'em slow."

In fevered agony, Hek twisted and turned despite his exhaustion. A pinch of snow would help, or a shot in the arm. But stronger than these cravings in the putrescent, spongy, fuzz-covered brain, was the desire to make Ruby, the mad plotting of that sexridden ego to best his preceptor in the game he taught. So strong was habit, *this* habit of mind, in Hek, so deep-worn those grooves of thought, that the all but automatic hysteria which would have brought a doctor with a needle to his side was postponed, and he finally slept, with a smile of cunning on the lips from which all beauty and tenderness had been burned.

## 4

CARL WADE telegraphed Bob. The message found him up, with protractor and pencil, making hieroglyphics of purely personal importance on a sheet of graph paper that covered the entire top of his desk. The desk had sent Florence to bed sadly-—hours before. The desk and Bob were so stubborn. You couldn't move them. That was it. Florence had suggested that they get rid of that old battered desk and make the front room a place to *live* in. It was her first major request, the first vital change she had attempted. Bob had said he was sorry.

The Western Union boy woke Florence with his pounding and the first thing she noticed—after reading the face of the clock on the dresser—was a pencil stuck in Bob's ear. "Haven't you been in bed? ... Oh, Bob, *why* do you stay up all night? Playing around with those figures!"

"It's a *telegram!*" said Bob.

BROTHER NEAR DEATH SHOULD BE WITH YOU CAN YOU COME

"A *telegram?*"

"About Hek."

"What about him? He—he isn't——"

Bob handed her the paper.

"I wonder——"

"What are you going to do?"

"I'm going—of course."

"Clear down there? It will take *days!*"

"He's my brother."

"Of course."

"Do you suppose your father would lend me the railroad fare? I've got to get it to-night."

"He will if he has it, Bob."

"I wouldn't like to wake any one else. Nearly four."

"It's *after* four, and you haven't had a wink of sleep."

"I'm all right. You go back to bed. I've got a lot to do."

"I'll pack—will you take that old kit-bag?"

"It's all I've got. You *could* do that."

# 5

So Harper was brought home to die. Funny how things work out. Ruby saw the brothers off at the station and wished to God she hadn't, wished she had shown Wade's good sense and pleaded a rehearsal. Hek would have been trouper enough to know that a rehearsal would come first. Because—Hek was unscrupulous enough, weak enough, to ask her to kiss him good-by. That wasn't according to Hoyle, of course. It hurt him dreadfully to have to ask. His technique had always inspired that desire in his women. He had never before needed to ask.

Hek realized, dimly but certainly, that the show was closing. The final curtain was being rung down—and they were carrying him off the stage. In this last encounter he'd been beaten. Ruby had average human intelligence. So—there was nothing to do but ask for it if he wanted the kiss, and he did. In such crises his expediency was Napoleonic, had always been. No pride, no sense of honor, no duty had ever kept Hek from achieving his ends with a woman. He had wept before them, demeaned and lowered himself in public; once he had allowed a cigarette to burn itself out in his palm (always the mummer)—all to convince young females that they must give themselves to him to preserve their own future happiness.

Since it was Ruby who had taught Hek why mouths are shaped as they are, it would have been meet and just for one of his less curable diseases to attach itself to her through the medium of that deathbed kiss; but thus it did *not* befall. Ruby kissed him—very briefly—revolted by the contact, and rushed to antiseptics and physic.

# CHAPTER NINE
# THE BOOK OF JUDGMENT

## 1

T HE desk was moved. There was nothing else to do. They had
to put him somewhere near light and air. Minnie's old bedroom was dark, an inside room. The desk was put in there. Doc
Smith, of course, attended him.

And there came to Bob a very strange mental aberration, an
aberration which recurred. It struck him first at dinner. He had
carried Hek's strained spinach and strained carrots and peas and
his glass of half milk and half cream to him on a tray; then he had
sat opposite Florence in the kitchen to eat his own sup—eh, *dinner*, now. With a laden fork lifted, he had paused. "Oh—" as if
he remembered something; then his mind was a blank.... "Gee,
that's funny."

"What is it?"

"I just thought of something——"

"What?"

"That's the funny part. I can't remember."

"Can't remember what you thought of?"

"No. Isn't that ridiculous?"

"You mean right now?"

"Yes. It was the strangest thing.... It seemed to be something
I had to tell you. Something I'd forgotten."

"Oh, well, you'll think of it again."

But he didn't. He didn't think of it again because he had not thought of anything in the first place. He had merely realized, suddenly, abruptly, realized that there was something he had forgotten.

It happened again while he was walking to work the next afternoon. He had rubbed Hek's back with alcohol, so Florence wouldn't have to, and had followed other orders left by the doctor, orders she could not follow. Then, on the street, he stopped suddenly. This time he knew definitely that he had forgotten something. What the devil? What *could* he have forgotten?

When Bob finally remembered what it was he had forgotten, he did not connect that phenomenon with the aberration, but from that time on he was not troubled again. What he remembered was Grandma Elling and her protracted illness. Yes, that was it. There was something about Hek and his condition and their relative situation which recalled that other siege. Hek was as incurably ill as ever Letitia had been. Every grain of medicine administered was given solely to stave off the end a few hours longer. While Bob played Minnie's part, with washcloth, syringe and hypodermic needle Florence was wedged between fate and fate, exactly as he had been; her life arrested, retarded, suspended, pending the consummation of a fatal and preordained event.

Bob hastened to think of something else. Implications, complications, beset that way. Hello! the Busy Bee was getting a new electric sign.

## 2

LIFE is extremely tenacious. Only consider how utterly fly or roach must be smashed; and Hek was no insect, not physically, at least. Death would not come, not while Doc Smith's conscience would permit him to continue the "treatments" which suited Hek best.

The doctor worried about that sometimes as he left the house. It rhymed ill with his personal code to continue this vain procedure. From time to time he tried to reduce the strength of the narcotics, but he couldn't fool Hek and he just had to get up in the middle of that night and give the boy what he might have had in the first place.

And Hek's mind followed Grandma Elling's for gradually lengthening periods, and the stories he told Bob and Florence were given a singularly convincing turn by the narrator's prime histrionics, even in delirium. Sometimes he was partly aware of what he was doing, but could not or did not wish to stop. On these occasions he thought of Dad Summers who was "always the actor—on or off, and always a good one". What do you suppose had become of the old man?

Twice Hek fooled Bob into going on long, wild-goose chases to other parts of Freeport, once to collect a debt, the circumstances of which Hek described in minute detail (all of them denied—to Bob's infinite chagrin and embarrassment—by the supposed debtor) and once to claim from a girl a locket containing his picture which Hek insisted he had given to the little one when they were in Sixth Grade together. Since she had married subsequently, she could not care to keep it, and he would like it back. The girl's husband, hearing Bob's plea over his wife's shoulder, was so impressed, so completely convinced, that to this day he makes a noise as if a shred of meat must be dislodged from between his teeth whenever lockets are mentioned. Both stories were as false as Hek's heart.

He couldn't fool Bob again, after the second one. The girl had cried and stamped her foot and finally screamed at them when she saw that both men, Bob *and* her husband, thought for all the world she was lying.

## 3

FLORENCE drooped. The double strain on her was cruelty carried beyond and below diabolism. She had not only to endure the unimpassioned, lackadaisical workaday *acceptance* of herself by Bob which had become the order even before. Hek's return, plus the extra labor caused by his presence and multiplied by his illness; she had not only to give up her home and her life for the boy, but she had also to suffer the constant and eternal dread of the day Hek should tell their story, in whispers to Bob alone, or loudly before a group of visitors. It would come. Sooner or later, no matter what, that would come.

Proof that he wandered, Bob's first-hand knowledge that his brother lied profusely—almost professionally—heartened her, heartened her until she recalled that Hek could fill in enough corroborative detail which Bob would remember to raise serious doubts in his mind. Good God! what was a *locket!*

All this strain showed in her face, her eyes, her manner. She never spoke unless she was addressed directly and she often started, pitiably, at the sound of her own name. To Bob, the generality, "what she was going through", was sufficient explanation. One thing he did not understand was why his attempts to comfort and soothe her should increase her nervousness. When he realized how tired she was and how much work she did, Bob arranged to have a Negro woman do the heavy laundry.

Florence could not avoid Hek, could not stay away from him. She must minister to his needs every day between Bob's morning departure and his return for lunch, between one o'clock and six. In these hours, Hek was almost always a totally different person from the boy in bed when Bob was in the house. His cruelty assumed a variety of forms, the simplest merely grasping her hand and holding it. That doesn't sound like much of anything, does it? Try grasping a leper's hand some time. Try grasping the hand of a leper with whom you have lain illicitly, a leper whose disease has also made him mad.

Hek knew she would avoid contact with his flesh, so he *snatched* for her, for the nearest piece of her, hand, shoulder, breast, chin. Then he smiled. And he devised other indignities, calling unnecessarily for the urinal and causing her to aid him. He knew she would not complain, dared not.

Other times he wished to talk, and always about the same thing, always about her sex life, with Bob—and before. Details he wanted, minute details—and she dared not cross him too much. He laughed at the truth, so she lied to humor him, inventing lovers and special nights in her past to make their single indiscretion the smaller, to dwarf it out of existence; instead, this incensed him and he speculated aloud upon Bob's possible reaction to their secret.

This torture had not been begun until Hek was sure Florence had no knowledge of Mercedes or Sister. Apparently the reverberations of that escapade had not carried far. Casually, he asked Pete: "How's Mers?" Trusting that time had dulled Pete's memory enough to make the man assume without definite knowledge that Mercedes and he had been friends.

"She's gettin' old," Pete had replied, "old and grouchy. Goes around with a chip on her shoulder all the time."

"She used to be all right."

"Yeah, she had some trouble. I never got it straight. I don't know what it was. She's livin' at the Baueschers' by herself."

"Yeah? What's become of her kid sister?"

"I don't know; I never fooled around with Mers myself. Did you?"

"No, not *me*. I just used to see her when I'd go in when Ma was workin' there."

"Oh, yeah."

"Cute kid—the sister."

"Yeah, I guess so. I never saw her. Somebody said she got into trouble, but they always say that."

"Sure."

"She's still workin' at the Mission. Like to see her? I'll tell her you're home."

"No—don't do that. Don't do that. I mean—don't bother. I'll have Bob stop in—if I want to see her. I never fooled around with her either."

4

EVENINGS in the flat were ghastly. They dared not leave him more than half an hour alone, and neither Bob nor Florence would go abroad without the other, save for short walks. Callers, numerous at first, dwindled until Pete, Master of Dust, was the only regular.

On his better days, Hek spoke with Bob of Life. "I never made much money but I had a hell of a lot of fun."

"Immolated and still impenitent," Bob murmured. "You built your own wheel and rack."

"Don't be so damned high-brow. Say it in English."

"It doesn't matter. I was just wondering if the fun was worth it."

"Worth a few pains? Hell, *yes*."

"It would have to be more fun than I've ever had, to pay me."

"Well, *you*; you never got anywhere, never did anything."

"No! I've—I've been pretty quiet."

"Don't you ever step out on Florence?" Hek spoke in a whisper and leered wisely.

Bob shook his head with a very slight resigned and tolerant smile.

"Never? Not once?"

"Never."

"You always were too good to be true."

"She wouldn't do that to me."

Hek looked at his brother for a moment, then turned away. He wouldn't tell him yet. It was too much fun to keep it.

Sometimes Hek got started on his adventures, real and imaginary. Bob had to listen. In this town, a husband would shoot him on sight. In another, a designing female had tried to blame her child on *him*. One day he would speak proudly of these exploits, another time he would revile himself and end in tears.

At the end of a month, the nerves of these three people were frayed to bleeding tatters, and Doc Smith chose that moment to get religion in the matter of more dope. He had tried several times to change his treatment in those thirty days to salve his Freeport conscience. Each attempt had failed because the patient immediately suffered a severe relapse. This time the doctor meant business.

Bob did not know what had happened. He was almost ready for bed himself—and Florence cried if he looked at her. Hek called weakly and the older boy carried his coffee to a chair at the side of the bed.

"I'm worse, Bob. I haven't been out of pain for three days and that son-of-a-bitch won't give me anything for it."

"Yes, he will, Hek. He's testing a new treatment."

"Testing, hell! I'm tired of being tested. He's been experimenting on me for a month. I'm sick of it."

"Try to be patient, Boy. He'll put you on your feet before you know it."

"Don't treat me like a damn' fool, Bob. I'll never get out o' this bed and you know it. I'm dying right now."

"You're *not*. You've retained more than half your food ever since the treatment was altered. That's better than you did before."

"I don't want to retain my food. I want to die. I want to get out o' this. I don't want to linger on and on like Grandma did, a burden to everybody, an eye-sore, a rotten, useless body.... Listen, Bob, do me this favor, this last favor. Get me some poison."

"You're not yourself, Kid. Don't talk like that." But Robert Ingersoll found the air suddenly thicker and too heavy to breathe. His throat contracted and he remembered a lullaby hummed to the stars as Minnie made up her mind.

"Listen, Bob, you're supposed to be sensible. You've always been the brains of the family. You know there's no heaven and no hell and no judgment seat. You and Ma taught me that when I was a kid. Listen, Bob, I'm in hell right now—and you can let me out. Get it for me, will you, Bob? Get me something that'll stop all this for good and all."

"I can't do that, Hek. It's wrong. You're getting better. You *know* you are. You feel stronger right now than you did this time last week."

"Stronger!—so's I can feel the pain that much more. Holy Christ, are you human? Don't you know what I go through night and day? My stomach is full of red-hot pokers. My brain dances with pictures that are driving me crazy. Every muscle and bone in my body aches like when a dentist takes a filling out to kill the nerve. Is it sensible to go on living like that?"

Bob bit his lip and waited.

"Haven't you got guts enough to live up to the stuff you've been preachin' all your life? Didn't you see anybody killed in

France? Get me something, Bob; carbolic acid, cyanide, I don't care what. Cut my wrists. Shoot me! Do *something!* I can't stand it any longer." His excitement threw him into a violent coughing spell and Bob grasped the boy's shoulders in a clumsy effort to relieve him.

What a mercy it would be if he should burst a blood vessel in a paroxysm like this—burst a blood vessel and know nothing more. Then Bob was instantly ashamed. If his reason told him that, and he had no better standard than that reason—poor as it was—what held his hand? What held his mind from decision? In the face of this suffering Minnie would never have suspended judgment so long. There had been no such urgent need to relieve Grandma Elling. She had been numb, insensible to physical pain. She had not begged to die. Was he afraid? Did he avoid dipping his hands in blood because it was his brother's? Because this man's usefulness to the world would be cut off? Because he shunned the bare possibility of being called to face an higher tribunal?

What held his hand? With Minnie's example before him, with Florence declining so rapidly that her endurance must snap, and soon; where was his strength?

He scrutinized the contorted face of the boy, his emaciated neck, the sore on his ear which iodoform would not heal, the ugly putty color of the skin. This figure was no longer a man. It was an animated *thing.* It should be killed.

Hek's dull, pain-misted eyes drooped nearly shut. "All right," his voice came in a whisper, "if you won't help me, I'll find a way to do it myself.... But it's a hell of a big laugh on you. You and your 'light of pure reason'."

That was Tuesday night. Florence was washing the dishes. "What does he want?" she asked in colorless disinterest. If Bob had never anwered she would not have noticed.

"He wants me to buy him poison. He wants to kill himself."

Florence, of course, was unreasonable. Hek's death was exactly what she needed, what she desired, but a Christian girl could not admit that. But Bob! Bob with his strange ideas, his lack of faith; Bob might do it. She set herself to dissuade him. "You mustn't, Bob. You—you couldn't!"

Robert Ingersoll closed his eyes. "Not yet I can't. Not yet."

"Bob!"

"Don't worry about it. God knows he'd be better off dead."

"But—*you* couldn't kill your brother, Bob. You couldn't."

"I went to France to kill Germans. That was all right."

"Oh, that was different."

"Healthy, young, ambitious German boys. Thank goodness I didn't have to—shoot any of them myself."

"That was different, Bob. They were trying to kill you."

Bob smiled at her as if she were six. "You have it all worked out too, haven't you? … I thought I had. I thought I believed in myself, in my mind. I thought I respected my mother as much as any one could."

"For *her* sake, Bob, don't do it."

"I didn't respect her half enough." He was thinking aloud, oblivious of his wife's presence. "I didn't know how much strength it required."

"What?"

"What?"

"What did you say?"

"I said—I think I'll take a walk." Dread came in her eyes. She would be alone with Hek. "Will you watch him?"

Florence had to swallow hard before the monosyllable would come. "Yes."

Bob walked a long time—and the next day was Wednesday. His boss saw him gazing, staring with hollow, weary eyes at a blank wall. "How's your brother, Bob?"

"Eh? ... He's dying. All we can do is wait."

The man shook his head. "You need some rest. Why don't you go home? We'll get along. Go ahead."

"All right! ... Thanks. I will."

He went to the cemetery. William Elling had a stone of some proportions. A metal emblem marked his father's grave. A MOTHER headstone had been all they could afford for Letitia. Minnie's grave was as yet unmarked. Bob studied the earth and wondered why he had come. At a level approximately six feet below him, four bodies in various stages of decay lay boxed as was the custom of his tribe. That was all. Living, they had represented something, each of them, each his individual code, and in life they were admirable or base, according to the strength they displayed when circumstance tested their tenets. Now Hek was coming here, to join them. His body would contaminate the ground. He would lie there next to Minnie, made her equal by death.

Bob went home uninspired. Why had he gone to the cemetery at all? Had he expected the sod over his mother's body to steel him, if all the instruction and precept of her life had not?

He entered the flat—unexpected. Florence leaned over Hek's bed and the boy seemed to be holding her, clutching her. At the sound of the door his hold was released. She whirled around in fright and panic. Bob tried to understand. "Oh—" he said.

"You're—you're home early. Lunch isn't ready yet."

She needn't be frightened. But he hadn't thought of such a thing before. The very nature of Hek's malady would keep sex uppermost in his distorted mind—and Florence was the only woman about. How long had she suffered *this* in silence? It was nearly ended now. Perhaps, in another twenty-four hours, he could do it. Perhaps; but *how*? Poison? Doc Smith would know. Doc Smith would know, no matter how it was done. There was just a chance, if Hek and he both talked to the doctor, there was just a bare possibility that *he* would do it.

"How do you feel, Kid?"

"Did you bring me that package?"

Bob turned quickly and went to the door. "I'll be back in half an hour."

"Bob!" Florence called, and ran after him. In the hall he quieted her fears.

"I just did that to keep him quiet, Honey. I'm not going to get it."

She leaned heavily against him. "Oh, Bob, how is it going to end? I'm almost crazy."

"There, there, Honey. It'll end soon. It's got to. I'm going to see Doc Smith." He drew away.

"He didn't come this morning."

When she returned to the flat, Hek whispered hoarsely: "He almost caught us; didn't he?"

Making *her* a party to his filthiness! "Us?"

"Oh—you like it."

Florence went into the kitchen…. No butter. No coffee. She'd have to go. "Will you be all right while I go to the store? It won't take me but a minute." She spoke from the door.

Hek nodded, sullenly, a scornful smirk on his lips.

They were out of the house. He was alone! Could he possibly reach the bath? Bob's old straight razor was there. Maybe, *maybe* he could make it. His puffy feet wabbled, his ankles twisted, he sank to his knees and crawled. The stool, the tub, the bowl gave him hand-holds and he saw his own face in the shaving mirror for the first time in two weeks. He shut the sight out with his lids.

"Miz Knott!"

The nigger! At the door with the wash. Coming in!

"Miz Knott?"

Hek tried to raise his voice. "In here, Zandra."

She set her basket in the hall and poked timidly toward the faint sound. Hek found the razor and turned with it in his hand.

Her pie-face smiled. "How feelin', Mister Hek?"

"I'm better. See? I'm up."

"I see you are."

"Will you help me here, Zandra? I'm trying to shave."

"Look out you don't cut yourself." She was very close. This would be a fitting exit, an appropriate curtain. He would rape this wench, then cut his throat. He would rape her if he was capable.

The suddenness of his lunge carried Zandra backward and Hek lay on top of her. The razor flashed in his hand. "Hold still, you black bitch, hold still or I'll cut you to pieces!"

She trembled, but did not attempt to rise. Keeping the razor gripped in his right hand, Hek raised her skirts with his left. But Hek had overestimated his own inner ability. Supine, a lump of fear, the laundress endured the futile prodding, murmuring, "Lord, oh, Lord. Lord have mercy on my soul"—until Hek thought he heard Florence on the stair.

"Quick," Hek coughed. "Bed." He crawled toward it, coughing. "Help——"

Wide-eyed, Zandra rose and adjusted herself.

"Help me—I'll kill you."

Shaking, sweating, babbling prayers, she helped Hek into bed. He put the razor under the pillow—and coughed and coughed.

## 5

PROBABLY that was just another Wednesday to most people in the world. It was the blackest day in Bob's life. But it passed.

Thursday, like eleven o'clock, is bound to come. And with Thursday, there came to Freeport, to play the last half at the Orpheum, three song birds who now sang whispering harmony—and the shrillest of these was named Geraldine, but not Farrar.

Geraldine, you may recall, came from Texas, and once she had mentioned a cannon pining for action in her trunk. Hek hadn't known he was sick at that time. He was, in Geraldine's case, innocent of evil intent. But that hadn't made the course of the disease any easier for the girl to bear and she nursed a hatred for that one actor which makes garden detestations fond attachments by comparison.

After his lunch, that Thursday, Bob had spoken to Hek, who had grown calmer since the day before. "You feel better. I can tell it."

"You're a piker."

"Please don't start that, Hek. I just can't do it. While"—Bob's tongue could hardly be forced to shape the words—"while there's life, there's hope."

Hek's sneer was hard to bear. "Well, all right. I've known all along you had no guts. Do *this* for me, will you? Go into the Mission on your way back and tell Mercedes Warburg I'd like to see her. She's a waitress."

"All right."

"Will you? Without fail?"

"Yes. What do you want Mercy for?"

"Because I think she has guts. She did have, once."

Mercedes happened to be standing near Geraldine's table when Bob found her. "Hello, Mercy, how are you?"

"I'm all right."

"Do you remember my brother, Hek?"

Geraldine stopped eating.

"Do I remember him?" Mercy said without smiling. "I do."

"He'd like to see you, Mercy. Can you go over to my flat some time to-day?"

"Is he in Freeport?"

And Geraldine wondered if there could be two people in the world named "Hek".

Mercedes nodded. "I can. I will. Are you sure he *wants* to see me?"

Geraldine studied the expression on the face of the waitress. It might indicate that—in a bacteriological sense—they were sisters under the skin.

"He's dying, Mercedes. He's *awfully* sick."

"Dying!"

"Yes."

"And he wants to see me?"

"Very much."

"I'll go. Thanks."

When Mercedes poured fresh water in Geraldine's glass, the songbird asked: "Are there any theatrical people living in Freeport? Any actors or actresses?"

"I don't know," the girl answered, scarcely hearing the question.

Dying, he was. Getting out of it, while those he'd hurt had to go on. Dying. Running away again, just as he had that Christmas. Getting out of it. The brother was nice. He'd grown up to be a fine man. Funny how different people in the same family went pht—different directions.

But Geraldine wanted to know. If *this* "Hek" was the same man, he shouldn't be allowed to die without seeing *her*. She studied the clean, sharp, almost hard jaw line of the tall, competent waitress. There was strength there, strength to admire. The girl from Texas admired Mercedes' strength.

"Look," said Geraldine. "I was told Freeport was the home of several theatrical stars. Don't you know anybody here—in show business?"

Mercedes noticed the songstress for the first time. "Stars? Humph. There's Hek Knott, but I don't think anybody ever called him a star!"

## 6

Bob had seen a movie once, wherein the plot concerned vengeance. He thought of that as he walked home. When the hero was about to visit some picturesque retributive violence on the villain, God had stricken the miscreant with lightning—and an ambitious director had caused the lightning flash to spell out: JUDGE NOT! *Vengeance is Mine!*

Bob thought of that as he walked home.

And he thought of a poem setting forth the narrative of an unbeliever in the African jungle, staked and surrounded by naked blacks with spears. A frying fire has been laid at his feet and the circle of fiends demands that he forswear his God—ironically, the God he has not acknowledged for years.

Bob thought of that as he walked home. Bob had a brother to kill. There was no way out of it. Bob walked home from his work, a man with a brother to kill. Bob walked, only half a man, only half an individual, only half strong enough to decide. The rest of him, the necessary balance of him was buried in a grave as yet unmarked. For they two had been but one. He opened the door softly. The scene he had discovered the previous morning had made him suspicious. If he found Hek annoying Florence that way again, his anger might serve to carry him through the commission of a deed his calm judgment seemed unable to support.

Florence was not in evidence. Hek seemed—dimly seen—to sleep. Bob went into his bedroom and looked at a snapshot of Minnie. The required strength must come from somewhere. It was odd that Florence was out. The kitchen, where meat should be frying, was silent. The whole house was a little too silent. He walked to Hek's bed.

The 'pane which should have been white was crimson as any rose. The bread knife, a long, sharp one, stood upright in Hek's chest. Bob's own razor lay on the floor at the side of the bed and it too was covered with blood.

Robert Ingersoll looked up at the familiar cracks in the ceiling to see if it was written there: *Vengeance is mine saith the Lord. Judge not!* His heart, relieved of its tremendous weight, beat faster and faster. It was done! He did not have to do it. But—by whom?

"Florence!" he called. "Florence!" and dashed frantically downstairs to the street.

# 7

IT could have been hushed up. Bob and the doctor could have got together and nothing need have been said, but under the strain of surprise and excitement, that idea was late in coming.

Henry Zupke, chief of police, had so few murders to handle that he was apt to make mysteries for himself to solve. The bread knife, upright in Hek's chest, gave him lots of material to work on.

The butcher who owned the building gave Zupke most of his information. "Mrs. Knott went out about three o'clock. I wasn't very busy. I don't think she come back at all. About four, maybe a little earlier, that Warburg girl from Schraeder's restaurant went in. I didn't see her leave, and I was sort of watchin', too.

"It couldn't o' been more than fifteen minutes later a colored man came along and *lie* went in.

"I was busy the rest o' the afternoon, but just after five I was gettin' a ham out o' the window when a woman I never seen before come out o' the stairway. She was kind of flighty lookin'. I don't know. I tell you; she looked a lot like a girl I see last night at the Orpheum. They could o' been sisters; about the same size too. That's all I know, until Mr. Knott come in, lookin' for his wife. It's awful, ain't it, him so sick and all."

But Zupke couldn't make a case out of it. He identified the visitors and talked to them, but he couldn't find a motive.

The nigger had come for the laundry. When no one answered his knock he had gone away without it.

Mercedes had found Hek alone, but alive and cheerful. She had talked for a few minutes—about old times, about his mother—and she had left.

Geraldine had called to pay a small debt; some six dollars he had given her once when they were on the bill together. She had received no answer to her knock. She had not tried the door.

Florence had gone away for a rest. Bob testified to that. He told the coroner it had been arranged between them. So Zupke's fun was spoiled.

The desk was moved back into the front room—and Bob found lots of time to read. He missed the home cooking, of course, but Mercedes always gave him the best cuts of meat at dinner in the Mission, and a sandwich was all he wanted at noon. A sandwich and coffee at the Pullman Lunch Room, a "diner" with a long row of stools.

The Pecatonica froze tight that winter, and when the first big thaw came in February it looked as if Stephenson Street Bridge would go sure enough. They had to blast the ice to save it.

As Bob entered the Pullman for his lunch, a class in explosives was in session. The Professor had seen the body rise. "They always do that. Dynamite will bring a drowned person to the surface every time."

"Who do you suppose she was?"

"I don't know. Some poor dame that got caught. The coroner's workin' on the case."

"She never fails, does she? That damn' creek gets somebody every year."

"I've changed my mind," Bob told the waiter. "I don't want anything to eat.... I beg your pardon, can you tell me where they took that body? that woman?"

THE END